THE FIGHTING TENDERFOOT

William MacLeod Raine, hailed in his later years by reviewers and contemporaries alike to be the "greatest living practitioner" of the genre and the "dean of Westerns," was born in London, England in 1871. Upon the death of his mother, Raine emigrated with his father to Arkansas in the United States where he was raised. He attended Sarcey College in Arkansas and received his Bachelor's degree from Oberlin College in 1894. After graduation, Raine traveled throughout the American West, taking odd jobs on ranches. He was troubled in his early years by a lung ailment that was eventually diagnosed as tuberculosis. He moved to Denver, Colorado in hopes that his health would improve, and worked as a reporter and editorial writer for a number of newspapers. He began writing Western short stories for the magazine market. His first Western novel was *Wyoming* (Dillingham, 1908), that proved so popular with readers that it was serialized in the first issues of Street & Smith's Western Story Magazine when that publication was launched in 1919. During World War I, Raine's Western fiction was so popular among British readers that 500,000 copies of his books were distributed among British troops. By his own admission, Raine concentrated on character in his Westerns. "I'm not very strong on plot. Some of my writing friends say you have to have the plot all laid out before you start. I don't see it that way. If you have it all laid out, your characters can't develop naturally as the story unfolds. Sometimes there's someone you start out as a minor character. By the time you're through, he's the major character of the book. I like to preside over it all, but to let the book do its own growing." It would appear that because of this focus on character Raine's stories have stood the test of time better than those of some of his contemporaries. It was his intimate knowledge of the American West that provides verisimilitude to all of his stories, whether in a large sense such as the booming industries of the West or the cruelties of nature—a flood in *Ironheart* (1923), blizzards in *Ridgway of Montana* (1909) and *The Yukon Trail* (1917), a fire in *Gunsight Pass* (1921). It is perhaps Raine's love of the West of his youth, the place and the people where there existed the "fine free feeling of man as an individual," glimmering in the pages of his books that will warrant the attention of readers always.

THE
FIGHTING TENDERFOOT

William MacLeod Raine

GUNSMOKE

First published in the UK by Hodder and Stoughton

This hardback edition 2012
by AudioGO Ltd
by arrangement with
Golden West Literary Agency

ISBN 978 1 445 88733 3

British Library Cataloguing in Publication Data available.

Printed and bound in Great Britain by
MPG Books Group Limited

CHAPTER I: *A Desert Greeting*

ON HORSE AND MAN the evidence was written plain that they had travelled far. Yellow dust, fine as powder, had sifted into every crease of the rider's trousers. It covered his boots, his black hat, his coat. It streaked the young fellow's face and caked his burning throat. The eyes of the man were sunken and bloodshot. As for the animal, sweat stains blotted flank and withers. Hoofs dragged and head drooped.

The road had deflected from the river flats and was wandering in haphazard fashion over a land rolling in waves toward the mountains. The chaparral was dense. It encroached upon the road as though Nature intended to win back to primitive desert this long trail ribbon wheels and hoofs had worn in man's westward trek. Thorns clutched at the sorrel's legs and at the rider's feet.

Garrett O'Hara nodded in the saddle. The heat of the sun made him sleepy. He wondered how long it would be till he reached the foothills that rose before him rooted at the edge of the desert. Not long now, he decided, for already the red slopes were beginning to be dotted with jack pines and cedar. He welcomed the change. Once he really reached the hills the dust would not be so irritating nor the heat so oppressive. No pressing engagement awaited him at Concho. Why not throw off among the trees and lie down in the shade for an hour? So, sleepily, he mused, hand on the horn to steady his lax body.

Out of the slumberous heat of the afternoon came sinister greeting. The traveller's hat, tilted to protect the face from the sun's rays, was lifted from his head as though by a sudden current of wind. The sound of an explosion boomed. From the chaparral smoke drifted skyward.

O'Hara's languor vanished—and so did he. Before the booming of the rifle had died, before the first thin shred of smoke had appeared, he had flung himself out of the saddle and was scuttling for the brush. As he ran he stooped to scoop up his hat.

Not till he had dodged past much greasewood and mesquite did he stop to reconnoitre. For one glance had shown him two holes in the hat.

The running man pulled up to consider ways and means. The position of the holes in the hat showed him that the shot had come from the right. What was the object of this attack? O'Hara was a stranger. He could have no enemies, not in this

5

frontier land. Since he was unknown, nobody could have acquired a grudge against him. Robbery, then, could have been the only motive. Somebody had tried to assassinate him to get his wallet, or else his horse and saddle. Who? O'Hara meant to find out, if it could be done without too much risk.

Slowly, with the greatest precaution against the snapping of twigs or the rustle of bushes, he moved toward the road, revolver in hand. He stopped. Something or someone was moving rapidly in the brush parallel to him. He could hear the thrashing of limbs thrust hurriedly aside.

A voice, two voices, came abruptly from the left.

The first, a rough, heavy one, startled by surprise. *"You, by cripes!"*

The other high and clear, on a note of excited resentment: "Who did you expect? Who were you trying to kill?"

"Why in Mexico do you ride around in them clothes?" The rough voice held both apology and exasperation.

"Suppose you mind your own business, Shep Sanderson," came swift, sharp answer. "What I want to know is why you shot at me?"

O'Hara, edging forward, could see them now from the cover of a cholla. They were in a draw. One, a light slender figure, stood against a bank, revolver in hand. The other, the big hulking man, carried a rifle.

"Why for do you go ridin' around in men's clothes?" the rough voice demanded defensively. "It ain't noways proper."

"I'm not in men's clothes, if you'd 'tend to your own affairs," the high voice retorted bitterly. "You answer me. How dare you shoot at me?"

The eavesdropper had a swift suspicion, which he verified by craning his neck around the cactus. The one who had spoken last was a young woman. She wore the shiny chaps of a cowboy, plain wide leathers into which she had contrived somehow to thrust her skirts.

"I ain't admittin' I shot at you, but if I did I had no way of knowin' it was a woman, let alone you. You got no license to wear that get-up." There was outraged virtue in the heavy growl.

"You shoot first and find out afterward who you're shootin' at. Is that it? I'll see what Dave Ingram has got to say about that. If you want to know, you're nothing but a low-down murdering wolf."

"That's no kinda way for a lady to talk," the big man told her, shocked into paternal reproof. "Say I made a mistake. I don't admit it, mind, but say I did——"

6

"Mistake!" she stormed. "Do you call it a mistake to shoot at a woman—at me? Do you reckon this country will stand it for a minute?"

"Now looky here, Miss Steelman, I didn't go for to shoot at you—if I did. I was aimin' at an antelope. I've done apologized. Cain't do anything more, can I?" he wheedled sulkily.

O'Hara slipped quietly forward and stepped down into the arroyo. The young woman saw him first. She stared at him, eyes wide with surprise. Her expression warned the big man. With unexpected swiftness he whirled, the rifle jumping to his hip.

"Who are you?" he demanded harshly.

The answer came smoothly and easily: "I'm the antelope you shot at, Mr. Sanderson."

The big man glared at him. Shep Sanderson was that unusual combination, a slow thinker and a fast shooter. He had a one-track mind and had no room in his brain for simultaneous cross currents. Either Barbara Steelman or this man was wrong. He had fired only one shot. As his mind functioned he knew, with considerable relief, that it had been the stranger at whom he had flung the bullet from his rifle. The girl must have been in the brush between him and the road. What was she doing here, anyhow? And how did this man know his name was Sanderson? What was the best thing to do now?

The face of the ambusher was a map of puzzled disturbance. He was thinking, and it did not come easily to him.

O'Hara lifted the hat from his head with a bow to the young woman. She caught sight of the holes in it and her eyes dilated.

"Did he do that just now?" she asked.

"Just now, miss, with his little bullet."

She felt the blood ebb from her heart as she stared at him. Somehow, in the rush of the moment, she had not been afraid when she thought Sanderson had fired at her. There had not been time for fear. But now, with the evidence that red tragedy had grazed so near, stamped in the hat, she was shaken.

"Why did he do it?"

"That's what I've come to ask him." The manner of the young man altered. Brown eyes and voice were no longer gentle. In his bearing was a certain poised inflexibility. Yet he did not raise his voice or change his attitude. The difference was of the spirit. "Why pick on me as a target, Mr. Sanderson?"

7

"I don't know you, fellow," Sanderson growled.

"Which makes your greeting to me all the stranger. Did you mistake me for one of your friends? Or was it my purse you fancied?"

Hoarsely, Sanderson murmured something about an antelope. In the presence of Barbara Steelman his gun was sealed even if he had wanted to argue further along that line.

The girl was puzzled at this young man who had dropped down upon them from the sky, as it were. She could not place him by type. He was not like any of the men she had known in her rather limited experience. "Tenderfoot" was written all over him. Clothes, manner, bearing, personality, all spoke of the city rather than the range. He was neither weather-beaten nor tanned, in spite of the signs of hard travel. She liked his vivid face, also the suggestion of shy deference he had shown when speaking with her. Slender he was, and graceful. The muscles seemed to ripple beneath his clothing when he moved.

Now she spoke quickly. "You're not Judge Warner?" The statement was a question.

"No," he replied.

She turned on Sanderson, and her words almost leaped at him. "I know why you tried to kill this man. You thought he was Judge Warner."

Though he denied it in words, the man stood convicted. There was confession in the blank, amazed look he turned on her.

"Why, I—I——Nothin' to that," he stammered. "I done told you I shot at an antelope."

"Who is paying you for this?" she cried. "Who hired you to do murder to prevent Judge Warner holdin' court to-morrow?"

Sharply she had flung out her questions, but O'Hara noticed that the assurance had died out of her before she finished speaking. Some thought had occurred to her that filled her with fear. She had asked for an answer, but perhaps she hoped not to get one.

"Tell you I shot at an antelope," the fellow insisted, shifting his feet uneasily. "In regards to that, if I made a mistake, no sense in all this belly-achin' about it."

"A trained antelope, one riding a horse," suggested O'Hara.

Sanderson turned sullenly a shifty eye on him. "Stranger man, you better fork yore fuzzy an' light out."

"Or you'll send another blue whistler at me," the young man said, brown eyes gleaming.

8

The girl spoke. She did not care to see the issue pressed too far. Sanderson had a bad reputation. "Talkin' about his horse, Shep, where is it? You'd better round it up for him."

"Me?" The big man glared at O'Hara. "I ain't been hired to wrangle for no tenderfoot."

"Don't you think, since it was your fault his horse got away, it would be decent to——?"

"For this *hombre?* Me? Say, I'm Shep Sanderson."

This seemed to be answer enough. His cold shallow eyes, light as skim milk, slid from O'Hara to Miss Steelman and back again. He moved away, his face toward the younger man, till he reached a dense clump of prickly pear. Behind this he vanished. They could hear his retreating footsteps.

The girl spoke, "First off, we better get our horses."

They found hers where she had left it when she slipped from the saddle to take refuge in the brush. It was grazing leisurely, picking up such forage as it could.

"We'll look for yours," she said, busying herself with a stirrup. She was disturbed that he should find her wearing leathers, using a man's saddle. Probably he would think she was some kind of wild creature who did not know any better. She wanted to explain to him that in such thorny chaparral one had to wear leathers to protect the clothes and flesh against cruel clutching spikes, that she was no crazy tomboy who raced around the country dressed up like a man. But any approach to the subject was embarrassing.

They moved through the brush toward the road, the man walking beside the horse.

"We want to be careful," the young woman said in a low voice. "He's a bad crowd, Shep Sanderson is. I think he has gone. With me here he probably wouldn't bother you, but you can't tell for sure what he'd do. . . . Which way did your horse go?"

They had reached the road. "There it is, back of that prickly pear," O'Hara said. I knew it wouldn't wander far. Too tired."

He reclaimed his horse and swung to the saddle.

"This way," said Miss Steelman, and swung her mount deeper into the chaparral.

For nearly half a mile she led the man silently in and out among the brush. Then she reined up to ride beside him.

Disapprovingly, she looked at his fancy boots. "They'll be ruined in all this cactus," she told him. "You have to wear leathers in this country. It's not a question of how you look."

9

He understood that this was not so much a criticism of him as a defense of herself.

"Yes, miss. I can see it's better," he agreed. "But I was expecting to stick to the road when I started."

"Started where from?"

"From Aurora."

"For Concho?"

"Yes, miss."

She was still puzzled to place him. Though in the mountains, Concho was in the heart of a cattle country. There men talked cows, worked them, lived them. It was the basic occupation upon which all others were dependent. It was an easy guess that this stranger had never ridden out the stampede of a trail herd. Yes, tenderfoot was sure enough the word for him.

But in asking him where he had come from she had already gone beyond the custom of the country. Where men came from was their own business. To ask questions about it was neither safe nor discreet. Too many men had left their former habitat three jumps ahead of a sheriff's posse. Yet her interest was not solely curiosity. She had a feeling that he was headed for trouble quite unconsciously and that he was poorly equipped to meet it. The combination of ignorance and courage is not a good one, not in a hard country like this into which he was riding.

He could not be a tinhorn gambler. He did not have the fishy eye. An itinerant preacher, maybe. No, she felt that was not a good guess, either.

He volunteered information timidly. "My name is Garrett O'Hara. I am a lawyer."

"A lawyer! Oh, you're going to Concho as one of Judge Warner's party."

"I'm going to live there."

She drew up her horse and looked at him in surprise. "Live there! What are you going to do?"

"Practise law."

"In Concho." A mouthful of white teeth flashed in laughter. There was, he thought, a note of ironic derision in her mirth.

"Don't you think I'd make a good lawyer?" he asked, too shy to let her comment pass unanswered.

"I don't know. But why Concho? Who wants a lawyer there?"

"Prosperous town, isn't it?"

"Yes."

"Then there must be business there—cattle, contracts, real estate, lands."

Abruptly she asked: "Who do you know there? Who sent for you? Whose man are you?"

It was the last query that snagged his attention.

"What do you mean, whose man am I?"

She did not answer that. Her reply was wholly unexpected. "Better turn round and ride back to Aurora to-morrow."

His eyes flashed interest, and something more than that. "Why, if the Court please?"

"Never mind why. Do as I say. It will be better."

"Better for me?"

"Yes."

He pondered that a moment. A sudden smile illumined his face. "I'm to take that sight unseen, am I, Miss Steelman?"

"It's not your kind of a country," she said.

"What kind of a country is it, where men shoot at strangers because they may be law officers?"

She flushed. "It's a good enough country, of its own kind. That Shep Sanderson is a low-down killer. You can't judge folks by him."

"I hope not, though I think you suggested that someone hired him."

"I don't know whether anyone did or not," she responded, and he noticed that at the thought her face clouded again.

His eyes rested on hers. Once more a warm smile lit his face. "You make me mighty anxious to see Concho, Miss Steelman. I expect it will be a very interesting town."

No smile met his. She was preoccupied and not to be diverted from her thoughts. Yet her next remark seemed to bear no relation to what had gone before.

"Do you know Dave Ingram? Or my father, Wesley Steelman?"

"No, miss."

Apparently she was a young person of abrupt transitions. "That hogleg you carry! Can you use it?"

"Hogleg?"

"Six-shooter," she said impatiently. "Do you carry it for show?"

"Mostly," he admitted. "I killed a rattlesnake with it to-day."

"Can you shoot?"

"I can hit a barn if I am near enough."

"Could you hit a man who was firing at you?"

"Don't think so. I'd hate to try."

"Then don't carry it. You'll be a shinin' mark for someone to bump you off."

"Do what to me?"

"Shoot you. I'd throw it away and play I was a preacher while I stayed at Concho. You'll be safe then."

"I'm much obliged for your interest." The colour was high in his cheeks. Clearly her suggestion insulted his pride.

"You're such a babe in the woods. You've got no license to practise law there."

"But I think I'll do my poor best to look out for myself," he went on, just as though she had not spoken.

"I didn't mean to cast a slur on you," she repented. "But the town is full of hard men, quick on the shoot. That's how they settle difficulties."

"I'd say what Concho needed was law," he said drily.

"Don't you understand?" she cried. "Men make their own law. They carry it in a holster by their side. Just now trouble is brewing—a lot of it. There's a feud on. Among such men a lawyer's arguments wouldn't last a minute."

"Or the lawyer either?" he asked.

"Go back where you came from," she begged.

He shook his head. "I'm headed for Concho, miss."

She threw up a hand with a gesture that waved aside responsibility. "All right. It's none of my business, anyhow. I'm interferin' where I shouldn't. Have it your own way, Mr. O'Hara."

"I'm sorry you want to hand me my hat before I've really started to call on your country," he said.

"Anyhow, look the ground over before you decide to stay. Talk with Steve Worrall. Say I sent you. He's in the freight business. You'll find him at the Longhorn Corral."

"I'll do that," he promised.

"Steve has a lot of horse sense, and you can trust him."

They had left the road and swung to the right. The land was rising toward the foothills. It was definitely, now, a country of jack pines and cedars, of cow-backed elevations and red hill shoulders. The water that poured down the arroyos was filled with the rust of iron ore in solution.

At the summit of a long climb Miss Steelman drew up her horse.

"Our ways part here," she said. "Take that trail to the left. It's about five miles to town. When you come to a creek go right through it. That's Squaw Crossing. You can't miss the road."

He hesitated, trying to find words to thank her for her kindness. He knew the colour was driving into his face, the effect of shyness. A quotation from *Jane Shore* came to his mind, and he blurted it out:

> " . . . Your bounty is beyond my speaking,
> But though my mouth be dumb, my heart shall thank you."

She flashed a quick look at him, gave a short laugh, and took the hill trail.

CHAPTER II: *At the "Baile"*

THE MEMORY of her scornful little laugh went down the trail with Garrett. He blushed with self-contempt. Why was it that with women he was so bashful and unsure of himself? He had no difficulty in saying to men whatever was in his mind. But when it came to a woman, and especially a young and pretty one, he never could be quite natural. His talk with Miss Steelman had been forced. Too shy to say "Thank you" simply, he had flung at her a tag of the old play. No wonder she thought he was a fool.

Barbara Steelman's vividness stayed with him. In spite of the leathers she breathed femininity. The slender figure so graceful and vigorous, the fresh softness of young flesh, the flash of dark, long-lashed eyes, the crisp wave of the chestnut hair, the low, clear voice, all denied any suggestion of coarseness. She was woman first, last, and all the time.

A safe guess was that she was the daughter of some rancher in the hills. She had come, he could swear, of a good family, one that held its head high. Why had she made so much of warning him against staying at Concho? What was this mystery at which she hinted, one which made it unsafe for him, an insignificant stranger, to practise his profession in the town? No doubt he would find out soon enough.

A steep trail dropped like a crooked rope down the mountain side to a village which nestled at its foot. As he descended he could see that Concho had one business street. From it, up draws and hollows, two or three winding roads started tentatively toward the adobe houses that formed the residence section.

The main street was not long but it teemed with life. There were saloons and gambling halls, a hotel, blacksmith shops, and two stores, one at each end of the street and on opposite sides of it. Men moved to and fro leisurely, stopping to talk to one another beside hitch racks or in the dusty road. All the men wore the costume of Cattleland. Many of them were armed. Most of them were big rangy fellows who walked with the rolling gait of the dismounted horseman.

O'Hara drew up in front of the Concho House and tied his sorrel to a snubbing post. This was an unnecessary precaution, for the horse was far too tired to ramble away. With saddlebags over his arm the young man mounted the porch steps and walked into the adobe hotel.

Three or four men were seated in the office, chairs comfortably tilted back. One of them was talking, his heels resting on a drum stove that had not been lit for many months. He continued to talk. Neither he nor any of the others paid the least attention to the entrance of the stranger.

"This Munz was a Pacific Sloper, a bully puss kind of a fellow. Claimed he was a curly wolf from the Mal Pais. Well, the old man drifts in an' speaks his li'l' piece, not wroppin' it up careful either. He looks straight at Munz. 'I'm cock-a-doodle-do here, an' if any son-of-a-gun don't like it he'd better pull his picket pin an' get on the prod pronto. Meanin' you in particular, Munz.' This slabsided Pacific Sloper looks mean an' says nobody can run a sandy on him. Me, personal, I jes' sat on my heels an' waited for the smoke signals."

A fat man who had preëmpted three chairs wheezed in an interruption: "Knowin' Dave Ingram like I do, if I'd been Munz I'd of been urgin' my bronc to scratch gravel about that time without waitin' to take my plunder along either."

"Munz was one of these wise pilgrims that don't know sic' 'em. Account of him havin' bumped off one-two fellows he figured he was a bad *hombre*. Well, one thing led to another till Munz reached for his .44, an' right then the old man drilled him. I never did know before what them shutters on the windows at the Diamond Tail was for. We carried this Munz out to the arroyo on one an' buried him there."

"Is the proprietor in?" O'Hara asked, the story evidently being finished.

14

The fat man looked at him. "I run this shebang."

"Can I get a room?"

"I reckon you can get a cot somewheres."

"Would you mind showing me where it is? I'd like to wash."

The fat man did not rise. "Go down that passage an' turn to the right. There's four beds in the second room. You can roost in one of them unless some guy squawks an' claims it's his. Wash basin back o' the house." His duties as host concluded, the chair dweller returned to unfinished business. "Well, if I was lookin' for a sure way to get filled with lead I'd run on Dave Ingram till he was sore as a toad on a skillet, an' I ain't criticizin' him either, y'understand. This Munz certainly suicided."

The long-legged man at the stove smiled, a smile of superior wisdom. "So Dave was sore, was he?"

O'Hara heard no more. He was heading down the long hall toward the bedroom of which he was to be part occupant. Upon one of the cots he dropped the saddlebags, after dusting them with a gunny sack which he found in one corner of the room. Back of the house he found a well, a tin wash basin, and a dirty towel.

A Chinese cook was in the kitchen and him O'Hara hailed.

"How about a clean towel, Charlie?"

"Him plenty good." The cook indicated with a thumb the soiled article.

The lawyer tossed him a quarter. "Not for me."

"Velly well." The siant-eyed one shuffled into a pantry and produced another towel.

With plenty of water and soap O'Hara made the most of such arrangements as were at hand. He finished just in time to answer the supper bell.

It was characteristic of Garrett O'Hara that he did not call at once on Steve Worrall at the Longhorn Corral. He wanted first to get his own impressions of the town. As much as he had seen of the place fascinated him. It was raw and crude, but the yeast of young and exuberant life worked in it. If it had not been wild and untamed he would have been disappointed.

His haphazard footsteps took him toward a sound of music. A Mexican *baile* was in progress. He paid the price of admission and stepped inside. A lithe, bright-eyed girl was doing a fandango with a young fellow in Spanish costume. The castanets rattled as they danced, and from the spectators came shouts of encouragement and approval. O'Hara watched the scene eagerly. This was the sort of thing he had come West to see. It had colour, the charm of the unusual.

There came a disturbance at the door, disputing voices, an irruption of men, not Mexicans. There were four of them, and at the head of the group one whom O'Hara at once recognized, the fellow whom he had met that afternoon, Shep Sanderson. They were intoxicated, primed for trouble. The Mexicans drew back, scowling at them.

O'Hara took one quick look around the room. There was no way out except by the front door unless he climbed through a window. His revolver was at the hotel in his saddlebags. He grinned, a foolish little smile. Probably he was in for a very unpleasant experience, to put the case mildly.

As yet Sanderson had not seen him. The fellow had seized hold of a girl and was dancing with her much against her will. The natives shouted protests and muttered oaths of anger, but they were not prepared for active resistance. The companions of Sanderson took the floor with other girls, two of them brushing aside the girls' escorts. O'Hara could see why the Anglo-Saxon race is not always popular with the Latins. Sanderson danced as gracefully as a bear, but what he lacked in technique he made up in vigour. He swung his partners so that their feet were usually off the floor.

The music stopped when Sanderson was close to O'Hara. The big man did not trouble to see that his partner reached her seat. He dropped her at once from his mind.

"Feed me a cigareet, fellow," he ordered, and then noticed to whom he was talking. "By cripes, it's the tenderfoot."

O'Hara felt his blood quicken. A little glow of excitement coursed through his veins. Danger always had that effect upon him.

"At your service," he replied.

"Who invited you to this *tendejón?*" the man demanded.

"Are you the floormaster, Mr. Sanderson?" Though he knew it was not safe, O'Hara could not keep a touch of jauntiness out of his retort.

The bad man's shallow eyes, a washed-out blue in colour, narrowed to points of savage cruelty. He had found a safe object upon which to expend his venom.

"Sa-ay, pilgrim, don't get funny with me. It ain't supposed to be safe. I aim to fix yore clock right now. After I've worked you over for a spell you hive off for parts unknown an' don't never let me see you again."

"Or you'll shoot straighter than you did this afternoon," suggested O'Hara.

16

"You don't have to get on the prod with me, fellow. I'm startin' to clean up on you right now."

A prize fighter had once given Garrett O'Hara six rules for rough-and-tumble fighting. He forgot the last five but remembered the first. It was to carry the attack rather than to wait for it. Now he reached for his foe's big outcropping ears, gripped them tightly, and jerked the unkempt head toward him. With all the force of his well-muscled arms O'Hara thrust back the head of the helpless giant, then leaped on him, twining his legs back of Sanderson's stocky ones. His feet moved up and down, swiftly and savagely.

The bully let out a yell of pain. "Take him off! Take him off! He's killin' me."

The dancers had pressed back from the fighting area. They stared at the entwined men, amazed at Sanderson's cry for help. For the stranger's hands still clung to the flapping ears. It was certain that he had not knifed the big man. Nor had he shot him. Why, then, was Sanderson bellowing like a frightened calf?

O'Hara felt a hand clutch his shirt and coat collar just back of the neck. He was snatched violently away from Sanderson and flung up against the wall of the room. A hard, low voice asked a question, not of him but of his antagonist.

"What you blattin' about, Shep? This little fellow's only a mouthful for you. . . . Get yore hand away from that gun."

A man had come into the room. He wore a blue flannel shirt, a broad-brimmed soft gray hat, an open vest, and no coat. His trousers were stuffed into the tops of high-heeled cowboy's boots. To the casual glance he was not a large man, certainly not compared with the bulky Sanderson. But he was powerfully built from the muscular slope of the neck down. The shoulders were broad and deep, the flesh on the body packed like ropes of steel, and he carried himself as one having authority. The light blue eyes were cool and flinty.

Reluctantly, Sanderson's hand fell away from the butt of the .44 which hung at his side. He glared at the newcomer. The urge struggled in him to defy the man, to wipe out with one swift lift of the arm and crook of the forefinger the tenderfoot who had discomfited him. But he was listening to his master's voice. He knew Dave Ingram too well to set himself against him.

The big bully looked down at the thighs of his legs. From them the trousers had been ripped and blood was dripping into the boots.

"His spurs rowelled me," Sanderson sputtered.

"Quite some," agreed the other drily. He turned to O'Hara, studying him for a moment. That he was a tenderfoot was palpable, yet he was wearing Mexican wheel spurs with long cruel rowels, a note in his costuming that seemed wholly incongruous.

O'Hara interpreted the question in the glance. "I bought them of a cowboy in Aurora who was hard up. He said they would be useful."

"He was right," agreed Ingram, smiling. "Good for man or beast."

"I'll get this pilgrim right one o' these days," Sanderson cut in vindictively.

"Very likely, but not now," his master said.

To Ingram a Mexican poured out a swift protest of flowing vowels. Other natives joined in, with much impulsive gesticulation. The cattle man listened, nodded, made answer in rapid and crisp Spanish. He turned to his henchmen.

"What d'you mean comin' here an' breakin' up the *baile?*" he demanded masterfully. "D'you want all the Mexicans against us, right at this time when we've got war enough on our hands? What's the matter with Pete's Paradise or the Gold Nugget? Can't you raise enough Cain in them without comin' here? Get outa here an' stay out!"

Ingram's voice was like the crack of a whip. The men to whom he spoke were hard fighting men, two of them at least "warriors" from Texas imported because they were known killers, but they had not a word to say for themselves except muttered excuses, sullen but restrained. They laughed to make the best of it and went swaggering out of the building. Sanderson whispered a word in his chief's ear before he left.

Garrett O'Hara had a capacity for hero worship. Looking at this bronzed Westerner, whose word had sent these ruffians trooping from the room, he recognized a leader of great force, strong, iron willed, master of himself as well as others.

"I'm in your debt, sir," the tenderfoot said.

"Who are you? Where d'you come from?" Ingram asked brusquely.

O'Hara told him.

"Here on business?"

"Expecting to settle somewhere in this country. Looking for a location. I'm a lawyer."

"A lawyer!" Ingram's voice expressed surprise.

"Yes, sir. Someone recommended Concho."

There was a moment of full silence before Ingram spoke.

18

"Come and see me at the store to-morrow—early," he ordered, then turned on his heel and walked out.

CHAPTER III: *"My Name Is O'Hara"*

GARRETT O'HARA walked slowly back to the Concho House. A thin sliver of moon rode the heavens. Ten thousand stars pricked a velvet sky. The dark outline of the hills rose close. The strumming of a banjo and the shuffling of feet came from Pete's Paradise. He could hear a raucous voice calling a dance. "Alemane left. Right hand to yore pardner an' grand right an' left. Ev'rybody swing."

The young man's thoughts raced excitedly as he tried to reduce them to order. Luck had certainly been with him, or he could not have escaped with any credit from a hand-to-hand scuffle with Shep Sanderson. He had been very fortunate, too, that Dave Ingram had come at the nick of time.

Who was this Ingram? Beyond question, he was important in the community. Judging by what he had heard at the hotel, the man was the owner of the Diamond Tail, or at least the manager of it. Also, he seemed to be proprietor of a store in town. He had said to meet him there next day, early. What hour was "early" here? He had not condescended to give his name or mention the location of the store. Evidently he expected people to know him, or if not to find out who he was. There was no doubt of his arrogance. It was unconscious rather than assumed. He had, to back it, good looks, a forceful personality, probably wealth, and no doubt power. One thing more O'Hara knew about him. Very recently he had killed a man for reasons unknown.

Decidedly, before keeping the appointment with Ingram it would be well to find out more about him. O'Hara did not turn in at the Concho House but kept on down the street to the Longhorn Corral. Of an attendant, a half-grown boy, he inquired for Mr. Stephen Worrall.

"I dunno where he's at," the wrangler answered. "He was here awhile ago. Might try the Gold Nugget. He bucks the tiger there sometimes."

O'Hara tried the Gold Nugget. It was crowded with men on pleasure bent. Some were playing faro, some keno, others fringed a roulette table. A young fellow pointed out Worrall to O'Hara.

Worrall was a tall lanky man with the look of the West stamped indelibly on him. Tiny crow's-feet radiated from his eyes, which were both shrewd and friendly. He was perhaps in his late twenties. As he was turning away from the wheel after cashing in his chips O'Hara accosted him.

"You don't know me, Mr. Worrall. My name is O'Hara. I'm a stranger here. This afternoon a young lady made me promise to introduce myself."

"A young lady?" the lank man repeated.

"Miss Steelman."

Worrall took him by the arm. "We'll get outa here," he said, and guided him toward the door. "I was leavin', anyhow. Picked up seventy-five bucks at the wheel. Enough for one night."

They walked down to the Longhorn Corral. Worrall asked his companion when he had arrived, what kind of trip he had had, and how he liked the town; but it was not until they were seated in the little office at the corral that he mentioned the name of the girl.

"Are you a friend of Miss Steelman's?" he asked, offering O'Hara a cigar while he himself bit the end from another.

"I can't claim that," the tenderfoot said. "I met her to-day for the first time. It was a question for a few minutes which one of us had been shot at."

"What's that?" demanded Worrall, a match burning in his hand. He stared at his guest while the flame travelled toward his fingers.

"Just as I say." O'Hara smiled. "I had conclusive evidence to settle the matter." He picked up his hat from the table and looked at the two holes in it.

"You mean some fellow shot at you an' hit yore hat?"

"Yes. To be definite, Shep Sanderson."

The owner of the corral dropped the match, shaking his scorched fingertips without looking at them. "Shep shot at you! Why?"

"That's what I came to have you tell me."

"You don't know why?"

"No."

"You an' him had any row?"

"Not then. We'd never seen each other. This evening we had a difference of opinion."

"How d'you know it was Shep?"

"He admits it. Claims he thought I was an antelope. That won't wash."

Worrall groped in his waistcoat pocket for another match. "Well, you got some idea why he shot at you, haven't you?"

"Miss Steelman had an idea. She told Sanderson he was

trying to kill Judge Warner and had mistaken me for him."

The lank man whistled. "Great jumpin' horn' toads! Could it be that? You do kinda favour the judge. About his size—an' store clothes. What did Shep say when she told him?"

"He denied it, but the way he denied it was a confession. He had no time to think up a good lie, because she was so quick about it. The fellow was flabbergasted. Of course he stuck to his antelope story."

"What d'you mean about Miss Steelman being shot at?"

"Perhaps I'd better tell you the whole story."

"All right. Hop to it." Worrall put his boots on the table and tilted back his chair.

He did not interrupt with a single question until O'Hara had finished, but there was at least one large one in his mind. What was Barbara Steelman doing on the edge of the flats so close to the entrance of Box Cañon? He thought he knew the answer, but did not want to believe it.

"So Miss Steelman wanted you to go back home where you come from? An' she wouldn't tell you why?"

"As I understand it, she sent me here to ask you why."

"Maybeso." The freighter rolled out some fat smoke rings and watched them. "You been here only a few hours. Likely you never heard of Dave Ingram."

O'Hara's answer came smilingly: "Heard of him, met him, got an appointment to meet him to-morrow at the store."

If the young man had expected this to bring an answering smile he was disappointed. The front legs of Worrall's chair came sharply to the floor. Into the long man's face had come an instant wariness. A blank film had taken all expression out of his eyes.

"Oh! You know Mr. Ingram."

"Not exactly. I met him for the first time to-night."

"But you've been in correspondence with him. He sent for you to come here."

"Wrong guess, Mr. Worrall. I never heard of him till to-day."

"I see. You an' he are strangers, but you jest happened to meet him an' get an appointment for to-morrow."

The young lawyer knew he had prejudiced his case and he tried to set himself right.

"I seem to be talking a good deal about myself, Mr. Worrall. Shall I tell you how I came to meet Mr. Ingram?"

The owner of the corral waved his cigar with a gesture which said plainly, "Do as you please about that."

O'Hara told the story of the evening's adventure. His account was a brief and modest one, but the salient fact could not be obscured that he had roughed it with Bully Sanderson and had not come out second best.

"He yelped for the boys to take you off after you had climbed his frame," Worrall repeated incredulously.

"I was tearing the flesh from his thighs with my spurs," explained the lawyer. "He couldn't shake me off and he couldn't stand the gaff."

Worrall looked at this stranger, shrewd eyes appraising him. He was neither tall nor stocky. There was no promise of unusual strength in the body, though it was easy to guess that he was an athlete. His movements were graceful, muscles smooth and pliant. It was possible he was one of those rare men whose fighting capacity could not be measured on the scales. Yet, in contrary testimony, there were the long-lashed soft brown eyes that would have made the fortune of a society débutante. Well, time would tell. The corral owner reflected that a man is like a watermelon: You can't tell how good he is till you thump him.

"Mr. O'Hara, I don't know you from Adam's off ox," Worrall said. "But if Miss Steelman sent you to me it goes as it lays. That young lady is fine as split silk, an' that's all there is to that. You look like a right limber young fellow, but you can't make Bully Sanderson look like a pore plugged· nickel an' get away with it. Seems to me like you've tackled more'n you can ride herd on."

"Likely enough," O'Hara agreed. "I was lucky this time. But there's no reason why he should hold a grudge against me. I was only defending myself."

"Hmp! He's p'ison mean. That's reason enough for him. You made him look like a two-spot. One of these days he'll get the dead wood on you an' do you a meanness. You can bank on that, sure as hell's hot. I know that bird. I've shared his blanket, beef, an' bread, an' I wouldn't trust him farther'n I could throw a bull. He may lay off you right now because Dave Ingram has given orders. That won't mean he's forgot, only that Dave is the big auger. Shep claims he was born in the Strip, raised on prickly pear, quarrelled with Comanches, an' played with grizzlies."

"He gives himself an appalling character," O'Hara said gaily. "Does he chew glass and swallow knives?"

"He's no false alarm," Worrall said gravely. "I don't know whether you savvy this country out here. It's a he-land with pants on. It ain't ever been curried. Sunday stops at the Missouri. When a fellow fills up with tarantula juice he's liable to run on the rope an' turn his cutter loose on the first guy he's sore at, especially this Shep Sanderson. Offhand, I'll bet you're no kind of a hand with a six-shooter."

"You win the watch on that bet," O'Hara admitted.

"My advice is for you to cut dirt back to the land of marshals, calabooses, an' plug hats."

"I think I'm going to like it here, Mr. Worrall."

"You're liable to rue yore decision if you stay. By the way, what's yore line, Mr. O'Hara?"

"I'm a lawyer."

"A lawyer. Great jumpin' horn' toads!" A thought stabbed the Westerner and brought his alert attention to another phase of the matter. "That's why Dave Ingram told you to come see him."

"Does Mr. Ingram need a lawyer?"

"I expect he does. To make his bluffs with so's to give them a lawful look." Again the freighter's shrewd eyes raked the other suspiciously. "Never saw him before to-day, you claim?"

"I'm still claiming just that," O'Hara replied, his mouth twitching with amusement. "Suppose you go a little deeper into this Machiavellian business. Is it a crime to know Mr. Ingram?"

Worrall slammed a hairy fist down on the table. "Young fellow, if I knew where you were at!"

"I'm a total stranger, as I told you before. Until to-day I never met a soul in this neck of the woods. I've had no correspondence with anyone. My purpose in coming was to find a good·town to hang out a shingle. Now my cards are on the table. I came to talk this over with you because I promised Miss Steelman I would. But since you doubt me——"

He rose and picked up his hat.

"Don't push on yore reins, Mr. O'Hara," the freighter told him. "Sit down. I'll tell you whatever you want to know."

Promptly, O'Hara tossed his hat on the table and sat down. "I want to know the inside politics of this town: who is fighting who and why, the reason Shep Sanderson wanted to kill Judge Warner, and the ground for Miss Steelman's advice that I had better not stay here to practise my profession. That will do to begin with."

The crow's-feet around Worrall's eyes crinkled to mirth. "You're sure enough a lawyer. Boy, if I answer those questions thorough you won't need to ask any more."

"I've got all night before me," the lawyer said.

23

Worrall made himself comfortable by resting his weight on the lower end of his spine and his shoulders. He talked.

CHAPTER IV: *The Man of a Few Hundred Thousand Words*

IF YOU WANT it in one word, short an' sweet, that word is 'cows,' " Worrall said. "Cows are the cause of all the trouble in this man's town."

O'Hara's eyes twinkled. "But I suppose it will take you about five thousand words to explain why they are the cause of trouble. Bossies look innocent enough to me."

"Goes clear back to the war. Down in Texas them days cattle ran wild, unbranded. All the men folks in the Confederate army. Well, when they come home, licked an' ragged, cows sure dotted the landscape. In a way of speakin' they belonged to the fellow threw the widest loop. Many a herd got its start in the next few months by real industrious brandin' of mavericks. Lots of cattle men sittin' pretty at the end of a few years far as cows went. Lots of cows, but no market for 'em. Last few years a market has been developing. Texas got crowded. The boys an' their herds began to emigrate. Some pushed into the San Marcos Valley. The one with the biggest herd was old Wes Steelman. Right now, today, he don't begin to know how many cows are carryin' the Hashknife brand."

"I've heard of the Hashknife brand. Didn't they use to call Steelman the king of the San Marcos?"

"Do yet," Worrall nodded. "The Lord sure blessed his herds an' they multiplied, if that's the way you want to look at it. Some folks didn't see it jest thataway. Other folks came into the San Marcos, mostly in the upper end of it an' in the hills above the valley. They were small cattle men, what they call nesters. Steelman didn't get along with them. He claimed they were rustlin' his calves an' hoggin' the water holes. They claimed his cowboys overrode their rights an' that the Hashknife waddies branded anything they run across. There was bickerin' at first, an' it got worse. A cowboy disappeared an' never did show up. Dry-gulched, likely. A small cattle man was found dead by a spring. Shot through the back of the head. He had been night-herdin'. It looked like hell was beginnin' to pop.

"I'm gettin' ahead of my story. The small cattle men drew together under the leadership of Dave Ingram. Dave owned

24

the Diamond Tail, a right numerous brand. If you listen to his enemies Dave usta be one of that kind of cow man that it would hurt his health to eat a critter with his own brand on it. You don't need to take that at par value. They say the same about everyone who has got ahead. Dave can see a dollar far as anyone. He started a store at Concho an' a freight outfit. He got in with the government officials an' secured fat beef contracts to supply the reservations. Small-fry nesters came to him an' he staked them. Dave got to be about the king pin up here in the mountains. What he said went.

"Well, Wes Steelman wasn't anyways pleased at the way things were shapin'. He had to go farther for markets. His range began to get crowded. Every which way he turned some nester had squatted, an' on top of that was Dave Ingram hornin' in on his markets. Time for him to get busy, he thought. So he started a store in Concho with Patrick McCarthy as his pardner. Then he bought out a fellow on Dead Horse Creek an' stocked a ranch of his own in the hills seventy miles above the main one in the valley."

"This was carrying the war into the enemy's country," O'Hara commented. "I suppose this didn't please Ingram."

"Not a li'l' bit. Both Dave an' Wes are what you might call arbitrary an' bullheaded. There's no compromise in either one of 'em, an' each thinks he ought to be chief. Consequence is, trouble. It grew to a head after a fellow called Shat Brown was killed. Shat was one of the li'l' hill ranchers up Jim Wilson Creek an' he was lined up with Ingram. You've got to understand that while Ingram an' Steelman are major-domos, as you might say, of their factions, they can't ride herd on every ornery waddy that trails along with them."

"I think I see," O'Hara said drily. "They reap the benefit of murder without being responsible for it. A convenient arrangement."

"That's no word to use, not in this country," Worrall told him severely. "If you aim to live long in the land you'll have to get educated. When folks have trouble out here they may have a difficulty resultin' in a shooting. I've been present at some killings, but that word of yours ain't either discreet or polite. There are some skunks it applies to, but we most generally hang them to the end of a propped-up wagon pole or a cottonwood."

"I'll have to learn the technical differences in homicides," the lawyer said.

Worrall detected a faint flavour of irony in this remark.

He dropped his feet from the table, and rested an arm upon it, leaning forward toward his guest.

"See here, young fellow, I'll offer you advice free gratis, seeing as Miss Steelman sent you to me an' seeing as I kinda cotton to you anyhow. Keep yore mouth padlocked. Folks fight here at the drop of the hat. Maybe you got sand in yore craw. I ain't sayin' no. Worse for you if you have, for you wouldn't last a split second when some low-down bird smokes up. Get this into yore coconut. Against a hos-tile bad man you're as harmless as a six-months-old baby. You've said enough, right here in this room, if the wrong parties heard it, to send you to hell on a shutter."

Garrett O'Hara smiled, that warm, friendly smile that was better than a letter of recommendation. "I haven't said as much as you have."

"I'm a darn fool about talkin'," admitted the freighter. "Some fellow onct got the laugh on me by sayin' I was a man of a few hundred thousand words. Probably I've been pretty frank with you, an' o' course you could throw down on me if you're that kind of bird. But I don't figure you are."

"I'm not," O'Hara reassured him. "I'm trying to show you that I choose my conversation to my company. I can be discreet when it is necessary."

"It's most always necessary here. Well, where was I at? After Shat Brown got killed Ingram an' his store pardner Tom Harvey began to bring in Texas warriors. So did Steelman an' McCarthy. Each side began to build its fences outside so as to get public opinion with it, including the territory authorities. A lot of newspaper ink has been slung, an' in the articles I notice one side is always black bad an' the other white good. I'm not tellin' any secret when I say that right soon now someone is gonna drop a match in a keg of powder an' our li'l' private war will begin to pop."

"You mean——"

"I mean that if Shep Sanderson hadn't made a mistake in his man to-day an' had shot straighter, if he had killed Judge Warner, the fat would already have been in the fire."

"How does Judge Warner come into it?"

"Another long story in that, but the upshot of it is that to-morrow he's expected to make Wes Steelman administrator of the estate of Jerry Hughes. Jerry was a friend of Ingram's an' his place is a sort of strategic point between the Diamond Tail an' the upper Hashknife ranch. Both Wes an' Dave want mighty bad to control it." Worrall added, to make the situa-

26

tion clearer: "Dave stepped in an' took charge of the place when Jerry died. He'd hate to give it up."

"So as a simple way out he decided to kill Judge Warner, an innocent party."

"Judge Warner is known to be friendly to the Steelman side, an' we don't know that Dave knew a thing about what Shep was aimin' to do. Myself, I don't hardly think he did."

"Don't you think it is possible you are so close to this feud that you are unconsciously exaggerating the danger? If it is as bad as you think surely the sheriff, the governor of the territory, or even the officer in charge of United States troops at the nearest fort, would take a hand."

The Westerner picked up his guest's hat and looked at the bullet holes in it. "Maybeso. Probably Shep was jest a-foolin' when he took a crack at you."

"sn't it possible he wanted to rob me?"

"If you think so go to Sheriff Banks an' see how far you get in swearin' out a complaint against Shep."

"The sheriff is a partisan, then. But surely the governor can't be. He derives his authority from Washington."

"I reckon the governor is human, too, but neither he nor Colonel Randolph at the fort will monkey with this dog fight if they can help it. Why should they? It's loaded with trouble for anyone who horns in. That's what Miss Steelman, outa the kindness of her heart, wanted you to know. Right now a fellow can hardly live here without takin' sides. There's no law business in Concho that won't tie you up with one side or the other. So there you are."

"If neither side has any respect for law why bother with judges and sheriffs and legal forms?"

"Hmp! Human nature is thataway. You can bet yore boots that sheriffs an' constables an' deputies an' J. P.'s will be right busy no matter what goes on. The story each side gives out will be that everything it has done was right an' lawful, regardless. So if you want to stay in Concho an' be Dave Ingram's man or Wes Steelman's why hop to it an' hang up yore shingle. I wouldn't wish to insure yore life, but that's neither here nor there, as the fellow said when his two wives met an' he lit out for the chaparral."

O'Hara rose. "If I hang out my shingle I'll be my own man."

The long man grinned. "You'll have a heap of time on yore hands to learn yore Blackstone thorough," he answered.

"And you, Mr. Worrall? I don't want to ask embarrassing questions, but——"

27

"No, I see you don't," the freighter drawled. "What other kind do you ask?"

"Don't answer this one if you'd rather not. Do you expect to sit on the fence and keep out of this fight?"

"I wish I knew," Worrall answered impulsively. "I'd like to, but here's where I'm at. Ingram an' Harvey have got their own freight outfit. I haul for Steelman's store an' for private parties. Looks to me like I'm gonna be drug in whether I want to or not, but you'll sure hear me yellin' for a while that I'm an innocent bystander."

Imps of mischief kicked up their heels in O'Hara's brown eyes. His remark apparently had no connection with anything that had gone before. "Yes, Miss Steelman is a very attractive young lady. As you say, if you're going to be dragged in anyhow——"

Worrall blushed beneath the tan. "Who said anything about Miss Steelman?"

The young lawyer fled, but he flung a grin back at the "innocent bystander."

CHAPTER V: *"If You're Not for Us You're Against Us"*

IT WAS IN the horoscope of Garrett O'Hara that he would plunge eagerly into life. He did everything with a zest. As he walked lightly along Concho's main street, the rays of the morning sun streaming down from a crotch in the hills, he knew that he was going to become absorbed in the drama of contending forces.

He had no difficulty finding the place for which he was looking. There were only two large stores in the town. The one at this end had a long sign along the front which read:

INGRAM & HARVEY

Into the big adobe building O'Hara walked.

Five or six men were lounging near the front of the store. They were in dusty cowboy boots, flannel shirts, and big wide-brimmed hats. All of them were openly armed. Some wore a holster swung low on the front thigh. One had his harnessed to the breast. Two carried a pair of revolvers. More than one had a rifle also.

O'Hara passed to the back of the store. It was difficult for him to believe that these genial youths, so smiling, casual, and indolent of manner, could be hired gunmen ready to embark on lawless war.

Two men were in the little office shut off from the rest of the store. One of them was Ingram. He called to O'Hara.

"Come in. Meet my partner, Mr. Harvey." To Harvey he said: "Tom, this is the man I was tellin' you about."

Harvey was a short, thickset man with hard, protruding eyes. His face was pallid, his mouth a slit narrowed by thin lips tightly pressed together. A ruthless man, one might guess, but without the character that gave his partner individuality.

"Glameechou," he unlocked his lips to say, all in one gulped word.

If he was glad he did not look it. There was no expression whatever in his chalky eyes.

"Where you from, Mr. O'Hara?" asked Ingram.

The Easterner told him. He answered other questions, put sharply and incisively. Where had he studied law? Whom did he know in Concho? Why had he come here?

O'Hara had taken an instant dislike to Harvey, but he did not feel the same toward his partner. It was odd, too, he reflected later. Evidently it was a matter of personality. This bronzed handsome man, who carried himself with such lithe ease, came none too well recommended. He could snuff out a human life with no regret. Undoubtedly he was unscrupulous, probably a cow thief. But he had the force that goes with a strong character, either good or bad. Masterful he was and always would be. The salient jaw, the resolute searching eyes, the close-shut lips, all certified as much. He would move to his end with direct, unfaltering energy, an egoist to the last hour of his life, and an imperious one.

"How come you to start trouble with Shep Sanderson?" asked Harvey, speaking for the first time since his word of gulped greeting at introduction.

"Did I start trouble with him, Mr. Harvey?" O'Hara replied, a steely note in his voice. "He shot at me from ambush while I was on the public road. Later he assaulted me in a dance hall. Afraid we differ in our points of view."

"I'm not chewin' words but talkin' turkey. Shep's ugly as galvanized sin when he's sore at anyone. Well, he's sore at you."

Ingram flung this aside with a gesture. "Forget about Shep. He'll lay off this young fellow. I'll see to that." He turned abruptly to the lawyer. "How about you, O'Hara? Can you live under yore own hat? Will you stand by yore boss long as there's a button on Jabe's coat? Have you got sand in yore craw?"

O'Hara answered, in the low, gentle voice that was sometimes so deceptive, since it led men to believe that he was meek, "To take your questions in order, Mr. Ingram: I do not talk about my clients' affairs, if that's what you mean. Nor do I sell out to the opposition when I engage to carry on legal business. Only time will tell whether I am too timid to live in Concho."

"You talk like a Boston lawyer," Harvey sneered. "This is the fightin' frontier. We're not lookin' for a fellow to split hairs but to do like we say. Will you go through? That's what we want to know."

"Perhaps you'd better be specific, Mr. Harvey. What do you want me to do?" O'Hara felt the Irish rising in him.

"Listen, O'Hara," said Ingram, looking straight at him. "You look like a smart young man. We can use one like that. But if you hook up with us we'll expect you to be for us first, last, and all the time. You'll work for our friends an' you'll work against our enemies. Do that, and you'll make yore fortune in this country." The cattle man lifted his strong brown hand to stop the lawyer from answering yet. "Wait, O'Hara, till I tell you the line-up. We're startin' a finish fight against Wes Steelman. He's run the San Marcos country long enough. He sure can't come up here into the hills and dictate what's what. It's a showdown. We're callin' his hand. Our friends are his enemies. His friends are our enemies. Everybody that amounts to a tinker's dam will have to choose which side he'll be on."

"Why? Why not be neutral?"

"If you're not for us you're against us."

O'Hara rose from the chair where he was sitting. "I don't accept that conclusion, Mr. Ingram. But let me first reply to your offer. I decline it. I won't be anybody's man and wear a collar round my neck. I'll not engage to support a cause beyond the point where it seems to me just. You want me to be your lawyer and yet tie me hand and foot. I can't do it. No man of spirit could."

"Then you'd better get right out of Concho. You're not wanted here," Ingram said bluntly.

"Why? I'm not in this fight. I've nothing to do with it. I don't intend to have."

"You chuckle-headed fool, you'll be in it an' out of it inside of three days if you stay," Harvey jeered. "Shep

Sanderson will take care of that. All we've got to do is say the word."

"Why should you say it?" asked O'Hara, his eyes steadily on Ingram. "I've done you no harm. I'm not in this fight against you. I'm a stranger here and intend to take no part in it."

Ingram gave a short scornful bark of laughter. "You're one of these fellows that know it all an' can't be told anything. All right. Play yore own hand. Suits me if it does you. But before you walk out of this room listen to me. It's good medicine, what I'm tellin' you. There's not a gather of beeves in this country that either Wes Steelman or I haven't a hand in, not a ton of freight moves that one of us ain't interested in directly or indirectly. If you can read yore title clear to practise law here an' not do business with the one or the other of us you'll sure have to be fed by the ravens. You got to make yore choice if you stay here—him or me, one."

The other partner cut in unpleasantly: "Maybe he's made it, Dave. I reckon he's already tied up with Steelman."

O'Hara looked at Harvey. "I've never even met him," he said with a touch of anger.

"You might of met his agent where you come from. We'll know right soon where you're at, young fellow." The jeering voice was an insult.

The lawyer's jaw set. "I don't have to explain my private business to you, Mr. Harvey. I'm a citizen of a free country."

At which Harvey laughed maliciously. "All right, Mr. Free Citizen, go right on down the road an' see where you head in."

There was something cruel, inhuman, about that laughter. It was without any of the milk of natural kindness in it. Later, remembering it, O'Hara was able better to understand some of the events that followed.

Ingram rose. "All right. 'Nough said. *Adiós,* Mr. O'Hara," he cut in by way of curt dismissal.

O'Hara turned away, not without regret. He had made the only choice possible to him. None the less, he was sorry. The personality of this strong fighting cattle man rather fascinated him. Under other circumstances he would have liked nothing better than to be an ally of David Ingram's.

CHAPTER VI: *The Belted Earl*

O'HARA CAUGHT SIGHT of the Innocent Bystander and stopped to say "Good-morning." Worrall was standing in the road, one foot on the hub of a wagon wheel. He was giving instructions to a mule skinner about to start on a two-hundred-and-fifty mile drive to the railroad.

"Hold on a minute," he called to the lawyer. He finished what he had to say to the teamster and then strolled over toward the Gold Nugget, in front of which O'Hara was waiting. "How's she comin' this glad mornin', stranger?"

"I've just had a little talk with Mr. Ingram and his partner," O'Hara said, smiling.

"Either of 'em say anything that interested you?"

"Both of them."

"Gonna line up with Dave?"

"Think not. By the way, he agrees with you—says there's no place here for an independent lawyer."

"Maybe you'll believe it after a while."

"I'm beginning to think there's something to it. First Miss Steelman, then you, then Mr. Ingram, not to mention his delightful partner Mr. Harvey."

Not a flicker of a smile touched Worrall's long serious face. "Took a shine to Tom, did you?"

"Who wouldn't? He gave me to understand, without exactly saying so, that he intended to sic' Shep Sanderson on me."

"That don't listen good to me. What did Ingram say about that?"

"Said he wouldn't let Sanderson start any more trouble, but that was before I had declined his offer. He may not feel the same about it now."

"Hmp! Well, the road's still open back to Aurora."

O'Hara shook his head. "Too hot and too dusty. Think I'll stay here."

"Don't like the notion of being run out by that scalawag Sanderson?" Worrall asked, with a shrewd sidelong look at him.

"No, I don't."

"Course you could stay here without practising law. There are other lines of business."

Out of the Gold Nugget came a young man. He was a slight boyish fellow in the garb of a cowboy: high-heeled boots, flannel shirt, open waistcoat, wide gray hat, and two six-shooters. His eyes were a very light cold blue, his chin receded, two prominent buck teeth showed. He seemed friendly and amiable, and on the whole was not bad-looking. O'Hara remembered him as one of the young fellows in Ingram's store.

He stopped to grin at Worrall. "How's the temperature up where you live, Shorty?"

The freighter smiled down at him from his six feet plus. "Meet Mr. O'Hara, Bob. Mr. O'Hara, shake hand with Bob Quantrell."

This ceremony concluded, Quantrell remarked that it was right hot for so early in the summer and continued, spurs trailing, on his casual way.

Worrall lowered his voice. "You may like to know that you've just shaken hands with a real killer. Bob Quantrell has bumped off a heap of men in his time."

O'Hara was amazed. "That boy? Why, he can't be more than nineteen or twenty."

"Eighteen last month. He told me so himself. I can name seven or eight he's killed, an' the story is that's not more'n half of those he has got."

"But he looks so mild and inoffensive, so—almost weak."

"Hmp! He's the coolest fightin' machine I know. I saw him on this very street, with two Mexicans an' a white pluggin' at him, keep those six-shooters busy till he'd got two an' the third was wearin' out a quirt on a bronc to get away."

"He doesn't look like a desperate character."

"I didn't say he was," Worrall demurred. "But he sure would make yore friend Shep Sanderson look like a nickel Mex if they got in a rumpus. Say, I got news for you. There's another stranger in town, an' the boys are expectin' some fun. He's a belted earl."

"A what?"

"That's what we call these rich Englishmen that maverick around. This one is a sure enough Britisher, so English he can't say 'hell' with his hands tied."

"What's he doing here?"

"I dunno. He'll go into the cattle an' drop a fortune. They all do. Conditions here ain't what they been used to. He parts his name in the middle. Smith-Beresford is what he calls himself."

At dinner, which of course was in the middle of the day, O'Hara had his first opportunity to see the Englishman. Smith-Beresford was a round ruddy man in riding boots and breeches. He had the clean scrubbed look characteristic of some of his race. It soon became apparent that he was a friendly sort, very enthusiastic about hunting and outdoor life in general.

Bob Quantrell came into the hotel to get dinner and sat down in the only vacant chair at the long table. It happened to be next to Smith-Beresford, and the Englishman at once engaged him in talk. He wanted to know about the hunting and the fishing. Particularly he was interested in the habits of grizzlies.

O'Hara noticed that Quantrell's voice was low and soft. At first he was inclined to be reserved, but evidently the overseas man took his fancy, for he warmed up and ceased to answer in monosyllables. Before dinner was over he and the Englishman had their heads together and were planning a bear hunt. Afterward the two disappeared. Smith-Beresford had taken the young fellow to his room to show him the collection of hunting guns he had brought. Later they came back to the lobby, the Britisher accompanying his guest to the front door.

"We'll have a jolly good hunt, old chap," he said. "I'll depend on you to look after the horses and that sort of thing. I suppose you know a good horse when you see one."

"I think so."

"Then, by Jove, we'll have a rippin' time."

Smith-Beresford came back into the room, where as usual several loafers had gathered. He smiled genially around at them.

"That boy is pretty young," he commented to the world at large. "I suppose he knows his way about—that sort of thing. Eh, what?"

For a moment nobody spoke, then the fat proprietor answered, cautiously but drily: "He's right competent, Bob Quantrell is."

"A nice boy—quiet, gentle, no bounce. Maybe I could use him when I get my ranch started."

Again the short silence before someone said, "Bob's a top hand with cows."

"At his age he probably wouldn't want full wages," Smith-Beresford ruminated aloud.

The fat man looked at him, started to speak, checked himself and said wheezily, "You'll find Bob's quite a he-man, mister."

"Glad to know it. Thought perhaps he was too young to depend on in a bear hunt."

A freckle-faced Texan drawled, again after that odd pause, as though he were weighing his answer, "I been told he's good in a bear fight."

"I'm going to like this country," the Englishman said in a high clipped voice. "By Jove, you know, when I woke up this morning the air was like champagne in my lungs."

"It's sure a right salubrious climate," the fat hotel keeper said noncommittally.

After Smith-Beresford had returned to his room the loungers spoke of him, rather guardedly. O'Hara judged that their remarks were less direct because of his presence.

"What's the belted earl figurin' on doin'? He spoke about a ranch. I'll sell him my place on Buck Creek real reasonable."

"Too late, Jess. He's done made arrangements to take the Widow Cress ranch."

"Oh!" Jess stopped to digest this. "He'll be a neighbour of Wes Steelman."

"So he will."

"Been in correspondence with Wes, he said." This contribution was from Brad Helm, the fat innkeeper, and it was dropped very casually.

Those present apparently did not think it called for comment. The Texan rose, stretched, yawned, remarked that he had not time to swap any more lies, and went on his musical way, dragging spurs jingling.

"Got lots of mazuma," Helm wheezed.

The reference was to the belted earl, of course.

"They all have. Money grows on trees in England. Looks to me like this whole country's gonna be mortgaged to the Rothschilds if someone don't look out," Jess said gloomily.

This started a political argument, somewhat coloured by misinformation and prejudice, during the course of which O'Hara departed. On the street he met Steve Worrall. The owner of the Longhorn Corral wasted no words in greeting.

"Judge Warner come through as expected an' appointed Wes Steelman administrator of the estate of Jerry Hughes. 'Most every man in the room was wearin' an arsenal. Wes had half a dozen gunmen with him an' so did Dave. Wouldn't have surprised me if war had started right there an' then, but I reckon the orders were for none of the boys to make a play. Well, soon now. That's my guess."

Worrall spoke in a low voice, for walls sometimes had ears. Concho was a town divided against itself. Spies and partisans were everywhere. A whisper at times carried to a far cow camp so fast that it seemed as though it had gone on the wings of the wind.

"Isn't there any way of stopping it? Couldn't they compromise?"

"They could, but they won't," Worrall answered. "Miss Barbara, she's worked on Wes consid'rable, but he's stubborn as a government mule." He hesitated before he added: "I reckon she's tried to fix it up with Dave, too, though I hadn't ought to say so, maybe. She was sittin' right beside her dad at the hearin', an' I shouldn't wonder but that was what kept the peace much as anything. We're mighty particular about women out here, not to annoy them any."

"Shep Sanderson and his friends did not seem to me so particular last night."

"Mexican girls don't count. I was referrin' to white women, an' straight ones at that. There's no place in the world where women of that kind are treated better than in the West. An' talkin' about angels, if we can't hear the rustle of their wings. Look who' sashayin' down the road."

O'Hara looked. A party of riders was coming down the dusty street. Those in advance were a grizzled, heavy-set man in his late forties and a young woman whom O'Hara at once recognized as Barbara Steelman.

Miss Steelman spoke to the man beside her and the party drew up beside Worrall and the lawyer. There were seven men in the group, all armed with rifles as well as six-shooters. Most of the revolvers were .44's, for the reason that these carried the same size bullet as the Winchester rifles used.

"This is Mr. O'Hara," the young woman said. "Mr. O'Hara, this is my father. I've been tellin' him about you."

Wesley Steelman's strong face had been tanned to a leathery brown by a thousand summer suns and winter winds. Deep blue eyes looked straight at the man to whom he was being introduced. He wore his clothes carelessly, but wrinkled though they were his coat and trousers fell into folds that seemed to express his individual ruggedness. He had fought his way up from the ranks, asking no man's favour, rising by sheer force of will and brain to the position he held of cattle king of the San Marcos. Looking at him, O'Hara could understand why. He was a man's man, with a frank and friendly manner, probably generous and kindly to those who supported him.

"Glad to have you with us, Mr. O'Hara," he said heartily, and swung from the saddle to shake hands with the lawyer.

36

"My daughter says you think of stayin' here. Hope you decide to do so. We can use some good citizens."

"That's not what I told him," Barbara said, smiling at the young man.

"Fact, just the same. Time this country was gettin' civilized. Mr. O'Hara, lemme make you acquainted with my friends. Shake hands with Jack Phillips an' Texas Jim."

While O'Hara's hand passed from one strong grip to another he became aware that another group of horsemen was approaching. They rode three abreast, in two rows. Ingram was in front, Harvey on his left, and Bob Quantrell on the right and nearest the other group.

As they passed, Quantrell laughed, insolently, gaily. "They're sayin' good-bye to each other," he murmured, just loud enough to be heard. "Well, you never can tell."

CHAPTER VII: *Bob Quantrell Buys Chips*

LYULPH HARCOURT SMITH-BERESFORD came down the street. He was on an English riding saddle and the cow pony to which it was fastened did not like the device. It slewed sideways and advanced like a crab when the Ingram party came close.

"D'you reckon he's been stuck to that postage stamp so he won't come off?" one young fellow drawled.

The cow pony bucked and its rider got off, unexpectedly and hurriedly. He picked himself out of the dust and caught at the bridle. The animal backed away, pricking up its ears.

"Ride him, cowboy," Quantrell called out with a friendly laugh.

The Englishman was sore and dusty but game. He grinned at the young fellow. "By Jove, you know, I can't ride him till I get in the saddle," he said.

He backed his mount against the wall of a building and swung on. The broncho arched its back and went into the air. But Smith-Beresford was ready this time and stuck. Then, again unexpectedly, the buckskin decided to be a model cow pony and behave.

"The brute has its moods, you know," the rider called to Quantrell as he went on his way at a canter.

He stopped fifty yards up the street to join the Steelman party. Already he had met the big cattle man and his daughter.

"Have you been givin' an exhibition?" the young woman asked him, a gleam of mirth in her eyes.

His face turned a deeper pink. "This bally saddle won't do for buckers, Miss Steelman. I see now why you put forty pound of leather on them, and a horn and a deep seat. Think I'll jolly well get one of your back breakers for this fellow."

"Think you'd better," she agreed. "I told you this mornin' there was a reason for everything our cowboys wear, from the bandanna to the high-heeled boots."

"I'm not converted to the boots yet," he said.

"You will be." Then, with a lift of the hand toward the lawyer, she added: "Make you acquainted with Mr. O'Hara, Mr. Smith-Beresford."

The two men shook hands.

"I'm another tenderfoot," O'Hara explained.

Steelman spoke: "We've got to be gettin' along home. Then we'll expect you out to-morrow mornin', Mr. Smith-Beresford. Better bring Mr. O'Hara with you. We'll show you some good huntin' and fishin'."

"Afraid I'd be some trouble, Mr. Steelman," O'Hara said, much desiring to accept the invitation.

"Not any in the world," the cattle man answered carelessly. "We don't ask you if we don't want you, Mr. O'Hara."

"Then I'll certainly come."

After the Steelman party had ridden away the Englishman dismounted and tied his horse to a hitch rack.

"I say. A deuced pretty girl that Miss Steelman. Eh, what?"

O'Hara agreed. "I'll make it unanimous."

"Jolly, too. Hear her rag me about my spill? Silly business, that fall."

"I expect they all get one now and then."

"I say, Mr. O'Hara, feel like a B. and S.?"

O'Hara did not, but he walked into the nearest saloon with the other tenderfoot. They sat down at a small table and the Easterner took a small glass of beer.

There was a very likable quality to the Englishman. He was enthusiastic and friendly and willing to learn. It occurred to O'Hara that Smith-Beresford would make friends, get along, and probably do well in the country.

They chatted for a few minutes. At first they were alone except for the bartender, but presently three or four men came in. One of them was young Bob Quantrell, another Shep Sanderson. From the table where he was sitting in a far corner of the room O'Hara watched the newcomers. It was apparent to him that the keen eyes of Quantrell had recognized both himself and the Englishman in the first sweeping glance, and he was equally sure that Sanderson had not even looked in their direction.

The Ingram men were standing at the bar, ready to drink. Sanderson became aware that there were two other men in the saloon. Scarcely looking in their direction, he waved them forward.

"On me. Everybody drink." There was arrogance in the invitation, which was almost a command.

The two men at the table did not move.

Sanderson swung his head. "Hear me? Come an' drink."

Then he recognized first O'Hara, and afterward the Englishman. His hand slid slowly toward the butt of his .44 and he moved a step or two toward the sitting men.

"So it's you, eh?" His shallow cruel eyes rested on O'Hara. They narrowed, taking on a curious glitter. "Well, you ain't teacher's pet any longer, young fellow, see, an' you're my meat. Me talkin'—Shep Sanderson. Understand?"

Smith-Beresford did not, at least. He rose to his feet. "See here, my man, you've been drinking. You mustn't come in and interrupt gentlemen——"

"What!" roared the gunman. "Who in hot Mexico are you to tell me what I must an' mustn't do? Call yoreself a belted earl, do you? Listen, fellow! I saw you pow-wowin' with old man Steelman a while ago. I'm gonna make it two right now. Both of you cash in, you an' the other tenderfoot, too, onless you talk me outa the notion, an' I'll bet my boots you ain't got a chance in the world to do it."

Still the Englishman failed to realize the perilous position in which he and O'Hara stood. He would not believe that in a fraction of a second the barrel of the revolver might be thrown down on him and a finger crooked that would send death roaring at him. This fellow Sanderson was a drunken bully and he did not propose to put up with it.

The plump little man strutted forward, his face flushed with annoyance. "See here, my man, if you think you can come in here and bully me——"

O'Hara interrupted, to cry out sharply, "He's not armed." At the same time he stepped forward and joined Smith-Beresford in front of the furious bad man. Once more he felt that curious singing of excited blood through his veins. He felt sure that Sanderson was working himself into a mad rage that would justify cold-blooded murder. The nearness of the

39

peril stirred every faculty in him to alertness. "Neither he nor I. Both of us unarmed."

His voice was a warning rather than an appeal. It served notice on the killer that to slay now would be outside the code, that even his own companions would disapprove and perhaps not protect him from Steelman's vengeance.

Sanderson sputtered. "You're packin' a gun somewheres an' you're scared to draw it. You're a liar when you claim——"

The man's .44 jerked up swiftly, for Smith-Beresford had done an amazing thing. The little man had thrust his head forward, so that now his eyes were not six inches from the end of the barrel.

"Shoot an' be hanged, you coward. You haven't the pluck to fire."

O'Hara thought that for one dreadful moment his heart had stopped pumping. To plunge forward, to make the least move, would be the signal for Sanderson to shoot. He could only wait helplessly in the heavy silence while the drama worked itself out.

It seemed forever before Sanderson's slow mind made its choice. He spoke hoarsely, savagely, "Go an' get heeled, both of you, an' when you see me, come a-shootin', fellows."

Quantrell's boyish laugh rang out and broke the tension. "He sure went for you all spraddled out, Shep, like he thought you was a big wind pudding. Another minute an' I reckon he would have crawled yore big frame the way his friend did last night. You don't have any luck with the pilgrims you pick to run on, Shep. I'll be doggoned if they don't make you look so bad yore ears flop."

Sanderson ignored his derision. "Like I said, get yore hoglegs, fellows. I'll shoot on sight from now on," he threatened.

"That would certainly be duck soup for you, Shep, wouldn't it?" young Quantrell said contemptuously. "Like takin' pennies from a blind greaser. Can't either of 'em shoot for sour apples, I reckon." He turned his smile on Smith-Beresford and mocked his accent and manner. "Eh, what? By Jove, you know!"

"I'm not so bally bad with a rifle," the Englishman said.

"Helpless as a pair of kids with a six-shooter," the lad announced. "Well, I'm buyin' chips, Shep. This gent has got sand in his crew, an' he's my friend. Lay off him."

"Since when has he been yore friend, Bob, seeing as he's Wes Steelman's friend, too?" the big man jeered.

"Don't drop questions like that around me, Shep," Quantrell warned him with a voice turned suddenly chilly. 'They're liable to explode an' hurt you."

"This other tenderfoot yore friend, too?" Sanderson asked sulkily.

The boy looked at O'Hara. He had watched this episode with wary, cool detachment, and he had seen the lawyer step forward to join his companion in front of the furious bad man. Tenderfoot he undoubtedly was, but like the other he had shown courage of a high order.

"Lay off him, too, Shep, an' see you do or I'll give you a game. I'm yore loadin' any jump in the road." Quantrell laid down the law to the other killer carelessly, almost casually, with the supreme confidence of one who knows himself chief.

"This O'Hara fellow has done me dirt," Sanderson complained bitterly. "He jumped me last night when I wasn't lookin', an'——"

"Yes, I heard about that," the boy grinned. "They sure keep busy showin' you up."

O'Hara's pride was touched. He did not want to hide behind an eighteen-year-old boy. "I don't know anything about a gun, but if you'll give me three weeks I'll get ready for this man," he said.

The young desperado's eyes lit. "Good enough, Shep. Lay off three weeks, an' then hop to it if you like. He'll give you a game his own self. Hooray!"

"Him! That pilgrim! Gimme a game—me, Shep Sanderson! Fool talk. That's all it is." The bad man snorted contemptuously.

"If it's fool talk maybe he's gauging it to the capacity of yore understandin', Shep. Sounds like fool talk to you. But is it? Those who saw him swarmin' over you last night, when you was hollerin' for someone to take him off, claim he looked like he could whip a stack of bobtailed wildcats."

"Jumped me when I wasn't lookin', I tell you," growled Shep.

"I heard you the first time, Shep. Well, the boys say he was certainly sailin'. I'd admire to see another performance."

"You'll see it. Soon's the bridle is off," Sanderson boasted.

"Which will be three weeks from to-day. Send me a front-seat ticket, Shep." Quantrell's voice drawled on insolently. "Did you say you had to light a shuck outa here? Well, so long, Shep. We mustn't keep you from any pressin' engagement that's shoutin' for you. *Adiós, compadre.*"

Sanderson looked venomously at the slender, jaunty boy.

41

He was being invited to walk out of the saloon and he bitterly resented it. It floated across his mind that it might be wise to jerk out his .44 and shoot down this impudent young devil who was taunting him and at the same time challenging him to call for a showdown. But Quantrell was like chain lightning on the trigger and amazingly accurate. That was why he still survived to stand there grinning after a dozen men had tried to down him.

"I ain't in any hurry to go," Shep snarled, his big body moving for the first step toward the door.

"My mistake," murmured the young killer. "Thought you were, Shep. I don't know how I got that notion. Oh, you're leavin' us, are you? Gonna scatter yore smiles somewheres else. See you later, Old Top, as our friend the belted earl says."

Sanderson slouched out.

The boy turned to O'Hara. "You've done wished on yoreself a man-size job. If you asked me personal I'd say you were gonna camp with Old Man Trouble."

"How long will it take me to learn to shoot?" O'Hara asked.

"If you practise real constant you'd ought to be a medium good shot in maybe twenty years. That is, if ever. Some fellows jest naturally never could be."

"But you're not that old, and they say——"

"I've got a gift thataway," Quantrell admitted modestly.

Smith-Beresford cut into the conversation: "Will you tell me, laddie, how you cut the crest of that big turkey cock? He's big enough to eat you in two mouthfuls."

"I've heard it said the Lord made us in many sizes but Colonel Colt made us all equal," the youngster replied. "Only some of us are more equal than others, you might say."

"If this Sanderson is just a bully who won't fight——"

"Don't make any mistake about that, sir. He'll fight," Quantrell said carelessly.

The bartender leaned forward and spoke to Smith-Beresford. "He's killed two-three men."

"But bless my soul, if he's so dangerous, why did he take all that talk from you, my lad?" the Englishman asked, much perplexed. "After all, you know, you're only a boy."

The man behind the bar coughed warningly. This was dangerous ground. But Quantrell only laughed.

"Oh, I reckon he didn't have his fightin' clothes on today," he said.

"What have his clothes got to do with it? I'm dashed if I understand you."

O'Hara laughed. "That's only an expression, Mr. Smith-Beresford. What Mr. Quantrell could tell you if he were not too modest is that Sanderson does not want to fight with him."

The plump Englishman took in the slight boyish figure, the receding chin, the amiable face of Quantrell. He could find no answer here. "I chuck it. Too deep for me," he admitted.

"One thing isn't too deep for us," O'Hara said. "The fellow would probably have killed us both if it hadn't been for Mr. Quantrell's interference. We both owe him our lives."

The young desperado shrugged this aside, a little annoyed, a good deal embarrassed. "Babes in the wood, both of you. An' anyhow, I happened to want to ride Shep some. He's too biggity. Let's drink."

This ceremony concluded, the lad sauntered out of the place. Then everybody began to speak to the Englishman at once. He learned that eighteen-year-old Bob Quantrell was the most notorious killer in the territory.

Chapter VIII: *The Tenderfoot Takes Lessons*

I'LL TELL YOU lads something," the bartender said confidentially, leaning forward on his forearms. "You won't ever be nearer crossin' the divide than you was right here ten minutes ago. I got no comments to make. Me, I stay healthy by mindin' my own business. But if I was you two pilgrims I'd drift outa the landscape kinda inconspicuous."

"But, my dear fellow, we're not looking for trouble with this bully," the Englishman explained. "We've done him no harm. Why should he bother us?"

The three of them were alone in the room. With a chamois rag the bartender polished the woodwork in front of him. "A nod is as good as a wink to a blind horse. I ain't sayin' another word." He began to hum "Good-bye, my lover, good-bye."

The two tenderfeet walked out of the place together.

"Sanderson's vanity has been affronted," O'Hara offered by way of explanation. "He's been made to sing small. Last night his own crowd laughed at him when he was calling to them to haul me off. He'll never rest till he has got even, and the only way he knows how to do that is to kill me."

43

"But bless my soul, isn't this a civilized community? Is there no law here? A chap can't go around murdering, you know. Why, deuce take it, the thing's not reasonable."

"Did Sanderson impress you as a reasonable person?" O'Hara asked drily.

"It's too much for me," the Englishman said, shaking his head. "That little chap now. By Jove, I can't believe he's a wholesale killer. At home he would be in school yet."

"You heard him say that Colt had made all men equal. His size doesn't matter. He's a dead shot, sure and swift. So I'm told. Which reminds me that I'd better use to advantage the three weeks of grace given me. Much of my time is going to be spent with Colonel Colt instead of with Blackstone. Let's step in here and buy some ammunition."

They had stopped at Steelman & McCarthy's store. In front of the adobe building sleepy-eyed horses drooped at the hitch rack. The two men passed inside.

From the rear of the store a small man beckoned to them. He had the hard, expressionless face of a gambler.

"Have a drink, gents," he invited.

The Englishman introduced him to O'Hara as McCarthy, one of the proprietors. In those days it was the custom to treat customers in the rear of the building. It was commonly done in the stores of Durango, Trinidad, Albuquerque, and other towns of the Southwest. For the Mexicans, tobacco in bulk was left in an empty cigar box. They could help themselves to "the makings."

They drank to Smith-Beresford's success in his new business venture. After which the two tenderfeet bought some shells, saddled their horses, and rode out of town to a wooded draw where they used up fifty rounds of ammunition each.

As soon as breakfast was over next morning they spent more time and powder practising. This time Steve Worrall went with them. He watched them for a few minutes before he ventured some suggestions.

"You've got the wrong idea," he told them. "When Shep gets in front of you fannin' smoke you'll have no time to draw a bead on him. With that bird it won't be any 'Gentlemen-are-you-ready?' stuff. No, sirree! He'll whang right away at you. It'll be strictly business, an' hurry-up business at that. Bob Quantrell, f'r instance, never takes aim. He looks at what he's shootin' at an' he hits it. I don't claim to be any expert, but if you'll watch me you can get the notion."

The lank freighter dragged a revolver from its scabbard and fired instantly from the hip. Shot after shot crashed out,

44

so closely spaced that the noise of the firing seemed almost to merge into one continuous crash rather than five distinct explosions. He had fired at a fir tree about fifteen yards distant. Three of the bullets had struck the trunk five feet or so from the ground.

"Don't see how you do it," O'Hara said. "You didn't take aim at all."

"That's not first-class shootin' by a jugful," Worrall answered. "If you'll notice I clean missed twice. The other three bullets are about a foot apart from each other. Say I'd been firing at some gent busy pumpin' lead my way. I'd of hit him once, or twice at most. I know a dozen fellows can beat that. Sanderson is one. Ingram is another. An' of course Bob Quantrell. But you get the point, which is that you've sure enough got to jump. A fellow doesn't often have to shoot, but when he does you may grab it from me that an *hombre* has got to be real sudden. Now you lads try again. It don't matter where yore bullets go. Let's see you empty a six-shooter in a second an' a half."

Neither of them could do it. The trigger finger simply refused to work fast enough.

"You're gettin' the hang of it," Worrall told them. "Keep on the job. This is right important business for you if you're gonna stay here an' pick enemies like Shep. It don't matter how wild yore shots went an' that you most killed an innocent bull. They'll steady down after a while. You're tryin' for speed now."

The three jogged back to town. At the hotel O'Hara and the Englishman packed their saddlebags. They rode with rifles strapped beside them. It was still a wild country. Occasionally Apaches left the reservation and went raiding. Others as bad as Indians had come in recently. But the real reason they carried rifles was that they expected to go hunting while at the ranch.

They struck Dead Horse Creek and turned up it, following a wagon road that meandered back and forth with the winding of the stream. For several miles it led by a steady ascent into the hills, then struck the rim of a park and plunged down. The park was two or three miles across, in some places wooded and in others open grazing ground. Here and there the riders could see bunches of cattle, one near enough so that they could make out the Hashknife brand.

The ranch houses lay below them, a cluster of a dozen buildings set back fifty yards from the stream. Two or three men were in a corral working a dozen calves that blatted

45

protest. At the blacksmith shop, which was outdoors under a tree, a young fellow was shoeing a horse.

The main house was a thick-walled Spanish house built of adobe bricks. A young woman was standing on the porch. She called a greeting to them. Smith-Beresford swung to the ground and went forward with the peculiar strut that characterized his walk.

"Well, we're here, Miss Steelman," he beamed. "All ready for the fatted calf, don't you know?"

"Are you the prodigal son—or Mr. O'Hara?" she asked.

"*Touché,*" he laughed. "The answer is that we're both prodigal in our admiration of Miss Steelman."

She glanced at O'Hara hanging shyly in the background. "Hadn't you better speak for yoreself only?" she suggested. "Mr. O'Hara doesn't seem to indorse that enthusiastically."

O'Hara blushed. He had never paid a compliment to a woman in his life. His gaze met her dark, long-lashed eyes then fled the meeting.

"I'm willing to leave him out of it," the Englishman amended. "Fact is, I can admire enough for two."

Beneath the tan in the girl's cheeks the colour moved. This young man's compliments were a little too pointed. She called to a red-headed cowboy who was passing:

"Will you take these gentlemen to the lower cabin, Red, and see they're made comfortable?" To her guests she added: "Supper at six if Dad doesn't see you before then. He's out somewhere just now with Jack Phillips, I think. Please make yoreselves at home."

To O'Hara, used to the small fenced farms of the East, the ranch was like some feudal demesne rather than a private home. At supper at least half a dozen guests put their feet under the table. One was a peddler passing through the country. Two were neighbouring ranchmen. The rest were cowboys riding the grubline. O'Hara was to discover later that the family never sat down without guests. Hospitality was the law of the land. Anyone not hostile to the Steelman interests was welcome to bed and board. To have offered to pay would have been an insult. A rider caught by night turned in as naturally as to a hotel.

The suggestion of feudal days was not only in the lavishness of the entertainment and the number of retainers but in the relation of the latter to their chief. They were less hired men than members of his clan. The Hashknife was their ranch as well as his, at least in the loyalty they manifested toward it. For that brand they rode out blizzards, endured

46

fatigue, went hungry. Some of them, no doubt, had rustled calves for it, very likely without the owner's knowledge. At his word they were prepared to go to private war without asking any questions as to the justice of it. The Ingram outfit was enemy to them one and all, but if any rider left the employment of Steelman the enmity automatically ceased.

The days that followed were pleasant ones to both the tenderfeet enjoying the hospitality of the ranch. The life they led was a stimulating outdoor one. With the Hashknife cowboys they rode the range, chasing wild longhorns through the fragrant chaparral thickets. They assisted at branding and cutting-out. They tried their hands at night-herding and trail-driving. When they so desired they hunted or fished the hill streams for trout. The dry lifeless desert had a charm for them no less than the hilltops among the pines fresh with dawn.

And every day, no matter what else they did, the two guests found time to practise with their Colts.

"It's a sure enough shame that Shep has got on the prod just because you jammed yore grappling irons into him that night at the *baile*," young Curt Steelman said, watching them fire industriously at a mark. "This community would be a heap better off without that bird. He's been fed on too much raw meat to suit me. It wouldn't hurt my feelin's none if he bucked out, croaked, cashed in, handed his checks to St. Peter, or otherwise became defunct. Not that I'm hankerin' after the job of ridin' herd on him, y' understand."

"It's been wished on me, this quarrel," O'Hara said lightly. "If you know anyone who would like to take it over——"

"I don't. But there's one thing. Threatened folks live long, they say."

It cannot be said that O'Hara was easy in his mind. He had the temperament which found exhilaration in immediate danger, but the thought of peril deferred brought disturbing moments. Though he was learning how to use a six-shooter, there was no use deceiving himself into the error of thinking he stood an even chance with Sanderson. Moreover, it was likely enough that the man would shoot him down from ambush as he had tried to do once before. The knowledge that one is marked for death in the mind of a callous killer makes for depression.

Also, his personal feud with Sanderson began to merge itself in the general one between the houses of Steelman

47

and Ingram. He had promised himself not to become a partisan, but he was one already in feeling. There was still none of the savage bitterness in his heart that animated the principals and those close to them. But the Steelmans had thrown wide open to him the door of their home. He had partaken of their generous hospitality. Why deny to himself that he wished them well in the conflict with Ingram and his supporters?

CHAPTER IX: *A Rendezvous*

"ME, IF I WAS LOOKIN'" for a nice plump blacktail I'd kinda drift up the creek an' across back of the Hughes place," Texas Jim suggested to the Englishman. "Two-three times I've seen some mule deer up thataway. Course I wouldn't go anywhere near the ranch, or some of Ingram's anxious boys might shoot you-all up. Keep well up in the hills, I'd say."

Smith-Beresford was watching Barbara Steelman. She was saddling her pony, though a wrangler was at hand doing nothing. A minute before she had roped the animal. That was like her. She had a self-reliant, independent streak in her. Usually she preferred to do her own catching and cinching. In this case the Britisher had offered to saddle for her and also to join her on the ride, and she had contrived without hurting his feelings to reject both proffers.

The Englishman joined O'Hara, who had just come out of their bunkhouse. "If you're ready, old chap, we'll be off," he called.

O'Hara was ready. Ten minutes later they took the trail up the creek. The wagon road ended at the ranch, but a zigzag path was well defined along the stream. They followed it out of the park to the rugged hills beyond. The country became rougher, the creek more rapid, the ascent more precipitous.

The hunters after a time struck across country to the west, dropping down one steep only to climb another.

"A bit tilted. Eh, what?"

O'Hara nodded. The other's remark needed no confirmation in words. "Must be above the Hughes place now," he said.

Toward noon they separated, Smith-Beresford working up toward the divide and his companion taking the shoulder of a hill that presently brought him above a wooded draw.

O'Hara dismounted and tied his horse. Rifle in hand, he crept forward through the brush. For he had heard the sound of breaking twigs. There was the chance of finding a deer feeding in the hill pocket below.

What he saw was even more surprising: two saddled horses grazing among the pines. Voices drifted to him from just below. He was on a bluff and he moved cautiously to the edge of it and looked down. A woman was talking. He could not at first see her face, but the figure was slender and graceful, the voice young and vibrant, just now passionately reproachful.

"I don't," she cried. "I don't. I don't. How could I when you're so—so hateful?"

"I'm hateful, am I? But you love me just the same." A man laughed, slowly, contentedly, as though he relished the fact.

"That's what you'd like—to make me love you anyhow," she went on resentfully. "It has to be all take an' no give with you, hasn't it? I'm just to be another triumph for you over my father. You want to take even his own daughter from him so as to gloat over him. Sometimes I hate you for being the kind of man you are."

The man looked down at her, his eyes close to hers. "An' sometimes you're wild about me for being like I am. Don't pull on yore picket pin, Barbara. Be reasonable. A man has got to play the hand that's dealt him. I'm not gonna lie down to Wes Steelman because he's yore dad. You know better than to ask it. But you're like a wild, high-steppin', unbroken colt that thinks it can have its own way. Now listen. It'll be like this when we're married. You'll be Dave Ingram's wife. I won't be Barbara Steelman's husband. I'm no stray cat for you to drag home."

"What do you mean, you won't be my husband?"

"I mean folks won't refer to me as Barbara Steelman's husband. I stand on my own feet. What kind of a man would I be if I knuckled down to yore dad because you asked me to quit an' throw down all my friends? You'd despise me for it."

"I don't ask that," she cried. "All I want is for you to let him see that you're ready to compromise."

"No," he answered harshly. "Let him come to me if he feels thataway."

"He won't. You know he won't." She flung out a hand in a little despairing gesture. "Why are men so—so obstinate and selfish? If you cared for me you'd do a little thing like

49

that for me. Any woman would do it for the man she loved."

"That's a woman's nature, to give way an' to be forgiving."

"And I suppose a man's nature is to bull through with any meanness he wants to. It's all right because he's a man. This poor fellow Munz. He gets in yore way an' you kill him."

"I killed him because he was a yellow dog and a traitor in Wes Steelman's pay. That's why I killed him," he said sternly.

Her eyes flashed. "That's not true. I don't believe it. If you're tellin' me Dad did anything underhanded——"

"Stop this foolishness, girl," he cut in harshly. "Leave my business lay. I'll run it. Stick to this one thing an' chew on it, that I'm to be yore man an' you're to be my mate. The Bible says a woman is to leave her father an' her mother an' her kin and cleave to her husband."

"You're not my husband. You never will be if you feel thataway. I wouldn't marry you if—if you were the last man on earth," she flung passionately at him.

"No sense in sayin' that." He caught her wrists in his strong fingers. "What has drawn us together in spite of hell an' high water? Why do you come to meet me, though you always fight an' quarrel against me because I'm like I am? Why do you think about me all the time you're not with me?"

"I don't," she denied. "I come to see you because I keep hopin' you'll patch up this dreadful trouble with Dad before it's too late."

"You're foolin' yourself, girl. You come because I'm the man you want for yore mate, because you get hungry to see me."

"No such thing," she flamed. "I s'pose you think you're so wonderful that any woman——"

He snatched her into his arms and kissed her, crushing her body to his. To O'Hara it seemed that the girl lay there a moment relaxed, drinking in his savage kiss, before she pushed him from her with all the energy of her strong arms. She flung one flaming look at him, then turned and ran toward the horses.

Ingram did not pursue her. He stood in his tracks, laughing triumphantly. "Wipe that out if you can," he called to her.

Barbara Steelman did not answer. She pulled the slip knot of her horse's bridle rein and climbed to the saddle. Swinging the animal around, she put it at the steep rocky ascent which led circuitously to the top of the bluff.

O'Hara woke up to action. Presently, emerging from the draw, she would reach the clump of pines where he had tied his horse. He was caught. He could not get away without being discovered. Perhaps he could deceive her into thinking that he had not known of her presence.

Swiftly he ran for the pines. Just before he reached his horse he could see her head and shoulders riding into view. With fingers all thumbs he uncinched and dragged the saddle from the cow pony's back. He did not look around, but made himself very busy examining a galled spot on the animal's back.

A stifled little cry made him turn. Barbara had apparently come almost upon him before becoming aware of him. She had drawn up her mount instinctively and was looking at him. That she had been weeping was so plain that he thought it better not to pretend to ignore it.

"What is it, Miss Steelman? Can I do anything for you?" he stammered.

"Where did you come from? Where have you been?" she demanded.

"We've been hunting. I left Mr. Smith-Beresford to see if there was a mule deer in the hollow maybe."

"And what did you see there?"

"I—I stopped to—to look at my horse's back," he said, turning a fiery red.

"You're a poor liar," she told him bluntly. "You saw us down there in the head of the hollow, Dave Ingram an' I."

He thought it characteristic of her that she flung the admission at him without attempting concealment. The lift of her head was a challenge, but even her pride could not keep the blood from flaming to her cheeks at the memory of what had taken place in the draw.

"I didn't mean to—to watch you," he stammered, then grew more embarrassed because his lame explanation was so badly worded that it implied there had been something to watch.

"Now you know what kind of a girl I am," she said bitterly, "that I rode nine miles to throw myself at the head of my father's enemy."

He was acutely distressed at her proud shame. Desperately he took the bit between his teeth and trod down his shyness.

"Yes, Miss Barbara, I know what kind of a girl you are, how bravely you've tried to keep peace between your father and Ingram. I—I honour you for everything I heard and saw."

Amazed, she looked at him, the stains of the tears still on her brown cheeks.

"You don't think I came because—because I had to see Dave Ingram, because I couldn't live without seeing him?" she demanded.

"No, I don't think that."

"Then you're a fool, for that's exactly why I came," Barbara blurted out in self-abasement.

He mumbled something inarticulate and turned to saddle his horse. She waited for him and they rode side by side along the hill shoulder. For a time neither of them spoke.

"I've met him alone seven times now," she said at last, her eyes full in his.

O'Hara was not sure whether she meant it as a confession or a defiance. He answered it as neither.

"Do you think it safe?" he asked gently.

"Safe! In what way?" she cried, ready for defense.

"Wouldn't it start trouble if your father found out?"

"Oh! That way. Yes. Right away. But he's not likely to hear—unless you think it yore duty to tell him."

The man winced. His look reproached her.

Impulsively her hand went out to him. "I'm sorry. But you're right. I'll not go again. I kept hoping that I could get him—Dave Ingram, I mean—to fix things up with Dad. But he won't. I see that now."

"Isn't there any way to stop this feud before it goes farther? Couldn't they meet to talk it over and come to a settlement?"

She shook her head hopelessly. "No way, I'm afraid. It's gone too far. But it's dreadful to admit I can do nothing."

"It wouldn't help if—if you married Mr. Ingram?"

No. The only way I could marry him would be to run away with him. Then my father would hate him ten times as much." Barbara lifted her hand from the saddle horn and let it fall again in a gesture of bitter despair. "I'm only a woman. What I want doesn't count. If Dave Ingram married me he'd brush me aside an' go right on with the feud."

"You—like him—very much?"

Her voice, in answer, held a furious note of feminine ferocity. "Sometimes I think I hate him."

Chapter X: *A Waddy on the Dodge*

DURING HIS FIRST WEEK at the ranch Smith-Beresford had several long private talks with Wes Steelman. After the last of these O'Hara was invited into conference.

The ranchman drew a cigar from his waistcoat pocket and offered it to the young man.

"Take a chair, O'Hara. Make yoreself comfortable. You've been with us now a week. What d'you think of ranch life?"

"Never enjoyed myself as much in my life before. It was good of you to ask me out."

Steelman waved that aside. "Question is, would you like to go into it as a business? You've got a little money, I understand. Here's the proposition. We've bought the Widow Cress place, our friend here an' I. Would you like to go in with us? I'll be a silent pardner. If you throw in with us I'll turn Jack Phillips over to you for a foreman. Jack knows cows. He's a good man every way. You'd ought to do well, though of course it's a gamble. I'm not givin' you any guarantee. I'll be riskin' my money along with you boys."

"You've got me interested," O'Hara admitted.

"Then I'll get down to cases." Steelman drew up to a table and gave facts and figures as to the cost of the land and the cattle with which to stock the range. Briefly and clearly he explained the situation. "If you throw in on the proposition it will be on the ground floor, O'Hara. No promoter's stock for me or Smith-Beresford."

O'Hara smiled. "I know what my answer is going to be, but I don't want to say 'Yes' until I pretend to myself that I've thought it all over carefully. Will you give me an hour or two to digest your offer?"

"Take yore time, boy," the brown cattle man told him.

"I've spent several years preparing to be a lawyer. If I go in with you on the ranch it must be understood that I'm to have the right to continue with my legal work. I may later want to set up an office at Concho."

"Suits me," acceded Steelman. "I can sometimes use a bright young lawyer in my business."

"And above all I'm a law-abiding citizen. I don't intend to get into this trouble with Ingram and his friends."

The ranchman's blue eyes crinkled to a smile. "That why you spend an hour a day practisin' with yore six-gun, because you're so crazy for peace you'll fight for it if you have to?"

"I'm not going to let Sanderson murder me if I can help it," O'Hara flung back.

"You're all right, boy. But don't make any mistake about this thing. You're in wrong with Ingram right now. If you stay in this country the only question is whether you play a lone hand an' get bumped off or throw in with us an' get a run for yore money."

"I'm not ready to accept that view of it. I've done Ingram no harm."

"Been livin' here a week, haven't you? Talkin' about going into pardnership with me, aren't you? Garrett, don't fool yoreself. They've got you labelled right now, an' you can't talk 'em out of it."

Within a week O'Hara had convincing proof that this was true. He was thrust into an adventure so grim and deadly that even to this day old-timers along the river and up the creeks in the hills tell the story of it when they grow garrulous with each other about early days.

The young lawyer drew up the papers of partnership and they were signed by the three parties to it. O'Hara and Smith-Beresford had their belongings moved from town to the log cabin vacated by the Widow Cress. Steelman shifted a bunch of cows to the range contiguous to Three Springs Creek and the two tenderfeet busied themselves helping their cowboys burn on the Circle S O brand.

A young fellow drifted up the creek one day looking for a job. He reached the round-up ground at supper time and was invited by Jack Phillips to fall off and rest. The cowboys, dust caked on their unshaven faces, squatted tailor fashion on the ground, a loaded tin plate and a steaming tin cup in front of each. Above a fire of juniper and piñon, the pungent smoke of which drifted toward an arrowweed thicket bordering the camp, the cook stooped and fished out strips of steak from a pot of boiling lard.

"Anything doing down Concho way?" Phillips asked casually of the visiting cowboy.

The lad hesitated, then spoke noncommittally. "There was a killin' last night. Fellow called Fitch shot Two-Ace Burke."

"Not Tom Fitch," the foreman said quickly.

"Yep."

"He's one of the waddies at our lower ranch," Phillips explained to O'Hara before he asked the cowboy what the trouble was.

"Some says one thing, some another. They had a rookus at the Gold Nugget an' bawled each other out. Friends inter-

54

fered. Burke was shot on the way home at the corner of the Longhorn Corral."

"Shot from ambush, you mean?"

"So they claim. Fitch was seen runnin' from the spot an was recognized. He forked a bronc an' lit outa town. That's what I hear. Can't prove it by me. This steak is sure good. Shove that plateful north by east, Shorty."

"Comin' up," Shorty answered. "Well, sir, I know Tom an' I don't believe it, that he lay in the brush waitin' for Two-Ace, I mean. That story sounds fishy to me. I'll bet Two-Ace got a show for his white alley."

"Y'betcha!" agreed Texas Jim. "Ingram's crowd has done fixed a story up like they always do."

"Much talk buzzin' around town since the shootin'?" Phillips asked.

The cowboy's eyes met those of the foreman. "Why, I slept late this mornin', Jack, havin' had consid'rable of a bun on, an' I left Concho almost right away, as you might say."

O'Hara saw the two in whispered talk an hour later. They appeared to be examining the tapaderos of a saddle. Phillips took occasion to report the result of this conversation to O'Hara and Smith-Beresford next morning.

"Hell will start poppin', looks like. Banks, the sheriff, is swearin' in a big posse to run down Tom Fitch. If they catch him he'll never reach Concho alive, not with the posse Banks is sendin' out. Ingram warriors, the whole caboodle. I'm sendin' word over to the Old Man by Shorty. I dunno as there's anything he can do about it, but I want him to know what's goin' on."

"Surely Sheriff Banks won't go out with a posse and let his men murder a prisoner," O'Hara said.

"Don't fool yoreself. Banks won't be in that posse himself. It will be made up of horse thieves like Shep Sanderson an' Bob Quantrell an' Hank Doty an' Billy Deever an' the Texas Kid. They'll be paid gunmen, all of 'em, an' Tom will last about as long as a snowball in Yuma on July fourth. That is, *if* they catch him. Me, if I was that lad, I'd do one of two things: make a bee line for Mexico or for Old Man Steelman. The Old Man might hide him out."

After breakfast the two partners left their riders and returned to the cabin which was their ranch headquarters. During the day another drive of cattle from the lower Hashknife ranch was expected to arrive, and they wanted to be at home to receive the herd.

As they rode up to the corral the two young men noticed a strange horse tied to the fence.

"Someone here already," O'Hara said.

"Don't see him. Must be in the house," his partner answered.

It was the custom of the country that if nobody was at home any rider who passed that way might cook himself a meal in the cabins used by the cowboys in temporary sleeping quarters on the range. By an extension of this right some cowboy might have made himself comfortable at the home ranch house. They could see smoke rising from the chimney.

The partners were talking together as they passed the window of the house and turned in at the front door. Abruptly they stopped on the threshold.

A man stood in the room, revolver in hand. The weapon covered them.

"Far enough," the man snarled. "Stop right where you're at."

He was a young man, almost a boy, but for the moment at least the look on his face was almost wolfish. His body was poised and crouched, knees bent, head thrust forward.

"Who are you?" he demanded.

Probably O'Hara did not think of the maxim: When in doubt tell the truth. He told it instinctively. "My name is O'Hara. This gentleman is Mr. Smith-Beresford. We've bought this place."

The point of the revolver dropped toward the floor. "You're the tenderfoots I been hearin' about. Stayin' with Old Man Steelman, wasn't you?"

"Yes. Till a week ago. What's the matter?"

"Sorry. I had to cover you, gents. Couldn't take a chance. My name's Tom Fitch, though that don't mean a thing to you."

"We've heard that you killed Two-Ace Burke yesterday."

"Heard that, have you? What's the story they're tellin'?"

"Put that gun away," ordered the Englishman sharply. "We don't care to talk with you when you've got a weapon in your hand."

The cowboy shoved the six-shooter back into its holster. "I wasn't drawin' on you gents," he explained apologetically. "How could I know but what it was some of Dave Ingram's killers?"

"The story we heard is that you had a quarrel with this Burke and later killed him from ambush," O'Hara said, looking straight at the man.

"I knew doggoned well they'd tell it thataway," Fitch broke out vehemently. "Nothin' like that. I don't claim I hadn't been drinkin'. I had. So when Two-Ace began ridin' me because I was a Hashknife waddy I come right back at him. Well, one thing led to another, an' I knocked him cold with my fist, me havin' given up my six-shooter at the bar. He tried to gun me from where he lay, but some of the boys stopped him. I was stayin' at old Manuel Chavez's house, an' on the way there I had to pass the Longhorn Corral. It was dark as the inside of Jonah's whale. That's howcome he to miss me, I reckon, for he was close as that window. I could see him by the flash of his gun, an' got Old Tried an' True into action *muy pronto*. My first shot hit him, an' two of the others I've been told since. I was too busy to know whether he got a second shot at me or not, an' I hadn't time to stick around, seeing as folks were headin' that way fast. So I lit outa town, lay doggo at Old Man Cowdery's in a haystack till I found out Two-Ace was sure enough dead, an' headed for the hills."

"I hope you are enjoying our hospitality," Smith-Beresford said, not without sarcasm.

"See here, mister, I didn't know the Widow Cress wasn't livin' here yet. She's a friend of mine's sister an' I figured she'd stake me to a breakfast."

"If this man's story is true——"

"Honest it's true. I'm no bad *hombre*."

"I was going to say that you'd better eat your breakfast and ride across to Steelman's," O'Hara went on. "If he thinks it's true he'll advise you what is best to do."

"You're shoutin'. The Old Man will tell me what to do. I been drug into this. If I'd started trouble I wouldn't make no holler, but I didn't do any such thing. Still an' all, I expect I'd better hive out for parts unknown."

"Your coffee is boiling over," Smith-Beresford said.

Fitch ate his breakfast, rolled and smoked a cigarette, and said he reckoned he would be going. As he stood at bow-legged ease, anxious to thank them for their kindness but a little embarrassed as to how to do it, his hosts saw in him only a boyish, good-natured cowboy. The wolfish snarl with which he had greeted them had vanished, had gone as completely as though it had never been.

He swung to the saddle, waved a hand in farewell, and rode over the hill. Not one of the three had any premonition of the desperate adventure into which they would be driven within the hour.

CHAPTER XI: *Garrett Holds the Fort*

FROM THE DOORWAY, where he sat smoking a placid pipe, Smith-Beresford drawled comment.

"Picture of a young man in a hurry," he said. "Study from life."

His partner walked to the door. O'Hara saw a rider coming over the hill. The Britisher had not overstated the case. If ever a man was in a hurry this one was. An arm moved up and down as he quirted his horse. The animal was jaded, but it stuck to a laboured lope.

"Fitch," O'Hara said.

"Righto! By Jove, he's not coming down here. He's heading for the clump of timber up there."

"They must be hard on his heels. That timber is no place for him. It's hemmed in on three sides by the bluff. There's no way to get through it."

"Wonder what's up, Garrett."

"Someone is after him. Maybe the posse headed him off."

Five minutes later horsemen came into view, a long straggling line of them. O'Hara counted twelve. They rode straight for the cabin. As they came closer he recognized Sanderson, Quantrell, Deever, and the youth known as the Texas Kid.

"We haven't seen anything of Fitch," O'Hara said to his companion. "We've both been in the cabin and didn't happen to look out as he passed."

"Count on me, Old Top."

"Think I'd better get my revolver. I don't trust Sanderson."

"You're speaking for me, too."

When they returned to the door at the cabin half a dozen members of the posse were dismounting. They were about a hundred yards from the house.

Sanderson shouted to them. "We want that bird Fitch an' we're gonna get him."

"Who?" called back O'Hara.

"Fitch. That's who. Send him out to us."

"There's nobody here but us. What's he done? What do you want with him?"

By this time the men were moving toward the house in a compact group.

"Don't think you can load us, young fellow," Deever

called. "Better send him out. If he starts any shenanigan we'll wipe out the whole outfit of you."

"Come and see for yourself," Smith-Beresford answered. "We're all alone."

The men approached cautiously, keeping the two at the door covered. For the first time Bob Quantrell spoke.

"Say, you pilgrims, don't try any funny business or we'll drill you through an' through."

The Ingram men moved past them, drooping spurs jingling, and poured into the house. Four or five stayed outside to keep an eye on the tenderfeet. Among these last was Quantrell.

"Who is this fellow and what's he done?" O'Hara asked.

"Fitch, the bird calls himself. He gunned Two-Ace Burke from ambush. I reckon you know all about it," Quantrell answered.

"I say, Old Top, be reasonable. How should we know about it when we haven't been to town for weeks?" Smith-Beresford asked innocently.

"How do you know it happened in town then?" demanded the young killer quickly.

For a second the Englishman was nonplussed. It was O'Hara who covered the slip.

"We don't," he said. "But this Two-Ace Burke is a gambler and lives at Concho. Where did it happen?"

"You guessed right first crack outa the box," Quantrell answered, his buck teeth showing in a grin.

"Is Burke badly hurt?"

"He'll never be deader," the lad replied callously. "We buried him in Boot Hill this mornin'."

Men trooped from the house. "Not there," one of them announced.

"No, but he's been there," the Texas Kid amended. "He had breakfast right in that room. Fitch never was thorough. I know that bird. He didn't wash his cup an' plate."

"Someone had breakfast here. You're right about that," O'Hara admitted. "We just got back from the camp where our boys are branding. Whoever this fellow was he'd gone before we got here."

O'Hara looked around on them, brown competent men, hard-visaged, ruthless. They had ridden hard and far for vengeance. He realized that they were not going to be particular where the blow fell. If they could not find Fitch they might strike at the men who they thought were protecting him. Any adherent of Wes Steelman's would do, given a reasonable excuse. He could not understand the psychology of such people. There was Bob Quantrell, for instance. He had been friendly with Smith-Beresford. He had protected them both. But Garrett knew that now he would not lift a hand to save them if Sanderson or the others moved to strike.

"Some of the cows their waddies are brandin' to-day were stolen from me," a weasel-eyed nester said bitterly. "They're aimin' to show us we've got to get off the earth."

"You're right, Houck, you an' Roche, too," Deever said. "Move we string these birds up to a limb an' make 'em talk anyhow."

"That's bally rot, you know," protested Smith-Beresford hotly. "I'm a British subject. You can't touch me. I've done nothing against your laws."

Bob Quantrell spoke. "Don't come the belted earl on us, fellow. We're free-born American citizens an' we'd just as lief twist the lion's tail as not an' hear him roar. But first off, I'm going up to that bunch of timber an' comb it. Three-four of you fellows come along with me. We'll take care of these gents when we get back."

Three men followed Quantrell to the horses. The four mounted and rode toward the grove.

O'Hara caught the eye of his partner and the two edged back toward the cabin. Very soon the riders would make a discovery, one which might have a disastrous reaction in precipitating trouble.

"We've nothing against any of you," O'Hara explained. "We have started here as peaceable ranchers. If we can we want to be friendly with our neighbours. There's room for all of us, a wide range, plenty of grass. Both of us would go a long way to remove any feeling against us there may be."

From the timber above a shot rang out, followed by a puff of smoke. The riders flung themselves from their horses and hunted such cover as the brush afforded.

"Dad gum it, they've got him!" the Texas Kid cried, and he started up the hill on foot.

Three men followed him. The others stayed to watch the partners. Among those who remained was Shep Sanderson.

"You knew he was there all the time," the big bully charged. "I've a mind to gun you right now."

Neither O'Hara nor Smith-Beresford answered him. They stood close to the door of the house, their eyes on their enemy. From above came the sound of firing, scattered shots at unequal intervals. Once Garrett flung a glance toward the battle ground and saw that the attackers were drawing closer to their prey. He heard voices in parley. The shots ceased.

A shout came down to them. "He's give up."

Men emerged from the timber. The one who moved in the centre of the little group, the prisoner, walked with a limp. Evidently he had been wounded.

Sanderson chose that moment, before his companions above could reach him to object, for his revenge. He fired from the hip. O'Hara felt the shock of the bullet. It had struck his cartridge belt at the buckle and glanced off, though he did not know until later that he was not severely wounded.

What followed came so rapidly that there was no orderly sequence to it in O'Hara's mind. He could hear the roar of guns, his own among them. A flash of flame seared his shoulder. His companion staggered, leaned against the door jamb, and cried, "I'm hit." He moved through lanes of fire. Figures loomed up in the smoke and vanished. Someone pushed close against him, striking with a knife. He pressed the revolver against yielding flesh and pulled the trigger. The man gave way with a groan that was half a scream.

O'Hara's revolver was empty. He was in the doorway now, astride the prostrate body of his partner, though how he had got there he did not know. Out of the fog of smoke a face loomed. He flung the empty weapon at it, stooped, and snatched up the six-shooter of his friend. There was no conscious volition on his part. The .45 began to roar.

One moment the day was filled with the fury of battle. The next the sound of it had died away. O'Hara's enemies were falling back, driven into retreat by the steadiness of his fire.

Once more his revolver hammer clicked on an empty chamber. Garrett dropped the weapon, stooped, and picked up his partner. He carried him into the house and laid him on a bed, then swiftly set about putting the cabin into a state of defense. Bolting the back door, he barricaded it with a trunk. He drew the window curtains. Another trunk he pushed into the front doorway, then dragged a mattress there and propped it up in front of the trunk as a protection against bullets.

All this had taken him scarcely a score of seconds. From a rack he drew rifles, a repeating Winchester for one, and two of Smith-Beresford's hunting guns brought with him from England. He examined them to make sure they were loaded.

A voice from outside hailed him. "Come outa there, you condemned pilgrims, or you'll go to hell on a shutter. You're bucked out, fellows. We ain't gonna monkey with you any longer. Come with yore hands up or we'll plug you full of holes." It was the hoarse raucous voice of Shep Sanderson.

From behind the trunk and mattress O'Hara took in the situation. Two men were wounded seriously. He could see them lying on the ground where their companions had dragged them. Most of the others were gathered in a group near the horses. Sanderson, waving a bandanna meant for a flag of truce, had stepped a few yards forward from the rest.

"We'll stay where we are. Dig us out if you feel ambitious," O'Hara shouted back.

From the bed, unexpectedly, came a faint murmur of approval.

"Righto! Hold the fort, Old Top."

"No use to give up. Sanderson would never let us get away alive. . . . Badly hurt, Lyulph?"

"About all I can carry, old chap. In the chest."

"Sorry. I'm hit in the shoulder and the stomach, but I feel pretty strong yet. Wonder if they'll rush the place."

Garrett could see the enemy grouped in consultation. Presently the men scattered. They were spreading out to surround the house. A bullet struck the trunk in front of him. Another ploughed into the mattress. The Winchester in his hands barked an answer.

Apparently they had settled down to a siege. O'Hara could count at least five foes in the fan-shaped open space in front of him. They were all behind cover, but the flashes of their weapons told him where they lay. Three or four were back of the stable with the horses and the prisoner. The others had disappeared. It was an easy guess that they were making a wide circuit to take him in the rear.

The besieged man slipped back from the doorway, leaving the barrel of a rifle showing beside the mattress. He dragged another of his partner's trunks to the back door and piled it on top of the first one. Lifting the table to the window, he put it on a box and nailed the top of it to the frame in such a way as to cover the glass entirely.

He hurried back to his place in the doorway, fired two shots, and withdrew again to give his friend water in a dipper. The firing of the attackers was sporadic but spirited. One bullet struck the stove. Others buried themselves in the log walls.

"How're you feeling?" Garrett asked.

His friend grinned feebly. "Boiler damaged. Can't get up steam." From time to time he coughed up blood.

Garrett went back to his post. There was nothing he could do for his companion and he could not leave the doorway for long at a time. He heard the sound of shots from the rear and the spat of the lead against the logs. The enemy had him completely surrounded now.

He waited for the next billow of smoke in front, fired at it, and put down the rifle. Unfastening the belt around his waist, he looked for the stomach wound. There was nothing there but a bruise where the metal buckle had been driven against the flesh. Undoubtedly the clasp had deflected the bullet and saved his life. Sanderson had fired with deadly accuracy at the most vulnerable spot. Only a miracle had frustrated his vengeance.

Hour after hour the siege dragged on. Beresford became delirious. The young lawyer knew that his own fever was mounting. The wound in his shoulder pained a good deal. It was his guess that the bullet had smashed a bone.

Grimly he recognized the fact that the attackers were paying him a compliment by their caution. They might have rushed the cabin and ended the affair in two minutes. Evidently they counted the cost as too great to pay. The men he had wounded were a sufficient object lesson to them.

What were they up to now? A wagon was being pushed from the back of the barn and headed toward the house. Four or five men were behind it. They were using it as a cover for their approach. Snipers from right and left kept up a steady fire to prevent his concentrating on the wagon.

The wheels of the wagon slewed to the right. A man crept forward to straighten them. Garrett drew a bead on him and fired. The man stumbled over his own foot and plunged to the ground. His body twitched and lay still. The others deserted the wagon and fled for the shelter of the barn.

The shot had been a lucky one for Garrett. But it decided the fate of the prisoner Fitch. One of the log rafters of the barn projected from the roof. The unfortunate man was led beneath this, a rope around his neck. The other end was thrown over the rafter. Before Garrett's eyes they hanged the cowboy.

It was a thing horrible to see. This boy they were hanging was no criminal. If he had killed it had been in self-defense. But he was no weakling. There was in him the stiff hardihood that frontier life begets. The rope already around his throat, he borrowed tobacco, rolled a cigarette, and smoked it. His horse was brought. He was helped into the saddle. As they started to lead the animal away he sprang into the air to make the fall of his body more violent.

Garrett turned away, sick at heart. He had to look again,

to see what the enemy was about. They were gathered in a group discussing something heatedly. Plainly they disagreed.

He heard a voice raised in sudden anger. A man detached himself from the group. "By cripes, I'll smoke the pilgrim out if I play a lone hand. What you birds need is sand in yore craws."

The speaker was Bob Quantrell. He walked to a horse and flung himself into a saddle. He reined the animal around savagely to face the cabin. The bronco went into the air sunfishing, came down, bucked up all humpbacked, and landed with legs as stiff as stakes. The rider had not yet found the stirrups. He lost his balance and shot through the air to the ground. Instantly he was on his feet again, running to catch the bridle.

Before he was in the saddle a second time an interruption occurred. Two riders, a man and a woman, galloped across the open toward the stable. The man was Dave Ingram, the woman Barbara Steelman.

Chapter XII: *Quantrell Talks*

RIDING THE CUT-OFF toward Squaw Crossing, Barbara Steelman became aware of a man below her. For a moment she saw him before he dipped into a draw. Presently he reappeared, climbing the trail toward her. As he drew nearer it became apparent that he was in a hurry. Instead of letting his horse take its time, he was urging the animal up the stiff grade.

She recognized the man as Steve Worrall and flung up a hand of greeting. "Aren't you off your reservation, Steve?" she called.

"Where's Wes?" demanded her lank friend.

"Why, at the ranch, I reckon. Was when I left an hour ago. Anything wrong?"

"One of his waddies at the lower ranch, Tom Fitch, killed Two-Ace Burke. They're out after him, Ingram's warriors are."

"Out to get him?" she asked quickly.

"Looks thataway. Sheriff Banks sent the posse out, but—well, you know Banks. I wouldn't trust that bunch farther than I could throw a bull by the tail."

"Where did this Fitch go?"

"Headed this way. Likely for the ranch. I'm some worried about him. Kid Quantrell an' Shep Sanderson led the posse

64

up Roubideau Creek. I shouldn't wonder but what they've got him headed off."

Barbara considered a moment. "What had we better do?"

"First off, get word to Wes, I'd say."

"I'm not worried so much about the cowboy. Probably they won't find him. But if they've gone up Roubideau they'll be mighty close to the Cress place. Shep will sure head that way lookin' for Fitch. What about our two tenderfeet? You know they've thrown in with Dad. If Shep an' his crowd are sore—and you know they will be if they don't find the cowboy—they're likely to harm those two babes in the woods."

"I've thought of that," Worrall admitted. "But they've got four-five riders with them, haven't they?"

"I don't know. The riders are brandin'. They may all be out on the range. Tell you what, Steve. I'll ride over to the Cress place an' warn them if they're at home. You go on an' tell Dad."

"What's the matter with you tellin' Wes an' me p'intin' for the Cress place?" he asked promptly.

"No," she vetoed. "I can go with no danger an' I can talk sense into that fool Englishman's head better than anyone else. If necessary, I can get him to leave the ranch thinkin' he's protectin' me."

"I don't reckon they're really in any danger," Steve ruminated aloud. "Still, you never can tell. Have it yore own way, Barbara. Drift over to the Cress place an' bring the lads back to yore ranch with you. At that, I kinda hate to let you go alone."

"What in the world could harm me?" the girl asked. "Maybe you think a cow might attack me unawares, or a bunch of antelopes."

"When you find those two pilgrims, close herd 'em straight to the ranch, Barbara. They hadn't ought to be let out alone without a nurse anyhow, those two lads."

Barbara swung away from the trail. She called back over her shoulder, "What started the trouble between Fitch an' Two-Ace?"

"Tarantula juice, I reckon. Fitch was ginned up an' wouldn't stand for Burke runnin' on him. Some say Burke shot at him first from behind a wall. I dunno the straight of it."

The girl rode over the hills and not once did she hesitate as to direction. None the less she was disturbed, since she knew how ruthless these hired killers could be. It would be like Smith-Beresford not to understand the danger and to stand upon his rights, and it would be like Shep Sanderson to let his passion blaze explosively.

Out of a gulch she emerged upon a plateau running to the down slope which marked the beginning of the Cress place. From a draw a horseman rode, caught sight of her, and at once headed his cow pony her way. The man was Dave Ingram.

"Where away?" he shouted.

She waited till he was nearer before she answered, "To the Cress place."

"Visitin' yore father's partners?" he asked, and she read into his voice a sneer.

"What if they are Dad's partners? Anything wrong about that?" she demanded acidly.

"Did I say there was anything wrong about it?"

"Your manner said it mighty loud. If you want to know, I'm going over there to make sure your friends haven't paid them a visit."

"Then I'll ride along. I want to wish 'em luck in their new business. They're goin' to need a lot of it."

"Meanin' what?" she flung at him.

"Looks like they might get in my way."

"Don't you start anything with them," Barbara flamed. "They're quiet young fellows not lookin' for any trouble. Why can't you let 'em alone?"

"If they're not lookin' for trouble they picked an unfortunate spot to begin ranchin'." He dismissed the subject as finished. "Why haven't I seen you lately?" he asked, his cool eyes on her.

"You're not going to see me any more, not the way I've been seeing you," she answered, forcing her gaze to meet his. The colour was hot in her cheeks. She felt her eyes burn.

"You've got it wrong, girl. I'm intendin' to see a lot more of you. What's the use of fightin' against yore own heart an' against me? You'll have to give in sooner or later."

"I'll not!" she cried. "An' I'm not 'fightin' against my heart. No such thing. I came to see you because I thought it would help to make peace between you and Dad. I was a fool. If I hadn't been I would of known you wouldn't let any —any—any——"

"Foolish sentiment," he suggested.

She refused to accept his words. "—any decent human feeling stand between you an' your bullheaded egotism."

"Which means I won't promise you to throw down my

66

friends an' my own interests to let Wes Steelman ride over me. Girl, if you marry me it will be as is. You can't make me over or run my life for me."

"I'm not goin' to marry you," she retorted, tears of vexation in her eyes. "I wouldn't dream of doin' so crazy a thing."

"You've dreamed of it a lot of times, Barbara. You've thought of it while you were lyin' in bed in the dark. You're due to think a lot more about it," he told her coolly.

"I never knew such conceit—never in the world," she flamed.

She was furious, more so because his words had touched the truth so closely.

They had come to the end of the plateau and could look down upon the ranch houses.

"What's doin'?" he asked himself sharply, and instantly put his pony to a gallop.

A puff of smoke from the cabin and the sound of a rifle had startled him.

Barbara looked and saw a group of men near the corral. She knew there was trouble afoot. Perhaps they had tracked Fitch to the ranch and the owners of the place were defending him. The shot from the house told her that her friends were not yet in the hands of the enemy. Even while she was making these deductions the girl was galloping hard on the heels of Ingram. She must save the men in the ranch house. How, she did not know.

Her eyes picked up another detail, a horrible picture never to be forgotten, of a body swaying in the wind. Her heart seemed to stop. She was too late, after all. Between her and the body hurtled a wildly bucking bronco. From the saddle a man flew, struck ground, and leaped to his feet.

She was close now to the stable, near enough to see that the swaying, suspended figure was neither O'Hara nor his partner.

Ingram dragged his pony to a halt and leaped to the ground.

"What's all this?" he demanded.

Deever moved forward. "These pilgrims have done killed Brad Sowers an' wounded three more of us. I don't reckon Pankey will make the grade."

"Who started it?" demanded Ingram.

The Texas Kid answered him. The young fellow had a blood-stained handkerchief tied around his arm. "We got to fannin' smoke all together, looks like."

The leader of the faction turned to Quantrell. "What was

you aimin' to do, Bob, when you put on this exhibition of fancy ridin'?"

"Smoke 'em out, by cripes! Show this bunch of quitters a tenderfoot can't bluff me out."

Ingram looked with an impassive face at the swaying body of the dead cowboy. "I see you got Fitch. Don't you reckon that's about enough for one gather? Suppose you leave this for me. Before we go any farther I'd like to know who got on the hook first. An' why?"

"They did," Sanderson blustered. "They fixed Tom Fitch up with breakfast an' then they hid him out on us. Soon as we found him that pilgrim O'Hara began to fan smoke right away. They got Brad Sowers an' they got Pankey an' they bust Jim's leg and hit the Kid here in the arm."

"How many in the cabin?"

Bob Quantrell answered, jeering at his companions and himself, "You got a surprise comin', Ingram. One live tenderfoot an' one dead one. The live pilgrim shot up consid'rable. Too much for the boys. They're allowin' to crawl off with their tails between their legs."

"We'll meet up with this bird some other day, won't we?" Deever contributed. "He's got cover there. What's the use of more of us gettin' shot up? Plum foolishness, I'd say."

Barbara waited to hear no more. One of her friends was dead and the other wounded. Her place was with them, not here. She touched her pony with the spur and the animal jumped to a canter. Straight toward the house she rode.

Too late Ingram understood her intention. Her horse had covered one third of the distance before he could make a move.

"Ladies' choice," murmured Quantrell insolently. "Right hands to yore pardners an' grand right an' left. Everybody waltz. I'll be doggoned if I don't begin to like the Hashknife outfit better than the Diamond Tail. No yellow in their stock, looks like."

Ingram looked at the young desperado coldly.

"Perhaps you'd like to join them," he said.

Unexpectedly Quantrell's answer jumped back at him, a sharp acceptance of the challenge, "You're damned whistlin' I would. No complaints against you, Ingram, but I don't like the company I'm keepin'."

He backed warily toward his horse, rifle in hand. The boy's buck teeth showed in a snarl as he drew up his lip. The cold light blue eyes passed in little stabbing glances from one

68

to another. He was ready at an instant's warning to begin flinging bullets.

No man moved to prevent him from going. They could shoot him down. That was certain. But not without loss. He was as quick, as accurate, and as deadly as a coiled rattlesnake.

"What's the use of going off half cocked, Quantrell?" the owner of the Diamond Tail asked evenly in a chill voice. "If you've not been treated right why don't you come to me like a man an' talk it over?"

"Nothin' to talk over. I just don't like this bully puss outfit of yours. If you want to know, Shep Sanderson started this rookus, an' by cripes! either one of those pilgrims was a better man than him. To jump a coupla tenderfoots an' have them stand us off at that, after one has been bumped off an' the other filled up with lead pills, sticks in my craw. I'm sayin' *adiós*, Ingram."

"You're liable to rue this, Quantrell," his employer said.

"Not none," the boy replied curtly.

He had reached his horse. Warily he edged behind it, not for one moment lifting his eyes from the group he had left. His hand felt for the bridle, his foot for the stirrup. He swung to the saddle, backed the horse behind the stable, whirled it in its tracks, and dashed for the pines, looking back as he rode.

CHAPTER XIII: *Barbara Declares Herself In*

GARRETT O'HARA watched with amazement as Barbara swung her cow pony and put it at a canter toward the cabin. His first impulse was to run out to meet her, under the delusion that perhaps he could protect her by so doing. But almost at once he saw that she was safe. None of the Ingram faction fired at her.

She slipped from the saddle and moved to the door while he dragged aside the mattress to make way for her.

Once inside, she looked at him, eyes dilating with fear. "Are you hurt—badly?" she asked.

"In the shoulder. I'll be all right. Afraid Lyulph is badly hurt. They hit him in the chest."

She looked at the bed where the delirious man lay tossing. "I'll take care of him. Watch out they don't rush the house. I don't think Mr. Ingram will let them, but I'm not sure."

Barbara made preparations to do what she could for the

69

man on the bed. Once more Garrett lay down back of his rampart and took stock of the enemy. Ingram appeared to be issuing orders to his men. They hitched horses to a wagon, put hay in the bed of it, and lifted the two most seriously wounded of the posse into the wagon, after which the team was driven away, followed by most of the riders. One man stayed with Ingram.

Garrett reported the proceedings to Barbara.

"Wonder what he's up to," she said, moistening a bandage.

"He's coming toward the house—alone."

The girl ran to the door. "He hasn't even drawn a six-shooter. He wants to talk."

When Ingram was twenty-five yards from the house O'Hara called to him, "That'll be far enough. Stay there and speak your piece."

Ingram did not even falter in his stride. "Don't be a condemned fool," he said impatiently. "If I was lookin' for trouble I'd come with my gun smokin'."

"Let him come in if he wants to," Barbara said in a low voice.

Garrett drew back and the cattle man pushed his way into the house.

With a glance of careless contempt Ingram's eyes swept the room. "Well, I told you what would happen if you stayed in this country," he said to O'Hara.

"Did you tell him what would happen to three or four of your killers when they tried to murder him?" Barbara asked, her eyes flashing indignation.

Ingram looked at her with an expressionless face. "Are you in this, girl?"

"Yes, I'm in it. They're my father's friends. Your hired men shot them for no cause." She stood straight and slender, quivering with indignation at the man whom she held responsible, with sympathy for the two victims of the outrage.

"Tried to obstruct a posse in performance of its duty. If they got hurt, don't blame me."

"That's not true," Garrett said quietly. He had slumped down in a chair, grown suddenly faint and weak.

"A posse!" Her voice was vibrant with feeling. "Would you call it a posse doing its duty to—to murder that poor boy at the barn an' this harmless man on the bed?"

"They carried arms in defense of a criminal wanted by the law. They started the trouble their own selves."

"I don't believe it—and what's more you don't, either, Dave Ingram. Would two young tenderfeet attack a dozen armed ruffians? It's not reasonable. That scalawag Shep Sanderson an' his friends started it."

"A sheriff's posse legally appointed to bring in a cold-blooded murderer," Ingram answered coldly. "Yore innocent friends here fed him an' hid him an' tried to defend him from arrest. An open-an'-shut case, I'd say."

"Did your legal posse have a judge an' jury an' try poor Tom Fitch before they hanged him?"

"They got excited when these scoundrels here shot up three-four of them. Who wouldn't? Why, it's common report that both these men here have been practisin' with guns ever since they came into the country. They were spoilin' for a fight. Dangerous killers like they are ought not to be allowed loose on a decent community."

Barbara read the faintest flicker of ironic mirth in Ingram's eyes. "You don't believe a word of what you're sayin'," she flung hotly at him.

"Facts talk," he went on evenly. "Add up the damages. One of the posse killed, an' three wounded, one of 'em desperately. Does it look like a bunch of ruffians had jumped a coupla innocent pilgrims? 'Innocent' was the word you used, wasn't it?"

"I'm not going to argue with you. What do you want here? Why have you come? I've got to get help to look after these wounded men. But I can't leave them like this."

"I've sent to town for both doctors. One of 'em can come here. Even criminals are entitled to medical attention. I'll look after them till he comes. Bring me fresh water from the spring."

Ingram rolled up the sleeves of his shirt and washed his hands before he approached Smith-Beresford. With his pocket knife he cut the shirt and undershirt from around the wound, then bathed it, using the cold water Barbara had brought from the spring.

Ingram turned to Garrett. "How about you, young fellow? Get yore coat off an' let's see where we're at."

Barbara helped the lawyer remove the coat.

The cattle man washed and examined the wound.

"Pain much?"

"I'm noticing it."

"Thought so. Bullet hit the bone likely. You're lucky it's no worse. From what the boys tell me a lot of good lead was wasted."

"They nearly murdered my friend, if not quite," O'Hara

71

said bitterly, in a low voice. "Isn't that enough to give you a little satisfaction?"

"Young fellow, if you know what's good for you don't insinuate that they did it by my orders," Ingram answered harshly. Then, curtly, "Fix me up a pad for this, Barbara. We'll not monkey with the lead pill till Doc comes."

A shadow from the doorway fell across the sunlit floor. Ingram looked up quickly and as he did so his hand slid toward his right hip and rested there. Bob Quantrell leaned negligently against the jamb.

"Come to see how yore sick friends are gettin' along, Bob?" the owner of the Diamond Tail brand asked ironically, his steady eyes on those of the young desperado. "I suppose, in a way of speakin', you might call them yore patients."

"No, sir. I reckon not. The band began to play before I got here. Credit Shep with the job. Does he get another notch on his gun?"

"Too early to tell yet. The only notch up to date goes to innocent Mr. O'Hara."

Quantrell laughed, slowly and insolently. "He sure tamed a bunch of wild wolves so's they was willin' to eat out of his hand. Never had been curried, by their tell of it. Chewed cholla spines, they was that tough. An' one lone tenderfoot, already shot up some at that, sent 'em to cover. My hat off to you, Mr. O'Hara. You're a sure enough wolf tamer."

"You ought to be gratified, O'Hara. This is praise from an expert," Ingram said grimly.

Barbara moved a step or two toward the young killer. She did not know why he had come and she intended to protect the wounded men if possible, provided he had any ill intent.

"What do you want here?" she demanded. "Why have you come?"

He swept the sombrero from his head. "Don't you worry, miss. I'm through with that bunch of wolves. I'll throw in with yore paw if he needs a top hand."

"Why? You fought these men. Half an hour ago you were tryin' to kill them."

"All in the way of business. Fact is, I like the way they called the turn on Shep's crowd. They've got sand in their craws, these two birds. A man can swap bosses, can't he?"

Ingram made comment. "I'll be glad to write to yore father, Barbara, recommendin' Quantrell's faithful services," he said.

The young killer's pale blue eyes rested on the cattle man. He understood the spirit of the remark though it was not obviously ironical.

"Meanin' anything in particular, Mr. Ingram?" he asked, very gently.

He smiled. "Let it ride as it lays, Bob. Like you say, a man can change his boss. No law against that. Since we're here we better make ourselves useful. I've sent for a doc. Till he shows up I'm subbin' for him. Take a look at yore patient's shoulder here. Nice clean flesh wound, wouldn't you say? Ought to heal in no time."

Quantrell looked at the wound. "Seems like it ought. Not my patient though, Ingram. Shep gets the credit, like I done told you."

"So you did. I forgot. Well, the main thing is that he'll be rollin' his tail high as ever right soon."

CHAPTER XIV: *Ingram Takes the Road*

THE SOUND of horses' hoofs came drumming down the wind. Barbara stepped to the door.

She spoke quietly, as though what she was mentioning had no special significance. "Father's here."

Neither Ingram nor Quantrell made any comment. Each of them became instantly alert without showing the least sign of apprehension. They were tying a strip of linen around O'Hara's shoulder to hold the bandage in place and they continued to work on this. But both of them shifted position in such a way as to face the door.

The galloping horses pulled up. A voice asked sharply, "The boys hurt, Barb?"

At the same time there were sounds of men dismounting.

Barbara spoke quickly. "Mr. Ingram is lookin' after them."

Wesley Steelman pushed past her and stood in the doorway. He glared at Ingram and in a voice hoarse with anger demanded, "Who did that?" His finger was pointing toward the body swaying in the wind.

Hard-eyed, Ingram met his furious gaze. "I wasn't here myself. A sheriff's posse, I'm told."

"Hired killers," Steelman corrected. "By God, someone will pay for this." His eyes swept the room and rested first on Smith-Beresford then on O'Hara. Of the latter he asked a question: "Both of you shot?"

"Both of us," Garrett answered, a gleam of wintry humour in his eyes. "I'm a botched job, but poor Lyulph is hit in the chest. Afraid he'll have a hard time of it."

"Who did it?"

"Sanderson and his friends. After we had been shot we backed into the house and stood them off."

Bob Quantrell laughed. "Not the way I noticed it. You picked the belted earl up an' carried him in. You stood us off by yore lone. Never saw the beat of it. One tenderfoot, some shot up at that. A dozen gunmen on the prod. An' by cripes! he stood us off two-three hours."

"So you were in this," Steelman said harshly to the young desperado.

"I was an' I wasn't," Quantrell answered, his buck teeth showing in a grin. "I didn't get in till after Mr. Tenderfoot holed up in the cabin, but I was one of the birds he made yell ''Nough!' He's sure the most eat-'em-alive pilgrim ever drifted into the San Marcos."

"I notice you're not worried about the health of any of the posse, Steelman," the leader of the other faction jeered. "But just so you'll get the record straight I'll tell you that yore young pardner here killed Brad Sowers, shot up Pankey so bad he won't live, probably, an' wounded two other members of the posse. All this whilst he was resistin' arrest, you understand."

"Resistin' arrest what for?"

"For aidin' an' abettin' the escape of a murderer wanted by the law."

"That's the way *you* wrop it up. Different here. Tom Fitch was murdered in cold blood. As for O'Hara here, I'm with him till the cows come home. If he did all you claim he did he's the best fightin' man on the San Marcos an' I'll be proud to ride the river alongside of him."

"Here, too," chimed in Quantrell.

"Bob is thinkin' of takin' you on for a boss, Steelman," Ingram drawled. "Glad to give him a recommend."

"I can speak for myself, Ingram," the boy said. "Far as that goes I don't reckon yore recommend would help me much with Mr. Steelman."

"Not none." Steelman spoke with emphasis. "An' comin' down to recommendations, Ingram, I'll make one right now. Get out. Hit the trail. Or my boys might follow the example you've set an' do some hangin' their own selves."

Coolly Ingram looked around. Steve Worrall had come into the room, and at his heels were Texas Jim and young

Curt Steelman. Two or three other Hashknife cowboys were grouped at the door.

Worrall spoke up. "Mr. Steelman does not mean quite that, Dave. Still an' all, that's good medicine about takin' the road while it's open."

"Good of you to have my interests at heart, Steve," the cattle man jeered. "I'll go when I'm ready to go an' there won't be any hangin', either."

"Not while I can fan a gun," Quantrell added. "We've come to different forks of the road, me an' Mr. Ingram. But I don't reckon anyone better get on the prod yet, not about to-day's rookus. He wasn't here during the trouble an' when he came he stayed to fix up these boys."

"Well, he's fixed 'em up," Steelman replied roughly. "After his hired men shot 'em. Nothin' more to stay for. I'm part owner here, an' I say he goes."

Barbara spoke in a low voice to Ingram. "I think you'd better go."

Ingram smiled hardily at her. "I'm comin' to that same notion myself. Looks like I'm being handed my hat. *Adiós,* Miss Steelman. So long, Wes. See you later. Better change yore mind, Bob, an' come along."

Young Quantrell shook his head. "No, sir. Too much Shep Sanderson in yore outfit. I quit."

The boss of the Diamond Tail sauntered to the door, spurs jingling as he moved. He passed through the group of cowboys as though they had not been there, superbly indifferent to them. Not once as he moved toward the stable did he turn to make sure that none of them was taking an impulsive shot at his back. When he reached his horse he swung to the saddle and rode leisurely away beside the man he had left with the two animals.

A hundred yards up the trail he met Dr. Holloway.

"Did Doc Manley go to my ranch?" Ingram asked.

"Yes, sir. I understand someone has been hurt here, too."

"Two wounded men, one of 'em shot up pretty badly."

"Who are they?"

"Couple of pardners of Wes Steelman—the belted earl an' that pilgrim O'Hara."

Holloway was a born gossip. He itched to know just what had taken place, but Dave Ingram was not the man upon whom to push home his curiosity.

"Well, I guess I'd better drift on down," he said.

"Do," the cattle man agreed. "An' when you're through

75

ride over to the ranch. Doc Manley may need some help. We've got quite a hospital there, too."

The doctor murmured that he was sorry there had been trouble.

Ingram smiled grimly. " 'Trouble' is not too strong a word for it, I reckon. We've had a right sanguinary mornin', takin' it by an' large. One man hanged, one killed, two more ready to cash in, three shot up more or less serious. Looks like there would be lively times on the San Marcos. I wouldn't wonder but what you had a good year, Doc. Don't let me keep you from yore patients, Rock along."

Chapter XV: *A Trip to Town*

AFTER THE BATTLE at the Cress ranch there was a lull in the Jefferson County War, as the conflict between the Ingram and the Steelman forces came to be called in later days. It was as though both sides were waiting to get their breath again. The less dangerously wounded men were afoot within a week. Pankey and Smith-Beresford hung for a few days between life and death, then very slowly began to mend, edging away from the gulf into which they had almost been plunged.

Meanwhile talk swept the countryside as a fire does a dry prairie. When men met at Concho or in some far hollow of the hills they talked about the feud if they were sure they could trust each other. Texas warriors rode grimly in and out of town, keeping always a sharp lookout against ambush.

The gossipers no longer smiled at the two young owners of the Cress place. They had gone through their baptism of fire, and they had to be taken seriously. That O'Hara had stood up to the blazing guns of Sanderson, Sowers, Deever, and others, had driven these notorious gunmen back out of range, and later had fought off the entire posse for hours could be classed only as a miracle, but a miracle made possible by the coolness, the courage, and the accurate fire of the tenderfoot. In a community where gameness was a matter of course, the one essential quality of anyone not a weakling, Garrett O'Hara had become set apart as one who had fought his way to fame. For no man in the history of Jefferson County had fought so unequal and so desperate a battle and survived.

The defection of Bob Quantrell from the Ingram faction was another detail that received much comment. It was known that he did not like Sanderson and Houck, and this was generally accepted as the reason for the transfer of his services. Few knew the deeper cause, that the callous young desperado had liked Smith-Beresford from the first, that he admired the courage of both Smith-Beresford and his partner O'Hara, and that he had signed up with them as a rider in order to protect them as well as he could.

The Circle S O ranch, as the Cress place was now called, had become a hive of industry. Cattle in large bunches had been shifted to the contiguous range and had to be worked. At all hours of the day and night cowboys drifted to and from the ranch. Just now half a dozen carpenters, imported from Aurora, were camped in the pasture. They had been engaged to build a new house.

The Lodge, as Smith-Beresford called it, was to be a commodious structure, rustic in type. The hewn-log walls were already up and the roof on. One of the chief features was to be a large open hall with an immense stone fireplace at one end. This hall extended to the roof, but a stairway wound to a second-floor gallery which extended around three sides of the hall. From this gallery opened the sleeping rooms. Rough slabs and logs had been used instead of sawn lumber wherever possible.

O'Hara passed the bunk house and stopped a moment. "Did Mr. Steelman say anything about that bunch of Bar B Y cows?" he asked Quantrell.

"Said he'd buy at a whack up if he could, but he wouldn't pay any big price. It's a sorry herd, cutbacks most of 'em. His notion is to push 'em back into the hills an' forget 'em till fall an' then work the bunch, cuttin' out the best to keep an' shovin' the rest down into Mexico. The Old Man said he wouldn't look at 'em twice if they weren't here already clutterin' up the range. At that, there's some good cows wearin' the Bar B Y. Kinda uneven, scrubs an' nice stock mixed. You'd be buyin' a bone yard to start with, but they'll take on flesh if they're put on a good range."

"More trouble than they're worth, I'd think."

"Maybeso." Quantrell showed his prominent teeth in a grin. "Up to you an' the Old Man. I ain't paid to do the buyin'. My forty per comes to me for forkin' broncs an' being an alleged top hand with cows."

"In about an hour I'm ridin' in to Concho. Want to go along?"

"Sure do." The cowboy got to his feet with one lithe twist of his body.

Presently the two men saddled and dropped down out of the hills. The cowboy noticed how easily O'Hara adjusted his body to the saddle.

"First you know you'll be a real cow man," the boy told his employer. "I notice you don't make the same mistake twice. I never see you ridin' that chestnut mare any more. Nobody but some run-down-at-the-heel nester ever rides anything but a gelding."

"Glad I'm improving. You must remember I didn't begin throwing my leg over the cantle of a saddle when I was a baby as you did. But the fact is, Bob, I want to be a good cow man. I like the life. Queer how I got into it. I came here to be a lawyer."

"Luck was certainly ridin' with you that time," the boy answered, much as though O'Hara had said he came out to be a sneak thief.

"The legal profession doesn't seem to be ace high with you," O'Hara suggested.

"Well, sir, if you want it short an' sweet, my notion of a lawyer is a fellow whose business is to make trouble an' beat a fellow outa what he's got. Gimme a chance an' I'll ride clear 'round one of them birds."

That was all. O'Hara was left to guess what had made him so decide. The cowboy retired within himself and began to hum softly,

> "Hush a-bye, baby,
> Punch a buckaroo,
> Daddy'll be home
> When the round-up is through."

They rode down the dusty main street of Concho past the store of Ingram & Harvey, past the *tendejón* where the tenderfoot had rowelled Sanderson with his spurs, past the Gold Nugget and the Concho House, to the Steelman store. Pat McCarthy came forward to meet them, his face as usual hard and wooden.

"Glad to see you, gents. How's everything up yore way?"

"Fine as silk," Quantrell answered. "Everything O. K. in Concho?"

"Far's I know. Hear you had some trouble at the ranch three-four weeks ago. You an' yore pardner all right now?"

This question was put to O'Hara.

"I am, and he soon will be. It's a great country to get well in."

"You were lucky, both of you."

Quantrell laughed. "We were some lucky, too. He's sudden death with a Winchester, referrin' to Mr. O'Hara here present. Next time I start to round him up I sure aim to carry a rabbit's foot."

McCarthy offered them liquor. Quantrell took a drink and departed. There was a Mexican girl in town he wanted to see.

He turned before he left the office to say, "Better stick around here till I get back, O'Hara. I saw Shep headin' into the Gold Nugget as we passed."

"I saw him, too, Bob. I'm not looking for him. My business won't take me into the Gold Nugget."

"I'd say stay right in this office till I get back. Won't be gone more'n a coupla hours." Quantrell was plainly a little uneasy about leaving him.

"Don't worry, Bob. I'll be here when you come back," his employer promised.

Into the store presently came Steve Worrall. He sat down in the office and chatted with McCarthy and O'Hara. The proprietor was called out by a clerk.

At once Worrall freed his mind. "You armed, O'Hara?"

"Yes. Any reason for asking me that right now?"

"I just came from the Gold Nugget. Shep Sanderson an' the Texas Kid were in there drinkin'. I'd be careful if I were you."

"What did they say?" asked Garrett.

"Not so much. Shep said you'd better let Bob Quantrell closeherd you while you were in town. They acted ugly, both of 'em. The Kid's been mean ever since you shot him up."

"What's the Kid like?"

"Got a bad rep. I've heard say he's a killer but yellow. May be nothin' to that. I'd lay off him an' Shep, too."

"I haven't lost either of them. It would suit me fine if I never laid eyes on them again."

"Thought I'd drop in an' tell you. Better stay here in the store. Where's Bob Quantrell?"

"I don't know." There was a flicker of a sardonic smile in Garrett's eyes. "If that boy wants me to look after him he'd better stay closer. Otherwise I can't be responsible for what happens to him. Come on, Steve. I've got to go to the post office."

Worrall hesitated for a fraction of a second then rose promptly. He had warned his friend. That was as far as he could go. On the frontier every man must play his own hand.

Brad Helm, the fat hotel keeper, was in the post office.

He nodded toward Worrall and O'Hara, got his mail, and as he passed out said in a wheezy voice audible to everybody present, "There's a letter for you at the hotel, Mr. O'Hara. It says 'Important' on it."

Passing the Concho House a few minutes later, Steve and Garrett dropped in to get the letter. Helm manœuvred the latter into a corner of the room and whispered a word of warning.

"Shep an' the Texas Kid are layin' for you." At the same time he handed O'Hara a whisky circular. "They're givin' you an hour to leave town."

"Much obliged. I've been looking for this letter."

Garrett and his friend stepped out to the sidewalk.

"Come on down to the corral with me," Steve proposed.

"Not now. You come to the Gold Nugget with me."

The long man flung a quick look at him. O'Hara's eyes were shining with excitement.

"All right. I'll throw in with you," he said.

Chapter XVI: *O'Hara Claims He Is One Scared Tenderfoot*

As Garrett O'Hara walked up the adobe-lined street beside the lank freighter he felt again that odd lift of the spirit that came to him when danger was near. He was going to meet it, audaciously, foolhardily. On the frontier a man did not lightly serve notice that he was "looking for" another. Such an announcement meant business.

Nor did he doubt that Sanderson would kill from ambush if he had a chance. No instinct for fair play would have any weight with him. He was of the wolf breed.

A short, thickset man came out of the Ingram store and down the street toward them. Out of a pallid face protruding fish eyes looked at O'Hara. Thin lips' opened to say insolently, "So you're still here."

"I'm still here, Mr. Harvey."

"Struttin' around, I reckon, because you've had a little luck."

More than once O'Hara had talked with Steelman about the posse which had attacked the cabin. It was the opinion of both of them that Harvey's hand had been back of the sheriff, his mind the dominating one. Ingram had been at the ranch and could not have known what was intended.

"Not your fault I'm strutting around, Mr. Harvey. I acquit you of blame. You did your best to make good the promise given in your store that I would not cumber the ground long." O'Hara's eyes bored into those of the merchant.

"Meanin' what?" demanded Harvey.

"Meaning that your hired men's intentions were better than their execution. Must be annoying to have them bungle a job the way they did."

"Say, young fellow, if you claim——"

O'Hara brushed rudely past him. There was always a chance that Harvey might be detaining him in the street while his killers were making ready.

The lanky owner of the Longhorn Corral looked at his friend, and in that look were both admiration and distress.

"Great jumpin' horn' toads, you sure go out a yore way to make enemies. Harvey ain't used to being treated thataway," he said.

"I didn't make Harvey my enemy. He was one already. Why not let him know I'm on to his dirty game? But there's no need to draw you into this. Suppose you leave me here."

Worrall flushed darkly. "S'pose I don't. Didn't I tell you I'd throw in with you? She goes as she lays. All I'm sayin' is that you're followin' a mighty dangerous trail. Don't fool yoreself any about that."

"This is the way I look at it, Steve," O'Hara answered, his glance sweeping doors and windows as he moved forward. "It's one thing for Sanderson to say he's going to get me. It's another for him to give me an hour to leave town. He thinks I'm hiding behind Bob Quantrell. I've got to show him I'm not. All you've got to do is to ask me that question when I give the signal."

"You mean the one you was speakin' about before we met Harvey?"

"Yes. You may not get time to ask it, but if you do I'll use it as a cue. If there's trouble, you keep out of it."

"Keep out of it? You sure bump into fool notions, boy. When the guns begin to smoke I've got to join in to save my own hide."

"I've a notion they're not going to smoke. Here we are."

They turned in at the Gold Nugget.

Sanderson and the Texas Kid were at the far end of the long bar. Both of them were drinking while Shep talked. He boasted of how bad he was and what he meant to do to O'Hara. The words died in his throat as he caught sight of

81

the two men who had just entered the place. His jaw dropped with astonishment.

O'Hara gave Shep's slow brain no time to guess what this meant. Lightly the young man walked to the bar, not more than five feet from his enemy. He ordered liquor which he did not intend to drink.

Sanderson glared at him, uncertain what to do. Was this a plant? Had he sat around drinking and boasting while his foes had gathered to ambush him? If not, why would this tenderfoot walk in so jauntily, knowing that he had no chance to beat the gunman to the draw?

The short red-headed cowboy known as the Texas Kid passed through much the same mental reaction, but he was decidedly more fearful than his companion. Why had he let the drink in him talk so loudly? Of a sudden he was sober, sick with terror.

"What makes you so white, Garrett?" asked Worrall, following instructions.

O'Hara did not look at him as he answered. His gaze was fastened on Sanderson. But in his voice there was a lilt of triumphant excitement. So far his plan had worked perfectly. Would it carry through?

"I'm scared to death, Steve, of two scalawags who are going to run me out of town. One of them is a big bully puss fellow ugly as sin, a he-wolf on the howl, to hear him tell it. The other is a hammered-down red-headed runt. If you see them let me know so that I can run, Steve."

O'Hara's mocking eyes looked straight into those of the big bully. They taunted him and defied him and made light of his prowess.

The question that Sanderson growled made clear his thoughts. "Where's Bob Quantrell at?"

"Bob had better hit the trail," O'Hara said to Worrall. "These fellows who have me so frightened will drive him out, too, probably."

Uneasily the bartender polished the top of the counter. He decided to drop to the floor before the shooting began. A patron of the house flitted inconspicuously out of the back door. Four cowboys at a poker table suspended their play and watched the antagonists alertly.

Sanderson spoke vehemently. "I never claimed I'd drive him out. Never gave out any such word. If anyone says I did he's a liar."

"You can tell Bob not to be frightened then, Steve,"

O'Hara said easily. "The scalawags I told you about don't intend to worry him."

"Where's Bob at?" reiterated Sanderson hoarsely.

"How should I know? I'm not his keeper. Stick to the business in hand, Mr. Sanderson. If you should meet either of those terrible bad men I've described tell them I'm one tenderfoot so scared that I'm shaking. This goes for you, too, Mr. Texas Kid."

"I—I'll tell 'em if I see 'em," the red-headed cowboy murmured.

"Say I'm staying in town because I'm too frightened to travel. Ask them not to be too hard on a poor tenderfoot."

"They was funnin', don't you reckon?" the Texas Kid offered by way of explanation.

"Better tell them not to scatter jokes like that around. They might explode and hurt someone. Don't you think so?"

"I'll be movin' along," the Texas Kid said from a dry throat. "I got to meet up with a fellow—with my brother Buck Grogan."

"Don't hurry. Stay and keep Mr. Sanderson company. He won't want to be left here alone."

"Say, fellow, lay off me," Sanderson growled. "If this here's a frame-up you can't start smokin' too soon to suit me. I don't scare worth a whoop. See?"

Nevertheless, his eyes left O'Hara for a moment to sweep toward door and window. He was plainly worried and anxious to be gone with a whole skin.

"You don't think I'd better get out of town, within the hour, say?" O'Hara asked.

Already the red-headed cowboy was moving toward the back door. Sanderson discovered himself deserted and began to follow, backing away slowly. His right hand hovered near the butt of a revolver but he made no motion to draw it.

"Don't ride me, fellow," the bully warned. "I can be pushed just so far. I'm not scared of you, not for a holy minute. Don't you think it."

"I understand that," O'Hara jeered. "You've got to meet up with a man, too, haven't you?"

"I'll meet up with you one of these days an' send you to hell on a shutter," the bad man boasted.

O'Hara's voice was a good imitation of that of the Texas Kid. "You're just funnin', don't you reckon, Mr. Sanderson?" he quavered.

"You or me, one, when we meet," Shep warned.

"Always to-morrow with you, isn't it? Well, it will be a thousand years till we meet, Mr. Sanderson."

The big man slid out of the back door. Outside, he whirled swiftly, at the same time dragging out his weapon. His eyes stabbed here and there looking for enemies. He saw nobody but the Texas Kid. That warrior was legging it on a run for the safety of Ingram & Harvey's store.

CHAPTER XVII: *Shep Makes His Play*

AFTER SANDERSON slid out of the half-open back door of the Gold Nugget there was a long moment of silence. The stage had been set for red tragedy. All present felt that it had been shaved by a narrow margin.

Steve Worrall let out a little whoop of delight. "Bluffed 'em out, by jinks—made 'em back down an' crawl off with their tails between their legs. Oh, boy, you're some wolf tamer."

One of the cowboys at the poker table slapped another a mighty blow on the back. "Made Shep take water, the tenderfoot did. Never saw the beat of it. Didn't think Shep would of quit for hell or high water. Well, you live an' learn, boys." He swept off his sombrero in a bow to O'Hara. "You're one sure enough bad-man buster. I'll be doggoned if Shep didn't tackle more'n he could ride herd on that time, an' you lookin' no more dangerous than a brush rabbit."

Now that the crisis was past O'Hara felt a little sick and faint. "Let's get outside," he said to his friend. His desire was to get back to the safety of the store. Excitement no longer buoyed him up. It shook his nerve to think what a chance he had taken, how he had staked his life on the audacity of a swift frontal attack. Not for a moment did he fool himself into the delusion that he was Sanderson's equal with a six-shooter. The big man had not been afraid of him, but of Bob Quantrell and his allies. Shep had been obsessed by the suspicion that they were trying to trap him into drawing his weapon in order to give them a plausible reason for shooting him down.

O'Hara and Worrall walked past Ingram & Harvey's on their way down the street. Harvey stood in the doorway talking with a big heavy-shouldered man.

"Friend Shep again," Worrall said quietly to his friend.

Sanderson raised his voice in resentful protest. "Tell you

they was layin' for me, Harvey. Ask the Kid. It was fixed to bump us both off if——"

The expression on Harvey's face stopped Sanderson. He turned, glared at O'Hara, and swallowed hard. His fingers itched for the butt of the .44 that rested so close to them.

"Don't shoot, Shep," Harvey said quickly.

O'Hara did not stop in his stride. Impudently he grinned at the storekeeper. "I had a little more luck, Mr. Harvey, and I'm still strutting around."

Nothing more was said. O'Hara and Worrall went on their way magnificently regardless of the furious bad man on the steps of the store. Neither of them turned to see whether, flinging restraint aside, he had snatched a six-shooter from its holster.

Forty yards farther down the street Worrall drew a deep breath of relief. "Whew, boy! I been feelin' Shep's lead pill right between my shoulder blades. I was plumb scared he'd turn his wolf loose regardless. Someone gimme a drink quick before I faint."

They turned in at Steelman & McCarthy's store. A little man sat on a dry-goods box talking excitedly to those present. He was ragged and unshaven. His boots were down at the heel, his hat coneshaped. He was the same Hank the lawyer had seen some cowboys making fun of once in Ingram's store.

"Right then I lit out," Hank narrated. "No place for me. Like I said, that doggoned tenderfoot stood there devillin' Shep to draw, crowdin' in on him, tellin' how scared he was of Shep, an' ridin' him all the time. You go order that pilgrim a coffin, Mr. McCarthy."

McCarthy was facing the door. His hard eyes did not change expression. "He can order it himself, Hank. Here he is now." The storekeeper spoke to O'Hara. "Hank has been worryin' about you. Glad to see it was not necessary."

Worrall sank down on the top of a barrel and mopped his face with a bandanna. "Someone worry about me awhile," he implored. "I'm wore to a frazzle worryin' about myself. This white-haired lad here is bullet-proof, I reckon. Different here. All I'm thankful for is you don't have to order a coffin for me, extra long size."

"Tell us about it, O'Hara," urged McCarthy. "Hank left in the middle of it."

"Not much to tell," O'Hara answered. "I had a little talk with Sanderson. That's all. It was a mistake about his wanting me to leave town. At least he did not mention it when we met."

"Lemme tell the story," Worrall said. "I was among those present, an innocent bystander who stood to get all shot up if trouble began. Garrett here gets what glory there is in being the prize jackass, though I qualify at the head of the list as a dumber one than he is. Someone feed me a cigarette, then listen an' tell me if we ain't both loco."

The lengthy owner of the Longhorn got his cigarette and told his story. He told it with humour, making the most of its drama. When he had finished a red-faced cowboy spoke.

"I don't savvy yet why Shep didn't come a-shootin'. Was he scared, do you reckon?"

"He was scared but bluffin' he wasn't," Worrall replied. "The Texas Kid didn't even make any claims he wasn't."

"What was they scared of?" the cowboy persisted. "Shep had better'n an even break, hadn't he?"

"Say, young fellow, how many men do you know who have stood off Shep an' Bob Quantrell an' Deever an' this Texas Kid an' 'steen other warriors for half a day? How many do you know who have crawled Shep's carcass an' branded him with grapplin' irons an' got away with it? I don't know so doggoned many myself." This contribution was from Worrall.

"Well, if anyone had told me you could run a sandy on Shep——"

"Question is, what will Shep do now?" interrupted McCarthy. "He'll have to make some kind of a play to explain why he didn't get on the peck. Right now he's sore at himself as a toad on a skillet."

"Yep. He'll make a play," Worrall agreed. "Soon, too. Got to do it or lose his rep with the crowd he trails with."

There came the sound of a shot, of several in quick succession, of another. The men in the store listened. More than one made sure that his revolver would slide easily from the holster. McCarthy stepped back of the desk in his office and came back with a rifle.

"From the other store, sounds to me," he said. "I'll go take a look up the street."

He moved a step or two toward the front, then stopped. A man had come into the store. He stood by the cigar case, a revolver in each hand. From the barrel of one of them a thin wisp of smoke lifted. The man was Quantrell.

"What's up, Bob?" asked McCarthy.

The eyes of the boy killer gleamed savagely. "They tried to get me—Shep an' Deever an' that Texas Kid."

"You hit?"

"Me? No." His buck teeth showed and his receding chin dropped as he laughed harshly. "Not me. Ask about them."

"What about 'em?"

"I got Shep an' the Kid. Say, let's go back right now an' clean out the whole outfit."

McCarthy shook his head. "Not enough of us here. Besides, we want the law with us. How was it, Bob? Did they jump you?"

"Came outa the store, all three of 'em. Shep called to me an' smoked right up. Right away all of us went to it. That's all, except that Shep an' his friend went to sleep in smoke an' Deever took cover in the store. Me, I skedaddled down the street *muy pronto*. I didn't know how many other guys were inside."

"Well, he's made his play, Shep has," Worrall said. "He was sure enough a bad picker. Off hand, looks like he might have had better luck with me an' Garrett. All I got to say is it might have been a lot worse—for us." He looked at O'Hara. "Am I right, old horn' toad?"

O'Hara nodded. "Quite right, I'd say."

CHAPTER XVIII: *The Shy Man Talks*

No THRILL as of wine raced through Barbara's veins these days when she rode the hilltops. Life had lost its savour. She did not at early morning drink in the air with unconscious joy because a new world had been born for her delight.

Until lately she had been queen of her little world with all the privileges that implies. The only daughter of Wesley Steelman, cattle king of the San Marcos, held an enviable position in that roughriding frontier country.

Now she rode with diminished head. An immovable force had brought her up short. It had seemed to her, not many weeks since, a fine thing to draw David Ingram and her father together. Eagerly she had adventured to that end. By her means friendliness would grow in that divided community where enmity had been. Signally she had failed. That, she recognized now, had been inevitable.

A bitter personal humiliation had accompanied the failure. It had come to pass soon that when they met she had moved toward Ingram with gifts in her eyes, and what she offered meant so little to him that self-will and stubbornness were more necessary to his life. Love! What was that to him? He had snatched at her roughly, not because he needed her and could not bear to do without her but as a weapon with which to wound her father. Not only her pride was hurt, but that deeper emotion which flowed like a strong stream from her to him. She was young enough to feel that what had happened to her was tragic. It was not yet within her experience that time mellows the sharpest sting of shame to a tender memory.

In the company of Garrett O'Hara she found comfort. In spite of his shyness he had a gift for companionship. She liked to explore his mind. He did not in the least object to being made fun of by her, for he sensed that she liked and respected him.

"You're the first good bad man I ever knew," she told him one day as they rode back to her father's ranch after he had roped and side-lined a cow. "Shep Sanderson was a bad bad man. I've known a good many like that. You've got a great reputation, but I suppose you don't shoot men often."

He answered in her own vein. "Not often. Once is usually enough," he said flippantly.

"Good gracious! Hear him boast. And after all he's only a tenderfoot. His rope missed the cow twice before she was caught."

He plucked a thrill from her raillery. She was the first young and attractive woman with whom he had ever felt at home. The important thing about their relationship to him was his conviction that she relied on him, that it was not necessary to put into words some sutble understanding between them.

A little later she referred to the secret that he knew. "Nice girls back East don't do what I've done. Down in yore heart what do you think of me? How much do you despise me?"

"I've known men who always played safe," he began hesitantly. "They never took a chance, always waited to see how the cat was going to jump. They didn't make friends because friendship is a risk. I've known others generous and eager and swift to give themselves and all they had. I suppose they weren't always wise, but even their folly was lovable." He stopped, flushing with embarrassment.

The girl let eyes tender and very bright rest on him for a moment. "I know a man just like that last kind," she said.

"Of course you do—probably several of them," he replied. "He's more liable to make mistakes than your cold selfish kind, but you don't blame him for them, at least not very

88

much." He looked away at broken line of the silhouetted hills pushing their crests skyward. Presently he added, as though the comment were a casual one, "I wouldn't think much of a man who couldn't do something foolish if—if he was fond of—of someone."

"You mean of a girl," she specified.

"Say of a girl," he admitted, and the colour came again into his face. Never before had he talked about such things to a woman.

"Yes, but a girl is different. You know that well enough. It's her place to be modest and wait. She mustn't show her feelings. If she's nice she's not supposed to have any—not till—till——"

He took this up shyly where she had dropped it. "I don't know anything about young ladies, but—I'd think that idea was contrary to nature. She has to be human, hasn't she? A young lady, I mean."

She shook her head. "Not what *Godey's Lady's Book* says. It's awful for a girl to be bold. That's true, too. If my mother had lived I might have been different."

O'Hara summoned his courage and blurted out what was in his mind. "You couldn't be anything but sweet and good. I wish—I wish you wouldn't talk that way. All you've done is what I'd want you to do if—if——"

He stopped. The hot blood stained his face from throat to forehead.

Barbara's soft and shining eyes thanked him.

"I'm glad you came here to live," she said softly.

He did not let his eyes meet hers, for he was afraid they might tell too much. She offered him only friendship, and already he knew that he wanted more than that.

CHAPTER XIX: *Peace Terms*

THE JEFFERSON COUNTY WAR had become more than a local issue. Both factions were justifying themselves in long letters to the newspapers. The territorial government favoured Steelman because of his business connections, and Sheriff Banks had been removed from office on a technicality connected with his bond. Rumours of the feud had even reached Washington and there was talk of national interference.

Ingram's warriors had "jumped" two of Steelman's cowboys while they were branding a calf claimed by the Diamond Tail. There had been a fight and the two Hashknife riders

89

had been left dead beside the fire they had started. That evening their bodies were found there by friends.

In reprisal the Hashknife forces had captured Houck, a notorious gunman from the Indian Territory employed by Ingram, and had left his body in a draw. The official report made to the new sheriff was that he had been killed while resisting arrest.

The active partners of the Circle S O ranch served notice to their employees that any discovered guilty of lawlessness would be discharged. Their cowboys grinned when they read this warning tacked on the door of the bunk house, but it was known later that some of them joined their allies of the Hashknife in night raids. Bob Quantrell stuck his tongue in his cheek. Very little of his time was spent at the home ranch, and what the bosses did not know would not hurt them, he told the cook cynically.

Smith-Beresford suggested compromise to Steelman.

"We've been talking it over, Garrett and I," he said. "Can't go on like this, you know. Something must be done. What say Garrett and I ride over and have a cozy little talk with Ingram? Might make the fellow see reason. Eh, what?"

Steelman reflected that it could do no harm. Moreover, it would be a good talking point later to be able to say that he and his partners had tried to arrange a compromise. Also, there was urgent need of peace financially if it could be brought about.

"Suits me," he said. "But I don't want you boys gettin' shot up. How you gonna arrange it to keep Ingram an' his friends from pluggin' you when you show up all full of peace an' Merry Christmas?"

"That's a stumper," admitted Smith-Beresford. "Our notion is to send someone over and ask for a peace conduct. If he says he'll talk with us we'll ride over to his ranch. Or if he'd rather we'll meet him in town."

"Better arrange it for town. Safer there than over at the ranch among his hired killers."

"Question is about a compromise. What can we offer him?"

"What had you thought of offering?" Steelman asked, a flicker of cynical humour in his eyes. He had no faith in the success of this mission.

O'Hara and Barbara came into the room. The eyes of the girl were shining.

"Mr. O'Hara has told me, Dad. You'll join in an' try to get peace, won't you?"

"Certainly," he answered promptly. "Anything in reason. I've always been ready to do the fair thing. Tell him to turn over to the law the killers he's shielding an' we'll talk turkey. If he'll drive a clean herd an' quit rustling my calves an' get off the Hughes place where he's got no business an' quit interferin' with my markets, why we'll be able to get along fine long as he keeps outa my sight."

"If that's what we're to tell him we'd better stay at home," O'Hara said, laughing.

"Oh, Dad, of course they can't tell him that. We've got to give up something for the sake of peace."

"Well, ain't I givin' up plenty?" demanded Steelman, a chip on his shoulder at once. "I could talk for an hour about the meannesses that fellow has done me, an' I'm willin' to put all that in the discard. All I'm askin' is what's right, an' not half of that."

"The trouble is, Ingram won't look at it that way," said Smith-Beresford. "He thinks he's been injured, too, all over the shop, you know. As I see it, question isn't who's wrong or who's right, but how to get a working agreement so that a fellow can step out in the morning without the chance of being shot down. Isn't there some way to adjust difficulties—ranges, markets, ownership of stock? A little give and a little take?"

"You're assumin' that Ingram an' I are equally in the wrong," Steelman replied harshly. "He's rustled my calves, an' underbid me on beef contracts because he can pick up my steers on the drive an' sell them for his. He's played underhanded politics to get his hangers-on into office where they could annoy me. He has hired gunmen to kill my cowboys. Right now he has got a bunch of his warriors over at the Jerry Hughes place after the court appointed me administrator. It's not a question of two honest men compromisin' a difficulty. He's a bad *hombre*, that fellow. You're damn whistlin'!"

"He's aggressive, high-handed, and lawless," admitted O'Hara. "I grant you that. But he'll stick to his word if he gives it. We ought to see if we can't work out some understanding with him. Things can't go on like this."

"He'll think you've come to tell him we've had enough an' want to quit," Steelman predicted. "But have it yore own way, boys. Go talk with him. Make yore proposition an' see what it gets you."

The three men talked terms while Barbara listened. She knew better than to say much, for fear her father might think

91

he was being "run" by a girl. One thing Steelman insisted upon. There could be no settlement of the trouble until Ingram moved his men bag and baggage from the Hughes place. If he would do that it would be evidence that he really wanted peace.

"Don't think he'll do it," O'Hara said. "That's one thing he's set on. Ingram feels that Hughes was one of his followers and that he rather than you ought to settle up things."

"Hasn't he got any respect for the courts?" demanded Steelman indignantly. "But why ask that? We know damn well he hasn't, or he wouldn't keep that bunch of warriors there. I won't stand for it. I'm gonna have Sheriff Graham send a posse to clean 'em out."

"Thought we were talking peace, Mr. Steelman," suggested O'Hara mildly.

"Well, we are. Like I said, I'm for peace if he'll come anywheres near doing the right thing. I'm willin' to keep my cows this side of the pass. If he can show that any of my riders ever ran the Hashknife brand on a Diamond Tail calf I'll send the guilty party down the road so quick he won't have time to say 'Billy be damn.' More than that, I'll keep outa the San Jacinto market if he'll agree to leave me the Indian agency at the fort an' not make any bids there. I'll get rid of my gunmen if he'll do the same. That's as far as I'll go an' he can take it or leave it."

O'Hara was of the opinion that he would leave it, but he did not say so. A peace mission, even though it did not succeed at first, might be an entering wedge that would later produce the desired results.

The three men drafted a letter and sent it to Ingram by one of the Hashknife riders. Word of what was in the air spread and Bob Quantrell suggested to O'Hara that he would be glad to go to town with him to meet Ingram.

"Much obliged, Bob, but I don't think that would be wise," O'Hara told him promptly. "Since our latest trip to town I expect you'd be like a red rag to a bull as far as Ingram goes. No, we'll leave you at home this time."

"Some of his warriors are liable to make trouble. Who do you aim to take along with you?"

"Nobody but Lyulph. We want to make it plain that this is to be a peace powwow. Perhaps we'll go absolutely unarmed."

"Hmp! You've still got a lot of those fool notions you brought West with you. There will be a dozen Ingram men in town, every last one of 'em armed. What guarantee you got that Ingram or his pardner Tom Harvey won't sic' some of 'em on you like Harvey did those fellows on me?"

"I'd trust Ingram's word."

"I'm not sayin' I wouldn't, but will Ingram's promise bind Deever or Roche or Harvey? You're shoutin' it won't, not if they get a notion to throw down on you with a cutter."

"We'll have to take a chance on that."

But after O'Hara had talked the matter over with his two partners it was decided that the envoys should wear their revolvers, not as a threat but because it was the habit of cowboys and cattle men to carry them. There was always a chance that the fact they had them in plain sight might save them from attack.

CHAPTER XX: *A Conference*

TO INGRAM AND HARVEY, sitting in the office of the store, came one of their clerks, a young fellow who had recently moved to the territory for lung trouble. His name was Millikan.

"They're alone," he reported. "Just rode up to the Concho House and have gone inside. They stopped for two-three minutes at the Longhorn Corral before they went to the hotel."

"Steelman not with them then?"

"No, sir."

"Drift out into the street an' make sure none of their men join 'em." After the clerk had gone Ingram turned to his partner. "We'll let 'em wait a while, Tom. Don't want 'em to get the notion we're anxious for a compromise."

Harvey agreed, but added a rider: "Just the same I reckon we better meet 'em halfway. Don't look good to me the way things are breakin'. If this war goes on much longer we'll be busted higher than a kite, you an' me."

Ingram looked out of the window at the red hill shoulder dotted with jack pines. Reluctantly he admitted to himself that what Harvey said was true. The expense of maintaining the little army of gunmen had been high. Trade had fallen off. It was a bad year for cattle from the market point of view. He had been forced to carry his allies, the small ranchers in the hills. Moreover, to meet Steelman's encroachments he had borrowed heavily and his short-time notes were falling due. He could borrow no more. The owner of the Hashknife had had business with most of the bankers in the territory and they were friendly to him rather than to his enemies in this feud. Add to all this the fact that there was talk of intervention from Washington. If soldiers came in from the fort there was little doubt that they would support Steelman, for he and Colonel Randolph had fought side by side in the Civil War.

In the field Ingram could hold his own. He was not disturbed about that, providing always that the United States troops did not come in. But he had read of generals who won every battle and lost the war. The thought of compromise was bitter to him, but he knew that if Steelman made a reasonable offer he must accept it.

Yet he was reluctant to admit even the possibility of defeat. "How about Steelman?" he said. "He must be near the end of his rope, too. His expenses are heavier than ours. It hasn't been any better year for cows for him than it has for us. He's borrowed more than we have, don't you reckon?"

"Maybeso. But he's got more money backing him than we have. Far as we can see, Dave, we're down to the blanket."

"Well, let's hear what these fellows have got to propose."

Ingram and Harvey walked down the street to the Concho House. The fat hotel keeper Brad Helm waddled forward and wheezed a greeting.

"The other gents are waitin' for you in the dining room," he added. "I'll see you're not interrupted."

The cattle man moved with light strong tread into the dining room. His cool flinty eyes fastened on the two men sitting at the table. The plump florid Englishman was smoking a cigar, his friend a pipe. Both of them rose to greet the newcomers, though neither of them offered to shake hands.

"Glad to see you, gentlemen," Smith-Beresford said genially. "Make yourselves comfortable. Cigars? Whisky? Beer?"

"Nothing, thanks," Ingram answered brusquely. "You have a proposition to make, I understand."

"About time we had a talk. Eh, what? Sit down, gentlemen, and let's make ourselves at home."

Ingram flung himself carelessly into a chair. He put a muscular forearm on the table. The lines of his thickset figure expressed strength no less than the powerful slope of the throat and the salient jaw.

"I'm ready to listen," he said.

O'Hara opened the conference. "I don't know what you think, Mr. Ingram, but as law-abiding citizens Mr. Smith-Beresford and I feel that the present conditions are outrageous and deplorable."

"Who made 'em that way?" demanded Harvey, an ugly look on his pallid face.

"I suppose we'd differ about that. The important question is how we can improve them."

"Are you talkin' for yoreselves or for Wes Steelman?" asked Ingram curtly.

"We're talking for him and for ourselves, too. He is ready to patch up a peace if you are."

"Had enough, has he?" jeered Harvey.

O'Hara looked at him. "If that's the spirit in which you are coming to this conference, Mr. Harvey, I'm afraid we won't get far," he said.

"Say, young fellow, you're a fine bird to come here preachin' to us," Ingram's partner retorted angrily. "Why, you've done more to make trouble than any other gunman on the range, except maybe yore sidekick Bob Quantrell. Who jumped pore Shep Sanderson an' devilled him an' finally got yore hired killer to bump off both him an' the Texas Kid? Who tried to stop a posse from doing its duty an' killed Brad Sowers an' shot up three more deputies? Who egged on Wes Steelman to all the deviltry that's been going on all over the range, dry-gulchin' an' what not?"

"That's bally nonsense, you know, Mr. Harvey," Smith-Beresford replied. "O'Hara is as peaceably inclined as I am. Both of us would go a long way to stop the wicked foolishness that has started simply because conflicting interests have not been sensibly adjusted. You know perfectly well that he wanted no trouble with that fellow Sanderson and that neither of us obstructed the posse in its duty. He fought for his life."

"Let that ride, Tom," Ingram spoke up. "Let's hear how these two quiet law-abidin' Christians propose to adjust the conflictin' interests referred to. Knowin' Wes Steelman like I do, I'd say he's perfectly willin' to lie down with the lamb— if it's inside of him."

"The only way to settle this thing is to start from now. If we get to discussing our wrongs our feelings will become involved. Steelman feels he has a good deal to complain of. So do you, I presume. Mr. Smith-Beresford and I think we have been dragged into this without any justification whatever. Let us forget all that and come to the actual business questions at issue. Does that sound reasonable to you, Mr. Ingram?" O'Hara asked.

The cattle man's smile was sarcastic, "You're a lawyer, O'Hara. It's yore business to make anything sound reasonable. Shoot yore proposition. I'll know then how reasonable it is."

O'Hara named, without argument, the concessions Steelman was willing to make. He would keep his cattle on the range east of the pass. He would leave the San Jacinto market to Ingram and his friends if they would not compete with him at the Indian agency. He would discharge any of his men against whom there was proof of rustling cattle. As to the lawlessness of the past few months, he was willing to let bygones be bygones.

Harvey laughed unpleasantly. "He's sure promisin' a lot. Has our friends shot up by hired killers an' then is willin' to call it off. Offers to keep outa the San Jacinto market when he knows Dave has got it corralled, but wants us to leave him lay at the agency where we've been outsellin' him right along. Yes, sir, I'd sure call that a Wes Steelman compromise."

"What about the Jerry Hughes place?" asked Ingram. "Will he quit gumshoein' around tryin' to euchre me out of it?"

"He's willing to leave that to the law," O'Hara answered.

"To the slick judge he bought to make him administrator. Not by a jugful. Understand me, young fellows. I'm for peace on any reasonable basis. There's no man livin' I'd put up with as much from as I have from him. I've never wanted trouble. I don't want it now. But neither Wes Steelman nor any other man can order me to get off the earth. The only compromise I'll discuss is one where he gives up all claim to the Hughes place. Jerry was my friend. He owed me money when he died. I've a right to run the place till I'm paid what he owes. Steelman butted in without any claim whatever, merely because he wanted to devil me. Well, he won't get away with it." Ingram slammed his heavy brown fist down on the table, his eyes gleaming savagely. "What business has he got up there in the hills, anyhow? Why did he buy that upper ranch? You know why well as I do. He couldn't stand to see anyone else gettin' ahead, anyone who wouldn't admit that Wes Steelman is the big auger. So he comes in to put me outa business. That's why he gets his hired-man judge to turn over the Jerry Hughes place to him. Thought that would fix my clock sure. Then, because I didn't light out like a brush rabbit scared of a lobo wolf, he begins bellyachin' around about how I'm a bad *hombre* an' all he wants is his rights. Hell's bells, if he had his rights he'd be wearin' stripes an' breakin' rocks. Law! That's a fine word for Steelman to use. He's for it strong as a shyster lawyer when it's for him, but I've

96

noticed that those who yell loudest for law are the ones would hate worst to have justice done to them. You tell him I aim to stay on the Hughes place till the cows come home, an' I don't allow to let any shorthorn cow man an' his warriors drive me away. Far as I'm concerned that's its shape."

Ingram looked O'Hara hard in the eye, and the younger man realized the ruthless force of him. In the current phrase, he would go through from hell to breakfast.

"If we make this a personal issue instead of a business one we'll not get very far in the way of compromise," O'Hara said. "Forget you don't like Steelman and tell us the very best you'll do, the concessions you are willing to make. Perhaps we can offer inducements to have you leave the Hughes place."

"No, sir, I'm stayin' right there, an' you can pass the word that he'll rue the day he an' his killers try to drive us out."

O'Hara smiled, the friendly flash of white teeth that made men like him. "I haven't got much yet from you that Steelman will enjoy hearing. Haven't you any compromise in your system at all? We're supposed to be talking peace and not war."

"I'm ready to talk it any time. All I want is my rights. This trouble is none of my startin'. All I've done is defend myself."

"That's so," his partner chimed in. "We're right an' Steelman is wrong all the way. But we're good citizens not lookin' for trouble even with him. If Dave's agreeable I'm willin' to leave him the Indian agency market. He's got no claim to it, but just to show where we stand."

"An' I'll accept his proposition about the pass an' keep my cows on the west side. If he really means business let him fire that bunch of killers he has got hired," Ingram said.

"Will you get rid of yours if he does his, Mr. Ingram?" asked Smith-Beresford.

"I've got no Bob Quantrells in my crowd, young fellow. But I'll admit I've been forced to protect my rights by armin' my men. I'll meet Steelman halfway there, too, an' turn off those I don't need as range riders."

The difficulties between the factions were talked over in detail. When the two Circle S O partners rose to go they felt that as a first conference it had not been entirely unsuccessful. Ingram had made concessions—ungraciously and reluctantly, to be sure, but the fact that he had made them at all was encouraging.

"He talks just like Steelman does," O'Hara said to his

friend, laughing ruefully. "You'd think to hear him that he was the most reasonable man in the world and that he never had wanted anything but the barest justice. One gathers, too, that he's a patient, law-abiding citizen driven at last by sheer necessity to defend his rights. But we've made a start. If we can keep the fire-eaters quiet long enough to come to an agreement we may succeed."

They rode out of Concho over the same trail O'Hara had followed the day he first saw the place. They climbed the steep ascent which led by way of a red hill shoulder into the jack pines and cedars. From this altitude the chaparral could not be seen. Manzanita and mesquite, sage and Spanish bayonet were wiped out by distance. The valley looked parched and lifeless, as level as a floor, all undulations smoothed away.

As they looked down upon it a rider dashed around the curve of the trail and at sight of them dragged his horse to a halt. He was a Mexican vaquero in a steeple straw hat and earrings. He wore a sash of green silk.

While his horse was still in motion the man flung up a rifle and fired. The horse went up into the air, bucking furiously. The rifle clattered to the ground.

The Mexican was a superb rider, but the trail was narrow. It looked as though the bucker would pitch down the slope. More than once its feet struck the edge and sent rubble clattering. To save himself the man flung his body from the saddle toward the hill, went clambering up a precipitous rocky outcrop of gneiss, lost his footing, and slid down again.

One of the hoofs of the plunging horse struck the man as he rose and sent him staggering backward. He stumbled over a piece of broken boulder and fell. Before he could regain his feet a sharp voice gave orders.

"Stick up your hands. No funny business."

O'Hara had slipped from the saddle and run forward, revolver in hand.

Up went the Mexican's arms. "*Si, señor,*" he answered submissively.

"Do you speak English?"

"Pretty good, *señor.*"

"You're one of Ingram's riders?"

"*Si, señor.*"

"What made you shoot at us? Have you been told to kill us at sight?"

The man broke into a torrent of Spanish, then interpreted it with excitable broken English. The Circle S O partners

98

understood from what he said that a battle was in progress at the Jerry Hughes ranch. A group of Hashknife warriors had made a surprise attack upon the place and he, Juan Garcia, returning from the pasture with a bunch of horses, had been fired upon by them and made his escape. He had recognized among the attackers Bob Quantrell and Texas Jim. When he had caught sight of the Circle S O partners he had jumped to the conclusion that they were there to cut off his retreat. Wherefore he had not waited for them to open hostilities.

"Did you see Steelman among the Hashknife men?" O'Hara asked.

Garcia said that he had not recognized him but that most of the riders had been too far away from him to tell who they were.

"Steelman told us this morning he was riding down to the valley ranch to-day," Smith-Beresford said.

"Yes," agreed O'Hara.

But the thought was in his mind that Steelman might have said this to divert suspicion. He might be with the attackers, or he might have ridden away, tongue in cheek, knowing that his men were going to try to seize the Hughes ranch. This latter alternative did not seem like him. Whatever else might be said of him, Wesley Steelman had the courage of his decisions. He would not leave his men to undertake what he would not attempt himself. More probably his hired gunmen had decided on their own initiative to force the issue.

CHAPTER XXI: *Quantrell's Posse Rides*

BOB QUANTRELL roped and saddled at the corral in a cloud of dust raised by milling horses. Others were roping at the same time. The young man swung astride of his horse and looked around.

"All caught?" he asked, and counted heads.

Five men were mounted in addition to himself.

"All caught," Texas Jim answered.

The riders cut across to the upper rim of the park and headed into the rough country beyond.

"Where at will Jake meet us?" asked Texas Jim.

"At Salt Springs. He camped there last night. Leastways that was the arrangement."

Another man spoke up, a squat cowboy in shiny leathers and costume much the worse for wear from the tattered hat to the dusty boots much run over at the heels. His name was

Owen, and he went by the sobriquet of Amen for some long-forgotten reason.

"The Old Man won't get sore, do you reckon?"

Quantrell looked at him. "Why should he? Didn't Judge Warner make him administrator? An' hasn't Ingram kept a bunch of gunmen on the place ever since? Wes has been leanin' backward so as not to get in bad with the territory authorities, seein' as he has them on his side now. Bet you my new saddle against a dollar. Mex he'll be plumb tickled to have us jump the ranch without his knowin' a thing about it. Jake is a deputy sheriff, ain't he? We'll all be sworn in as special deputies. Everything legal an' aboveboard. The Old Man won't have a thing to kick about. With no trouble a-tall to him the sheriff executes the order of the court. He'll come back from the lower ranch to find himself sittin' in the saddle high, wide, an' pretty."

"How do you aim to make yore play, Bob?" another of the party wanted to know. He had an eager boyish face which looked odd beneath a heavy thatch of prematurely white hair.

"Depends on this an' that, Whitey. My notion is to slip into that clump of timber above the ranch house an' lie doggo till we see where we're at. Chances are these warrior-waddies will be kinda careless by this time an' we'd ought to be able to surprise 'em. Course we hope they'll see reason right away, but if they don't—well, that'll be too bad."

They were crossing difficult country, filled with ravines, gulches, and steep ascents. Hills rose and fell precipitously. They wound around some of these. Others they climbed.

"Salt Springs," Texas Jim called back from the forefront of the line. "An' some lone bird is sure enough roostin' down there before a fire of nigger-heads."

The lone bird turned out to be Jake Sommers, and at sight of the approaching horsemen he at once put himself in a position for defense. From the cottonwood behind which he had taken shelter he sang out a greeting which was also a challenge.

" 'Lo, you fellows!"

Bob nodded greeting. " 'Lo, Jake! How's yore corporate sagacity this glad mornin'?"

"I been waitin' here quite some time," he complained. "You told me you'd be along either last night or before daybreak."

Sommers was a hard-eyed, frozen-faced specimen. He had been a professional gambler until recently.

"I said, barrin' accidents," Quantrell corrected. "We were

held up at the ranch. The belted earl an his friend O'Hara were over there with the Old Man. When they hit the trail I had to stick around till the Old Man had got off for the lower ranch. We didn't get started till ten o'clock. We been shovin' our broomies right along since. What's yore sweat, old man? Nobody's gonna walk off with the Hughes place before we get there."

"I thought the idea was to surprise these birds—hold 'em up as they came out of the bunk house in the mornin'," Sommers replied sourly.

"It's been wished on us this way." The boy grinned at him, intrepidly gay-hearted. "Who cares? We got a better light to shoot by, old sockdolager."

"The light ain't any better for us than it is for them, is it?" asked the deputy.

"I been tellin' Bob we're liable to have trouble," Owen put in.

"For an old bronco peeler who usta sit the buck you're certainly a cautious guy, Amen," Quantrell said jauntily. "An' you're the same hellamiler that fought his way out of Martin Dunn's saloon in Tascosa with four rangers on the shoot at him."

"Hmp!" snorted the cowboy. "I was fed on raw meat in those kid days. Usta fool myself into thinkin' I wouldn't ask odds of old John Wesley Hardin himself if I met him. After I got shot up two-three times I got more sense."

"Oh, well, you never can tell. Here's hopin'."

As they drew closer to the timber above the Hughes place conversation ceased. The men rode warily. They might by chance come at any moment on some of the enemy.

In the timber, near the upper edge of it, the men dismounted. Boy though he was, Quantrell by common consent took command.

"You stay here with the horses, Joe," he ordered. "The rest of us will move forward through the pines. It's not likely we've been seen. But don't let yoreself be surprised, Joe. We'll come a-runnin' if we hear yore six-shooter bark. I don't reckon I need to tell you other bow-legged bipeds to keep yore tongues padlocked. No Fourth of July orations go where we're headed for."

They stole forward through the grove, Quantrell and the deputy in the lead. From a bluff well sheltered by brush they could look down on the Hughes ranch house, not more than two hundred yards away.

A couple of men were at the stable, sitting in the shade cast by the building. One of them was whittling, the other oiling a revolver. A third man was at the brook which ran back of the house. He was washing some socks and hanging them on the branches of some willows that fringed the stream.

"Looks like we'll have to disturb a right happy home," Quantrell murmured ironically to the deputy.

"I'd give a plug of tobacco to know where the rest of 'em are at," Sommers said.

"We're gonna find out mighty soon. Get yore artillery ready, boys, an' we'll send some lead plums down there. Soon as we do we're liable to hear the other curly wolves howl. I'll take the fellow by the creek. The two sociable guys will be yore meat." The young killer glanced around at his men. "Are you all ready?"

Someone misunderstood. He was either too anxious or he was nervous. A shot rang out from the bluff and the three men below scrambled into instant motion. The one at the creek scudded for the house. The other two ran around the barn to find safety there.

Instantly Quantrell's rifle cracked. Other weapons boomed out. The man running from the brook stumbled, almost fell, recovered himself, and disappeared limping into the house. The other two vanished into the stable.

Quantrell was disgusted. "You spilled the beans proper, Mac. We had three of 'em salted an' we didn't get a one. What's the idea? Did you get buck fever?"

"You asked was we ready," Mac defended.

"Oh, well, no use beefin' about it now. We've probably got 'em scared into the notion that there's a million of us. Right now we'll rush the stable. Come on, boys, before they get time to get set."

He slid down into a brushy draw, ran through it, and emerged into the open. Straight for the stable he ran, the others at his heels. If they had had time to talk him out of it they would have done so, for this was a reckless business. But he had given them no time to argue. They had to follow or let him go alone.

The boy had covered more than half the distance before the first shot of the enemy rang out. It came from the house. At the same time two men emerged from the stable and fled through the willows at the creek toward the bunk house. They were the same ones who had been driven into the stable a minute earlier. Almost simultaneously a rider came into sight over the brow of a hill. He was a Mexican, and he was driving a bunch of horses. Texas Jim took a shot at him. He wheeled his horse and fled.

From the ranch house guns spat bullets at the running men. Quantrell reached the stable. Texas Jim and Whitey and Mac were at his heels. The deputy sheriff came panting in twenty yards back of them. He was a heavy man in the late forties, not used to doing a two-hundred-yard sprint.

Quantrell counted heads. "Where's Amen?" he asked.

"I dunno. He was right behind me when we started," Whitey said.

There was an opening in the rear of the stable originally intended for a window. Texas Jim stepped back and looked out.

"They done got him, Bob. He's out there twenty-thirty yards from the house." He added presently: "He moved, so he ain't dead."

Young Quantrell called to the cowboy. "How about it, Amen? Can you crawl to this window so's we can help you in?"

Owen crept a yard or two on hands and knees, then sank down. "I don't reckon I can," he answered.

A bullet flung up a spit of dirt a foot from the wounded man's head. Another struck the heel of his boot.

"Cripes, all they got to do is keep pluggin' at old Amen till they finish him," Quantrell said. "Damfidon't take a whirl at gettin' him in, boys. Try to keep the guys in the house busy while I make my play."

He propped his rifle against the wall, put one leg over the window sill, and in a moment had wriggled out. Across the open he ran toward the man on the ground.

A bullet whistled past him. A second struck him in the thigh. He either fell or flung himself down beside the squat cowboy.

CHAPTER XXII: *Besieged*

QUANTRELL ROSE to his knees, crouching low. Sand flew where a bullet struck the ground beside him.

"Gotta get to cover pronto, Amen," he snarled. "Those sidewinders will bump us off sure. Climb on my back, fellow. Hell's coughing fire here."

He helped the other to his feet. Owen wavered and almost fell.

"On my back, Amen." The boy's cold eyes glittered. His

voice had an ugly rasp. "We'll beat the flop-eared devils yet."

Owen put his arms around the boy's neck and Quantrell staggered toward the stable. The feet of the older man dragged along the ground. A few yards from the building Quantrell collapsed and went down. He lay where he had fallen, pinned down by the weight of the other.

Someone dragged Owen's body from on top of him. Quantrell looked around. Texas Jim was carrying the helpless man toward the corner of the stable.

"Come on, Bob," the Texan yelled.

Guns roared. Whether the shots were being fired at him Quantrell did not know. He followed Texas Jim and passed the corner of the log building to temporary safety.

The man called Mac came out of the front of the barn and helped carry Owen inside. They put him down on the hay.

"Looks like he's hurt bad," the white-haired cowboy said, lowering his voice.

Owen opened his eyes. "Betcha I make the grade, Whitey," he said feebly.

"Sure you will. Where you hit, Amen?"

The wounded cowboy put his hand to his stomach and clamped his jaws to suppress a groan. He was suffering severe pain.

Quantrell sat down on a feed box and cursed bitterly and fluently. The object of his maledictions was the party of Ingram's gunmen at the ranch house. The adventure he had planned and led had gone wrong. Scarcely more than five minutes since the odds had been all in favour of his side. In that five minutes the situation had been wholly reversed. The Hashknife men were the ones now in a hole. Quantrell did not need anyone to point out to him how badly he had blundered in charging down the hill. He had acted under impulse like a fool boy.

"Where do we go from here?" asked Whitey.

The deputy sheriff was watching the house from a chink between the logs of the wall. Without looking around he growled an answer.

"We don't go anywhere. We stay right here till they smoke us out."

Quantrell answered what he chose to read into the man's words. "Light out soon as you've a mind to, Jake. Nobody has got you hog-tied."

"Where would I head for, Bob?—on foot, with all them killers pluggin' at me."

"You could explain you're a deputy," the boy jeered.

"I'm a plumb fool for being in this trap, but seein' as I am I'll do what explainin' I got to do with old Tried an' True here." Sommers patted the barrel of his rifle with his hand.

The boy desperado was examining his wound. He looked up to drawl out a question carelessly, almost insolently. "What's yore kick anyhow? Course I'm sorry Amen got shot up, but outside of that we're sittin' pretty. You're a gambler, you claim. What odds you want, Jake? Heard about the Circle S O fracas, haven't you? Well, if two babes in the woods can stand off a dozen gunmen an' make 'em quit how long can five husky he-men hold out against maybe seven or eight guys who can't hardly hit the side of a barn, looks like?"

"Hit you an' Amen, didn't they?"

"Outa how many shots? If they'd known their business they would have picked off 'most all of us as we came down the hill."

The young man tied up his wound with a bandanna he had taken from his neck. Texas Jim and Mac were ministering to Owen. There was not much they could do for him. The bullet had passed through the lower intestines, apparently.

"Wish we had a doc here," Mac said to Quantrell, speaking in a low voice.

"Hmp! While you're wishin', Mac, don't quit at one doc. Wish for seven or eight good fightin' men to help us stomp out that nest of rattlers that stung pore Amen."

All firing had ceased. Those at the ranch house made no immediate attempt to molest the invaders. Presently Whitey made an announcement.

"Fellow just got on a horse the other side the house an' rode off."

"Gone to let Ingram know," Texas Jim guessed.

"An' after a while Dave will be back here with a whole passle of warriors," Sommers added.

Quantrell made no comment, unless it was one to hum his favourite refrain:

> "Rock a-bye, baby,
> Punch a buckaroo,
> Daddy'll be home
> When the round-up is through."

"It'll be a round-up of Hashknife waddies, looks like," Mac said.

"You never can tell till you've ridden circle an' brought the longhorns in," Quantrell contributed blithely. "Before they get this beef rounded up it sure will go on the hook an' annoy Ingram considerable. I've a notion there will be a chance of his warriors checking in first."

During the next hour or two there was desultory firing on both sides, though it was plain that the men in the ranch house were waiting for reënforcements before they forced the fighting.

Once Quantrell stooped and asked Owen a question.

"How are they comin', old-timer?"

"Not so bad. Wisht I had a drink, Bob. I'm sure burnin' up." Owen added gamely: "But I'm makin' it fine. Don't you worry about me."

The boy considered making a dash for the creek after water, but gave up the idea reluctantly. He would have to limp down and would probably be shot either going or coming.

"Coupla fellows on horses comin' through the willows," announced the white-headed cowboy abruptly.

Quantrell picked up his rifle and went to the door. What he saw was certainly unexpected. Two men were riding along the edge of the creek among the willows. They had with them a led horse. The riders splashed through the creek and made a dash for the stable.

"Dad gum my skin if it ain't the belted earl an' his friend the good bad man," exclaimed Texas Jim excitedly. "What in Mexico are they doin' here?"

The young desperado laughed, his voice when he spoke filled with gay and careless mirth. "Where else would they be? Don't they always head straight for trouble, those lads?"

A moment, and O'Hara and his partner were in the stable.

Chapter XXIII: *A Rescue*

The Circle S O partners consulted with each other.

"Nothing to do but ride over to the Hughes ranch and call off the Hashknife boys. If they've got Ingram's men penned up we'll probably be in time," O'Hara said.

"What shall we do with Garcia?" asked Smith-Beresford.

"Better take him along. He can guide us over the hills and get us there quicker."

The ruddy-faced Englishman turned to the Mexican. "Fork your horse, my man, and lead the way. And don't forget, by Jove, that I'm learning the tricks of the frontier. If you betray us I'll pump you full of lead."

"*Sí, señor*," Garcia agreed. "I will be true."

The Mexican rode in front of them. He was covered by his own rifle in the hands of Smith-Beresford. This was none of his fight. He had been hired by Ingram as a cowboy at regular wages and not as a gunman. Naturally, he had no intention of offering himself as a target for the Englishman if he could help it.

Unerringly Garcia led them through a maze of hilltops.

"Quantrell must have left the horses somewhere," O'Hara told his partner. "Juan says they came down from the rim rock on foot. Likely they left someone with the mounts. Hadn't we better swing around that way and see if he's still there?"

"Not a bad idea, Old Top. He could give us the latest developments. It would be deuced awkward if we met Ingram's men before we did our own."

"The Hashknife men are in the stable," Garcia said.

"They were when you left, if you're telling the truth. But that doesn't prove they're still there. Eh, Garrett?"

"No. We can't be too careful. Take us around by the rim rock."

They skirted the edge of the park. Garcia pulled up to listen, lifting a hand for silence. Someone was riding toward them. They could hear the hoofs of horses striking rocks.

The three men waited. Garcia's heart died under his ribs. He was between two fires. If these should prove to be Ingram's men he would be in a bad way.

Riderless horses came over the brow of a hill. Behind them rode a single man. The man was Joe, one of Steelman's cowboys. At sight of Garcia and the others he stopped and wheeled abruptly, driving in a spur for flight.

O'Hara called to him by name. Joe jerked his horse to its hind feet, so sharply did he check it.

The Circle S O partners joined him. In three sentences Joe made clear the situation.

"The boys are in the stable. One of 'em is wounded bad, looked like. Quantrell carried him in."

"Has there been a lot of shooting?" Smith-Beresford asked.

"Quite a lot. Someone rode away from the ranch hour an' a half ago. Gone for help, I'd say. I'm movin' the horses. Figured they might come up to collect 'em soon as they got around to it."

The partners talked together and afterward O'Hara gave Joe instructions. "We'll leave Juan here with you. Hold him

107

till we see you again. In about half an hour move the horses to the south end of the meadow, to the place where the creek runs out. We're going to try to follow the creek through the willows to the stable. We'll take a lead horse along for the wounded man. If our plan works out we'll join you as soon as we can."

"What if I'm jumped by Ingram or someone else?"

"Then you'll have to look after yourself. But I don't think he can get here before night."

The partners rode back to the creek, by way of the park rim, dropping down to the meadow land over a pine-clad hill. Smith-Beresford carried the rifle, O'Hara led the extra horse. They moved up the creek, keeping on the far side from the house and using the willows as a screen. They understood the dangers of their undertaking. Some of the enemy scouts might see them. Even if they reached the stable it might mean only that they would have to remain besieged with their comrades.

"Getting close to the stable," Smith-Beresford whispered over his shoulder to his friend. "There's a sort of ford where the horses drink just ahead. Think we'd better splash over and make a run for it?"

O'Hara's gaze swept the field—the stable, the open space between it and the creek, the house a hundred yards away where the riflemen of the Ingram forces were waiting.

"Might as well," he agreed.

The horses waded through the little creek and climbed the slope beyond. They broke into a canter, headed straight for the stable. Just before they reached it a single shot rang out from the house. The bullet cut its way through the foliage of the young willows.

Quantrell let out a yell of glee as the two men swung to the ground. "Made it, by cripes, you doggoned old hellamilers."

O'Hara did not share his enthusiasm. He had come to get the raiders out of trouble if he could, but he did not intend to condone their offense.

"Who has been hurt?" he asked coldly.

"Amen is shot up right bad. I'm carryin' one pill in my leg as a souvenir. How did you find out we was here?"

"Met a Mexican you drove away. How many of Ingram's men at the house?"

"Don't know."

"Any hurt?"

"One. I got him before we came down here."

O'Hara walked across to the place where Owen lay on the hay. "Can he ride?" he asked Texas Jim.

The Lone Star State man scratched his head. "I dunno. Doubt it. He's a mighty sick man."

Apparently Owen had been dozing. He opened his eyes. "Sure I could ride, if I was put on a horse," he said.

"Then we'd better get out before Ingram's reënforcements arrive. The rest of the horses are at the entrance to the park. The question is whether we can get away from here without being shot down. If we slip around and keep the stable between us and the house we might make it."

Quantrell's eyes gleamed. "You're damn shoutin', O'Hara. You fellows go. I'll stay an' hold 'em back till you cross the creek. Then I'll light out after you."

"That's good medicine," Texas Jim agreed. "I'll stay with Bob. Hop right along when you get started. You took 'em by surprise when you came in. They didn't hardly know whether you were friend or foe. But they'll be ready for business now."

The deputy sheriff spoke up. "There's an old door boarded up this side. If we break that down we can slip out an' not be seen at all."

Five minutes later the door had been knocked to pieces with an ax. Owen was lifted to the saddle of a horse. He clung to the pommel, teeth clenched.

O'Hara turned to Quantrell. "You take my horse. With that hurt leg you can't make a run for it if you have to. I'll stay with Texas."

Already the white-haired cowboy was leading Owen's horse through the broken doorway. Mac walked beside the saddle to steady the wounded man.

"No, sir," answered Quantrell. "It's liable to be hotter'n hell with the blower on here. I wished this on myself. Besides, I want to give some of these Ingram bad men a ticket to Kingdom Come."

"Get on that horse," O'Hara ordered quietly, looking straight at the young desperado. His voice had a ring of command, his brown eyes blazed.

Quantrell laughed. " 'I'm wagon boss here,' says he. All right. Have it yore own way. But understand, everybody, I'm not to blame if they collect him." The boy limped to the horse and pulled himself into the saddle. "*Adiós*," he called back with a jaunty wave of the hand as he rode out of the building.

The deputy sheriff was already on his way. Only Smith-

Beresford remained. He was reluctant to leave his friend and he argued the point, but O'Hara brushed aside his objections.

"I've got a better idea than yours, Garrett," he said, consenting at last. "I'll leave my horse here. You two may be in a hurry when you start. He'll carry double till you reach us. Good hunting, Old Top."

The Englishman followed the others. Hidden by the stable, the little cavalcade got some distance before it was seen by those in the house. Then men poured out of the house as seeds are squirted from an orange. One of them, leading the pursuit toward the stable, gave a yell compounded of triumph and rage. O'Hara recognized him as Deever.

Already O'Hara had given orders to his companion but he reënforced them by a reminder. "Remember, Texas, you're not to hit any of them unless we can't drive them back otherwise."

The firing from the stable took the Ingram men by surprise. They wavered. Deever pulled up abruptly, hesitated a fraction of a second, then ran for the shelter of the willows by the creek. Two of the others followed him, the rest broke back for the house.

"If we can give our boys fifteen minutes' start they ought to make it," O'Hara said.

"Can't do it," the Texan answered. "Just about now it's gonna strike those fellows to slap saddles on their horses an' swing round to cut the boys off from the mouth of the park."

Texas Jim anticipated their thoughts by less than five minutes. Presently they could see Deever and the others slipping up from the creek to the hitch rack by the house.

"Time to say '*Adiós*' if we don't aim to be cut off," the cowboy said.

"Right you are," agreed O'Hara.

A moment later he was on Smith-Beresford's horse, with the Texan behind him. They dashed into the open at a gallop. A bullet whistled past them.

"Cut for the creek an' get acrost it," Texas Jim advised.

O'Hara swung to the left and sent the horse plunging into the young willows. They crashed through, the supple branches whipping their faces. The animal lost its footing as it went down into the creek and both men were flung into the water. Texas Jim caught the bridle and dragged the bronco to its feet. The riders were soaked, but O'Hara had managed to keep the rifle out of the water when he made his dive into the stream's shallow depth.

Into the saddle the Texan dragged himself. He stiffened

his foot and O'Hara used it for a step to swing himself behind. A moment, and the horse was charging through the saplings fringing the opposite bank.

Glancing back, O'Hara could hear the excited voices of the pursuers. They were too far away for him to make out the words, but he realized that they were already in motion.

Someone shouted to them. O'Hara caught sight of young Quantrell riding down the creek.

"Came back to chew over old times," he called gaily to them. "I figured you boys had just naturally wore out yore welcome at the Hughes ranch about now."

"Where are the others?" asked O'Hara.

"They're humpin' right along. We can hold these roosters back if we have to. If they get on the prod we'll educate 'em proper."

"We're not looking for trouble, Bob. What we're trying to do is to get away with our skins whole. Don't forget that. I won't have any unnecessary shooting. We've had more than enough. Later I'll have a word to say about that."

The voices of the pursuers came closer. Quantrell grinned cheerfully. "What shooting I will do will be necessary, looks like."

"If we can only reach the gateway of the park." O'Hara said, glancing back.

"Sure enough. If my toes only reach the ground when they hang me it won't hurt much," Quantrell jeered.

The riders behind swung into sight. By way of warning O'Hara dropped a bullet in front of them. The Ingram gunmen opened up into loose formation, each man riding wide of his neighbour. But they kept coming. Shots sounded. A bullet cut off the branch of a willow five feet from O'Hara.

"Another half mile, boys, an' we'll make it," Texas Jim said anxiously. "Onct we reach the boulder field there we can stand 'em off."

Bob Quantrell slid from his horse. "I'm gonna stop those birds."

He rested his rifle across the branch of a willow, took careful aim, and fired. A man tumbled from a horse.

CHAPTER XXIV: *Between the Devil and the Deep Sea*

QUANTRELL LET OUT a "Hi-yi" of triumph. "Got that fellow good," he called across to Texas Jim. "Guess they won't push on their reins to get any closer."

He was right. The pursuers made for such cover as was available. One object lesson at a time was enough.

The fugitives took advantage of this to increase the distance between them and the Ingram men.

"They ain't such curly wolves as they think they are," Quantrell shouted gleefully to his two companions. "I'll show this bully puss bunch whether they can push me more'n so fur."

The hills that fenced in the park grew closer. Not far ahead was the cleft through which ran the creek. Into this the horses galloped. They passed to a boulder-strewn field beyond which was a gulch.

At the upper end of this they found the rest of their party. With them were Joe and the horses he had brought to the rendezvous.

Owen, his face drained of blood, looked like a man ready to collapse and sustained only by a resolute will.

"Can you go on?" O'Hara asked him.

Both of his hands clung to the saddle horn. He nodded, not wasting the energy to answer in words.

"We'll try to make the Circle S O," O'Hara said. "It's less than four miles by the mesa."

He rode on one side of Owen, his partner on the other. Quantrell and Texas Jim brought up the rear, watching alertly for the pursuers.

"Betcha Ingram's warriors have had enough," the young desperado called to O'Hara. "Betcha we don't see hide or hair of 'em before we reach the ranch."

The deputy sheriff and Joe rode in the van of the procession. Joe was an old-timer and picked with a sure eye the easiest way across the hills to the ranch.

Owen drooped in the saddle more and more.

"Look out he doesn't fall, Lyulph," O'Hara cautioned his partner.

"I'm gonna make it," the cowboy said, spacing his words between clenched teeth. "Not far now."

He succumbed within sight of the ranch, slipping from the saddle into O'Hara's arms. One of the men rode forward at a gallop and brought back a buckboard into which he was lifted. A few minutes later he was carried unconscious into the house.

O'Hara sent a messenger for a doctor and another for Steelman. That the attack upon the Hughes ranch would be interpreted as a challenge he was quite sure. Coming as it did on the heels of the offer to compromise, Ingram would be justified in considering it black treachery. He would retaliate swiftly, probably with deadly efficiency, unless it was possible to get him to see the affair in its true light. Quantrell and the men who had ridden with him on the raid must be discharged. It must be made clear that neither Steelman nor his partners of the Circle S O ranch countenanced in any way what had been done.

He talked it over with Smith-Beresford. The Englishman suggested a difficulty.

"It's all very well talking about getting rid of Quantrell and the other young devils who rode with him on this raid, but let's not go too fast about it, old chap," he said. "The Assyrian may come down like the wolf on the fold, and it would be deuced convenient to have a few of these wild hellions around to repel boarders, you know. We can't discharge Quantrell until we know what Ingram means to do, even if he did spill the apple cart for us. It's no fun being between the devil and the deep sea, but that's just where we are. Better wait till Steelman gets here."

Steelman arrived the evening of the next day. He was accompanied by half a dozen armed men. O'Hara's messenger had found him at the lower ranch and he had returned as soon as horses could be roped and saddled. He had ridden since daybreak.

After he had talked with his partners the owner of the Hashknife sent for Bob Quantrell. That young man came in sheepishly, expecting to be raked over the coals. He was wearing a Mexican sombrero and as a gesture of independence he left it on his head.

"You've certainly spilled the frijoles, young man," Steelman said bluntly. "What have you got to say for yoreself?"

Quantrell showed his buck teeth in a grin. "I didn't cut the mustard, boss. Better luck next time."

"Who asked you to raid the Hughes place?"

"Me! Oh, I was kinda playin' a lone hand. Would you call it a raid when we was a sheriff's posse all swore in regular an' proper?"

"At the very hour you were pullin' off this fool business my two partners here were tryin' to arrange a compromise with Ingram. What do you suppose he'll think about us?"

"He'll probably onload his private can of cuss words." The boy put one thigh over the edge of the table and sat on it by way of showing that he was at ease. "What's the use of compromisin' with him? We've got him whopped, looks to me. The banks are closin' in on him like buzzards on a dead cow at a water hole. That's the story I hear."

"Of course, if you're runnin' this campaign, Bob," the old cattle man suggested satirically.

"Lemme ask you a question," Quantrell cut back. "Say I'd made my play good. Would you have bawled me out then or would you have figured it good medicine?"

For a moment Steelman was taken aback. It was not just the question he wanted asked at the moment.

O'Hara answered for him. "You could not have made it good without making me and my partners liars, Bob. We either went to Ingram in good faith or else we didn't. What'll his opinion be?"

"Do you care?" drawled the young killer insolently. "If Ingram's any Sunday-school superintendent I never heard tell of it. He started this war to win it regardless. That's the kind of a bird he is."

"It's not the kind we are, Bob," cut in Smith-Beresford. "We went to Ingram in good faith to settle our difficulties with him. We offered concessions and so did he. Then he learns that at the very time we're talking with him our men are attacking his."

"Let's say yore plans had worked out the way you originally expected, Bob," said Steelman. "You'd have surprised Ingram's warriors early in the mornin'. Say word had reached him while he an' our friends here had been talkin' compromise. What do you reckon he would have done to them? Would they have had a dead man's chance to get out of town alive?"

"Maybe not. But I didn't aim to let any of his warriors get away to town for to have a powwow with Ingram. My notion was to make a clean round-up of them for a summer Christmas present for you-all. I'd heard you belly-achin' about how Ingram was hangin' on to the Hughes place contrary to law an' how you aimed to drive him out. Well, I figured I'd save you the trouble."

"Instead of which you have involved us in fresh trouble," O'Hara said curtly. "You've put us in the wrong in the most flagrant way. There's just one thing for us to do, and that is to show Ingram if we can, that this attack took place without our knowledge and against our wishes. We can't keep you in our employ, Quantrell."

The brown eyes of O'Hara met steadily the light blue shallow ones of the young killer.

"Scared of Ingram, eh?" the boy sneered. "Suits me if it

114

does you, Mr. O'Hara. I'm to get the gate because you want to play up to this fellow, you not havin' sand in yore craw enough to go through with what you started. All right 'Nough said. I'll ride down the river to-day."

"Understand, Bob, we've got no personal feeling against you," Steelman explained. "I'll go farther than that. I've still got cattle in Texas, an' I'll give you a note to my foreman there to take you on at once at the same wages. You won't lose a day's pay. After we get things straightened out here you can come back an' ride for me on the river."

"I don't aim to go to Texas, but to stay right here, Steelman," the young fellow answered. "I wouldn't wonder none but there'll be times a-plenty when you wished I was in Texas."

O'Hara tried again to get him to understand. "You've forced our hand, Bob. We don't want to lose you, but——"

"But you've got to do it to save yore face with Ingram," interrupted the boy rudely. "No need to explain to me. I understand what you're drivin' at. I don't need any church to fall on me before I take a hint."

"We want to part friends," O'Hara said. "There's no reason why we shouldn't. You're too—impulsive, let's say, to ride for us just now, but——"

"Friends," interrupted Quantrell, his cold blue eyes narrowed to slits, his voice filled with scornful anger. "Me, I was ready to ride the river with you. I'd have gone with you to the end of the trail, through, under, between, or over. An' you drop me like a hot potato because you're scared of what Ingram will think. Don't talk to me about friends, fellow. I'm through with you, but you'll find you're not through with me by a hell of a lot."

"Let's be reasonable," Smith-Beresford said. "It's not Ingram that's involved so much as our good faith. We've got to play our cards aboveboard, you know. Can't let you go raiding his men while we're talking peace to him. But we're deuced sorry to lose you, and our personal feeling isn't changed at all. Some day we'll laugh about this together, and to show our appreciation of your services we want you to accept this little bonus from us."

Quantrell took the check handed him and tore it into twenty pieces. He turned on his heel and clumped out of the room. Fifteen minutes later he disappeared over the hill on horseback.

"Well, we sure turned a good friend into a bad enemy,"

Steelman said ruefully, lighting his pipe with a live coal at the blacksmith's fire.

O'Hara felt that Steelman left a criticism implied if not expressed. The old cattle man would not have let Quantrell go, but would have credited the young fellow's action to excessive zeal and let him off with a reproof. But then Steelman had no hope in the success of the negotiations with Ingram and was not interested in demonstrating good faith.

"I don't see what else we could have done," Smith-Beresford said despondently. Like O'Hara, he regretted very much the necessity that had driven them. Quantrell had probably saved both their lives on one occasion. He had been loyal to their interests as he interpreted them, but he was headstrong and implacable to a degree that made it impossible to retain him. Undoubtedly some day he would have broken out again if he had stayed. He was a killer. The lust to slay had become a fever in his blood likely to flare up any time.

Steelman voiced the same thought. "I reckon he would have made us trouble finally, though I'd have liked to keep him till this war is over. But I've seen his kind too often. When a cowboy goes bad he goes bad to stay. Quantrell is a killer an' a cow thief, an' he'll never be anything else, though he's certainly true to the man that hires him. I reckon now he'll nest up in the hills an' rustle our stock." He puffed at his pipe for a few moments, then changed the subject. "Looks like Amen might make the grade, Doc says. Those old toughfoot cowboys sure take a lot of killin'."

"Yes," agreed O'Hara absently.

Chapter XXV: *"If You Care as Much as That"*

At the Hughes ranch all was busy preparation. Guns were being examined, horses saddled. Ingram himself grimly supervised his men as they made ready.

Deever called to him: "Guy comin' up the creek, Dave."

The approaching rider was a Mexican. As he drew nearer they saw that he wore a steeple hat and earrings. Around his waist was a green silk sash.

"Juan Garcia," said Harvey. "Where's he been at since the fireworks began day before yesterday?"

"I'd been wonderin' if Steelman's warriors hadn't collected on him. The boys say he didn't give 'em much chance; went down the creek like he had wings." Ingram spoke indifferently. One Mexican more or less was nothing in his life.

116

Garcia rode up, fumbled in his sash, drew out an envelope, and handed it to Ingram. The owner of the Diamond Tail tore it open and read it with an impassive face. Meanwhile Garcia was busy answering questions. He had been captured by the enemy, taken to the Circle S O ranch, and had less than two hours before made his escape. All this he explained in Spanish.

Ingram drew him to one side. "Did Miss Steelman give you this letter herself?"

"*Sí, señor.*"

"An' then she helped you make yore getaway?"

The Mexican hesitated, then decided it was better to tell the truth. "Señor Steelman he tell me *vamos*."

"Did he know about this letter—see her give it to you?"

He had not, Garcia explained. She had slipped it to him and begged him to deliver it to Señor Ingram.

Ingram's strong brown hand closed viselike on the shoulder muscles of the vaquero, the ones that sloped up to the neck. "If you're lying to me, you greaser, I'll cut yore heart out when I come back."

The little brown man shrieked with agony. He protested, *por Dios,* that it was the truth he told, nothing more nor less.

Ingram dragged the Mexican from his horse and flung him into the arms of a man standing near. "Keep him till I come back," he ordered. Then, to Harvey, he said: "I'm postponin' this expedition a few hours, Tom. Got to see someone first."

"Who have you got to see, Dave?" asked Harvey.

"Private business of my own," Ingram answered curtly.

"Hmp!" Harvey would have liked to make comment about that private business but he thought it wiser not to do so. His partner's high-handed ways irritated him at times. He did not enjoy being treated like a junior clerk.

Ingram chose a fast horse and cut across the park to the eastern rim of it. From here he pushed into the hills, heading farther to the north. Apparently he knew exactly where he was going. But after he had travelled three or four miles he swung sharply to the left and made a wide circuit by way of a gulch and a pine-clad slope beyond. At the summit of a wooded ridge he dismounted and tied the horse, then moved forward cautiously, rifle in hand. His keen eyes scanned the terrain carefully. At times he stopped and stood perfectly still for minutes at a stretch, then once more crept through the brush toward a small arroyo that dropped swiftly to a mesa below. He followed the descent of the arroyo through some jack pines to a ledge. It was the spot where he and Barbara Steelman had been used to meet before the feud had flamed into open warfare.

He did not, however, advance into the open but sat down behind a boulder with his rifle in both hands. It would be too much to say that he suspected treachery. If he had done so he would not have come alone, but there was a chance that his enemies had bribed the Mexican and were lying in wait to ambush him.

Ingram had been there only a few minutes when a lone rider emerged from a draw. The approaching horse clambered up to the ledge plateau and Barbara Steelman drew the animal to a halt. She looked around, then slipped down from the saddle and arranged her skirts, which had become disordered from riding.

Out of the brush came Ingram to meet her. He walked with lightness and strength, a deep-chested powerful man in the prime of life. No words were wasted by him in greeting. Before he spoke his flinty light blue eyes searched her for a moment.

"I got yore note, an' I'm here," he said.

She plunged at once into what she had to say. "I had to talk with you. I had to tell you how it was about the attack on the Hughes place. My father had nothing to do with that, neither he nor his partners."

There was bitter irony in his answer. "Of course not. Wouldn't be reasonable, would it? Just a bunch of stray waddies dropped in to pay us their compliments."

"I know what you think," she cried. "You would, of course. But it's true, what I am sayin'. My father had started for the river ranch after a conference with Mr. O'Hara an' Mr. Smith-Beresford. It was agreed they should start negotiations with you to stop this dreadful war. Bob Quantrell was to blame for the attack, an' he has been discharged since. We're all so sorry about it."

"I'll bet you are," the cattle man grimly replied. "Sorry Quantrell fell down on his end of it after it had all been fixed so pretty. A nice alibi arranged for everybody, an' those two pilgrims in town drawin' the wool over my eyes. You tell 'em from me that the first time I meet either of 'em he'll have a hide so full of holes it wouldn't hold hay."

"But you're wrong," she persisted desperately. "I've got to make you see that. It's true what I say, every word of it. My father didn't know what Bob Quantrell meant to do. Neither did the others, his partners at the Circle S O.

118

They've always wanted peace, an' they talked Father into offering a compromise. You know Bob Quantrell, how he is. I should think you'd understand."

"Are you here from them? Or from Steelman?" he demanded.

"Nobody knows I'm here. I thought you'd believe me if I told you how it was. So I had to come."

"Why, girl, those two fellows, O'Hara an' the Englishman, rode straight from town to the Hughes place an' joined Quantrell's gang. Three-four of the boys recognized 'em."

"They met a Mexican who told them about the attack. The only reason they went there was to stop bloodshed."

"Was that why they killed one of my men as they were leavin' the park?"

"That was Bob Quantrell, too. You know how he is. There's no stoppin' him when he gets started."

"It's certainly lucky you've got Quantrell to blame everything on," Ingram said with a flash of anger. "Everybody innocent but him, that sounds to me."

"But just the same it's the truth."

He looked long into her eyes, then spoke harshly. "All right. Say it is. You want peace, you claim. How much do you want it?"

She knew that he was about to make an offer, and that it would be a personal one. Her pulses began to flutter, but she held her gaze to his.

"I'm listening," she said in a low voice.

"You can have it, soon as you like—if you'll take it on my terms."

"And they are?"

"Marry me. Do that, an' I'll agree to make peace with Wes Steelman an' these young squirts he has taken up with."

She felt the blood beating into her face. "If I ran away with you an' married you Father would be furious. It would make any settlement of yore troubles impossible."

"I'll make peace first. Gimme yore word you'll marry me afterward." He said it almost savagely, no suggestion of tenderness in voice or manner.

"You want to make a bargain with me," she cried bitterly. "I'm to sell myself to you in order to get you to do what a reasonable man would be glad to do because it is right. That's no way to—to ask a girl to marry you. It's an insult. Even if there was a chance for a girl to be happy that would ruin it to start with."

"If you want me to look at you like a sick calf——"

119

"It's so much better to look at me as though you'd beat me with a quirt if I didn't knuckle under to you," she interrupted passionately. "That's a sure way to make a girl fond of you. Bully her an' trade on her fear an' her dread of the evil things you'll do if she doesn't give way. What a good start for a happy married life!"

"What makes you always quarrel with me?" he asked impatiently. "Why do you twist what I say an' put something in my mind that's not there? Girl, I want to marry you. I've always wanted to since I first saw you. What's the sense of always rowellin' me with yore spitfire words?"

"Why do you want to marry me?" she flamed at him. "Because it would madden Father. Because you'd have the whip hand. Because you'd like to break my spirit."

His hands went out and caught her arms just above the elbow. She could feel the pressure of his strong fingers on the firm flesh of her forearms. Somehow, though the grip did not hurt her, she felt the force of his vital strength coursing through her blood, and with the feel of it excitement pounded in her veins.

"No, by God!" he cried in a low hoarse voice. "Because I want you for my mate an' mean to have you. Because there's no girl like you on the river—no, nor anywhere else. Because"—he gulped the words out, almost savagely—"I wouldn't give yore li'l' finger for any other woman I've ever known."

She looked at him, eyes dilated, breathing as though she had been running fast. This was what her heart had ached for, a rush of vehement passion that trampled down the pride and policy that ruled him. Her pulses throbbed. A glow pervaded her body. She knew the rapture of having evoked from the man she loved an emotion that would not be dammed.

He snatched her into his arms and held her close, looking down hungrily into the dark eyes which now denied him nothing, which in their soft and shining depth held gifts never before offered to any man.

There was a little rustling movement of her body toward him. Perhaps it was only an unconscious sigh of happiness. She felt love pouring through her quivering being.

Ingram kissed the palpitant brown throat, the glowing eyes, the red lips between which gleamed perfect ivory teeth. The touch of love had awakened her. She was a flaming flower, incomparably desirable in her soft and joyous vitality. From her surrender, so full of innocent and passionate

120

abandon, the man plucked an emotion new to his experience.

Shyly she withdrew from his embrace, her cheek flying a flag of colour. "We're all alike, we women," she laughed tremulously. "We want our man and—a home."

He came to earth and the less important business of the day. "Tell yore father it's to be peace between us. I'll sure be easy to do business with."

"I can't tell Dad. He mustn't know I've been here. It's to be a secret yet—about us. You'll have to make friends with him first. I'll tell Mr. O'Hara, an' he'll meet you."

"There's a lot between us all, girl. We'll have to bury the hatchet mighty deep or someone will dig it out again. I'll do my share. That's all I can say."

"An' I'll do mine. There can't be more trouble if you an' I say there won't be."

CHAPTER XXVI: *Ingram Uses a Quirt*

As INGRAM RODE UP to the Hughes ranch he recognized a claybank cow pony at the hitch rack near the house. Several men were sitting on the porch, including Harvey, Deever, and Roche. Leaning against one of the end posts, a rifle across his legs, sat Bob Quantrell, smoking a cigarette insolently but warily.

"What are you doing here?" demanded Ingram harshly.

Harvey started to explain. "Why, he came here, Dave——"

"I'm askin' him," interrupted the senior partner, frowning at Quantrell.

The lad took the cigarette from his mouth and blew out a fat smoke wreath lazily. "The short an' sweet of it is that I'm here lookin' for a job. I'm through with that other outfit. I don't like their ways an' they don't like mine."

"You've got the nerve to come here, after what you did the day before yesterday," Ingram said blackly.

"All in the way of business, Dave," the boy replied airily. "What would you expect? I was workin' for Steelman's crowd then. Like I said, I've quit 'em. If you're needin' a top hand, either with a bunch of cows or a six-shooter, why just say the word. I'm yore gooseberry. Any of the boys here can recommend me."

He spoke with apparent indifference as he lounged carelessly against the post, but never a pair of eyes watched another man more closely than his did Ingram. In coming here at all he had taken his life in his hands, and he knew it. Before he reached the house, before he could open his lips to explain why he had come, he might be shot down. That risk was a part of the game he played. Even if they let him talk, the fury of these men might blaze out at him. Only two days ago he had wounded one of their comrades and killed another. He had counted on the impudence of his approach, on the fear his reputation bred, on the fact that most of them were hired gunmen who counted killing all in the day's work. So far his foolhardiness had served him well. What about Ingram?

The big cattle man did not lift his eyes from the slim lad with the receding chin. This youngster grinning at him with his buck teeth showing was the most notorious bad man in the territory. His six-shooters had blazed a way for him to infamy already more than local. In time men would come from afar to write books about his wild career, though none of those present could guess that his repute would some day be nationwide.

Ingram was not afraid of him. He was afraid of no man alive. His pride was too arrogant and domineering to leave room for fear.

"You're an insolent young devil, Quantrell," he said, measuring his words carefully. "You've run on the rope all yore life till you think you're chief. You're not—not on this range. Trouble with you is that you weren't wore to a frazzle with a hickory when you first reached for a gun."

"Me?" broke out Quantrell, his cold shallow eyes narrowing to slits of glittering anger. "Wear *me* to a frazzle?"

"Listen," ordered Ingram harshly. "You're through with this country. Get out. Push on yore reins an' shove. I ought to have you arrested right now for murder. If I didn't know you'd break jail that's just what I'd do. Serve you right if we shot you down here on the spot. But I'm servin' notice on you. If you stay in this country I'll have you hunted down like a wolf."

"You're the big auger, are you?" jeered Quantrell. "Big talk, with all yore men sittin' around here to back yore play. You listen awhile, Dave Ingram. There ain't men enough in all yore wolf pack to drive me out."

He had risen and stood beside the porch, the rifle held in both hands close to his right side. Ingram had likened him to a wolf, and as he stood there crouched, lips drawn back and buck teeth showing, the parallel was obvious. A cornered wolf was never more dangerous.

The cowboy Roche, standing near him with a coiled rope in his hands, watched him with eyes that never lifted. He had spent the past ten minutes hating the young outlaw impotently, for the man whom Quantrell had shot as he left the park had been a close friend of his. They had slept under the same tarp many a night.

Ingram took a step forward. When he spoke his voice rang out sharply. "Don't raise that gun to me, you young fool. We'll fill you with lead sure."

Quantrell glared at him. What was in the lad's mind nobody knew. Apparently he did not move, but there was a sort of ripple of tensed muscles that foretold motion of some sort. In the same breath the loop of Roche's lariat snaked forward. It dropped over Quantrell's shoulders as low as his waist. Instantly the cowboy drew the rope tight with a savage jerk, pinning the other's arms to his side.

Before Quantrell could free himself enough to use the rifle Ingram closed with him. In the hands of the big cattle man the killer was like a child. Ingram wrenched the rifle from his grip and sent it flying through the air. Struggling desperately, the boy was flung to the ground and his hands were pinned down by one of Ingram's. The six-shooters of the gunman were wrenched from their scabbards and tossed aside.

The cattle man caught his shirt at the throat and dragged him to his feet. They stood for an instant glaring at each other, the youngster held at arm's length by the powerful grip of the Diamond Tail owner.

"I'll kill you for this," Quantrell cried with a furious oath, his voice breaking into a boyish falsetto.

Ingram did not answer. He was not through. His eyes had fallen on a quirt hanging from a nail driven into the wall of the house. Toward this he propelled his victim, forcing him up the steps to the porch. The boy tried savagely to fight himself free.

As Ingram reached for the whip Quantrell realized what he meant to do and shrieked protest.

"Don't you dass touch me! Don't you! Don't you!"

The cattle man paid no attention. His muscular forearm held the boy off while the lash hissed through the air and coiled itself around the slender body protected only by a flannel shirt. Six—nine—twelve times the quirt rose and fell. Quantrell fought to escape the torture, snarling and biting like an animal.

Those watching the scene stood silent, startled at what

123

they saw. There were no sounds except the swish of the lash, the scuffle of the shifting feet, and the whine of wild-beast fury issuing from the throat of the writhing man.

Ingram stopped, flung away the whip.

"Gather those guns," he ordered Roche.

When the cowboy had done this the cattle man threw the young outlaw down the steps.

"Get out of here," he ordered. "Out of this country or I'll hunt you down like I promised."

Quantrell rose to his feet. He was sobbing with the fury of uncontrollable humiliation and pain. His voice was so broken that he could hardly make coherent the dreadful threats he poured out.

Grimly, Ingram looked down at him. He did not answer the man's ravings. Standing there, straight and stern, he was a picture of masterful strength.

The young killer limped to his horse, dragged himself to the saddle, and rode away.

Harvey was the first to speak. "I'll say you're thorough, Dave."

"The young ruffian has run on the rope long enough," Ingram answered. "Time he learned he's no ace in the pack."

"He's sure learned it—temporary. But if I was you I'd go mighty careful. He'll lie in the brush for you."

"I'll run him outa the country." Ingram turned to the others. "Boys, our party is off for to-day. The Jefferson County war is about over, looks like. Wes Steelman an' I are gonna patch up our troubles. Don't any of you get on the prod with any of the Hashknife warriors for a day or two till we see what's what. Come on into the house, Tom. I want to talk it over with you."

Chapter XXVII: *Garrett O'Hara Loses*

BARBARA DID NOT RIDE straight home after her talk with Ingram but turned aside to the Circle S O ranch. She wanted to talk with Garrett O'Hara before she saw her father. As she travelled the hills and the gulches between the creeks on which the ranches lay her heart was lifted as it had not been for many days. Yet back of the excitement and the joy that thrilled her was a premonition of disaster. It was not in the cards, so some deep instinct told her, that she and her lover should be happy together. Too much lay between them, too many gulfs of separation. Too many wrongs had been done, too much hatred stirred up. Wes Steelman and Dave Ingram would mix no better than oil and water.

Moreover, though a rising tide of emotion had swept this away for the time, she knew that his ways were not her ways. They were temperamentally at war, in spite of the fact that he fascinated and allured her. Just now she was willing to hope, passionately eager to believe, that love would fuse their spirits to harmony. It must be so, she told herself. His cry for her had been wholly genuine. Surely, beneath the hard surface, she had found at last the real man.

Smith-Beresford caught sight of her as she rode forward and came to meet her. He helped her from the saddle and they moved together toward the house. Barbara waited on the porch while he went in to get his partner.

When O'Hara joined her the girl moved with him, as though unconsciously, toward the hitch rack. It was like her to begin without devious explanation.

"I've just left David Ingram. He's ready to make peace on any reasonable terms," she said.

He looked quickly at her. A crimson stain streamed through her cheeks.

"I sent him a note by that Mexican Garcia," she went on. "I asked him to meet me. We've talked it all over. He'll do whatever's right."

"In spite of Quantrell's attack?"

"Yes. I can't go to Father yet. I'm not ready to explain everything. Will you meet Mr. Ingram and then take his message to Father?"

"Of course I will." He felt as though the bottom had dropped out of his heart. There was more to this than she had told him. Something had transformed the girl, had given her frankness a touch of shy mystery. In her soft and shining eyes was the light of a dear dream come true.

"We . . . had a talk," she said, almost in a murmur, dropping her long lashes.

It seemed to him that he had never seen her so beautiful as in this mood of flushed gentleness. Like all men, selfish in his love, it stabbed him that not he but another had inspired this radiance. Before he spoke again he made sure that none of the emotion which surged in him would show in his voice.

"When am I to meet him—and where?" she asked.

She gave him directions, and while she did so a tide of tenderness toward him flowed through her. Just now, in her

125

new-found happiness, she wanted to hurt nobody, least of all him. She knew his secret and was much touched by it. Love was so rare and desirable that it hurt her to think his must end in frustration.

Neither of them referred to what was in both their minds, his love for her and hers for another man. They discussed the peace terms between Steelman and Ingram. He saddled a horse and rode with her until the path forked. Before they separated she had one last word to say to him, and she said it with her hand on his coat sleeve.

"I want peace more than anything else in the world, Garrett. You *will* do yore best, won't you?"

His brown eyes rested on hers as he promised. "I'll do my best, Barbara." Perhaps his smile was a little wistful as he added: "I want you to have what you want more than anything else in the world."

"Would you want me to have it if you thought it wasn't best for me?" she asked.

"No, but I wouldn't want to stand in the way of your having it."

He thought many times later of that last remark of Barbara. Had she some prescience in her mind of short-lived happiness, some intuition that her love craft was likely to be wrecked by stormy seas? In the light of subsequent events he came to think so.

The peace negotiations, now that Ingram had made up his mind to them, turned out to be absurdly simply. Confronted by this new situation, a foe willing to make concessions, Wes Steelman made a mental right-about-face. He did not want to be outdone in generosity. The promiscuous killings of the past months did not rest easily on his conscience, even though he acquitted himself of blame. Financial ruin lay ahead if the feud continued long enough. Therefore he met his foe at least halfway.

"I'll never like the man," Steelman confided to his son. "He's hard as nails an' none too scrupulous as to how he wins. But you've got to respect him. He's got guts, an' he'll not rue back on any deal he makes."

Within four months of the date of the treaty Wesley Steelman had to swallow a bitter pill. He stood up beside his only daughter, the child he idolized, and saw her married to David Ingram. One aspect of the matter troubled Barbara. She had thought it would be a great blow to his pride, but she saw it was his love that was hit. He grieved because he was sure that she would be unhappy in her marriage.

And before she had been David Ingram's wife two weeks Barbara knew he was right. She summoned her pride and her courage to keep him and others from finding out.

CHAPTER XXVIII: *"A Man With Sand in His Craw"*

IT WAS AGREED in a conference attended by the governor of the territory, the sheriff of the county, Ingram, Steelman, and the United States marshal, that the slate should be wiped clean of all offenses committed during the Jefferson County War unless indictments had already been found against the law breakers. In the event that any of these latter were convicted the governor promised a pardon. This was a sorry vindication of the supremacy of law. but even the authorities at Washington connived at it; for to attempt to enforce exact justice would be to make outlaws of scores of ranchers and cowboys and very likely would result in re-opening the feud.

Bob Quantrell was no party to the armistice. Tacitly he refused to recognize the new conditions. He went on the dodge and disappeared into the chaparral, emerging from it only to get food and supplies or to raid some ranch and rustle stock. Three or four desperate characters had rallied around him, men who preferred to steal rather than to work for a living. Deever was one of these. Pankey was another. It was thought Jake Sommers and the cowboy known as Mac belonged to the gang, though as yet there was no positive evidence of this. The depredations of the Quantrell Gang, as the outlaws came to be called by common consent. were high-handed and flagrant. They killed a clerk at the Indian agency, an innocent youth from the East who chanced to come on them as they were driving away a bunch of horses belonging to the government. They preyed particularly upon cattle bearing the Diamond Tail, the Hashknife. or the Circle S O brands.

The outlaws were protected by their friends. Young Quantrell was popular among the Mexicans. He had once saved the life of Manuel Gomez, a leader among the natives, and it was known he cast amorous glances at Dolores, the daughter of Manuel. The more ignorant of them liked him because of a certain easy camaraderie he possessed, and they ascribed to him the qualities of a modern Robin Hood. Some of the

American ranchers nesting in the hills also aided him, either out of personal good will or because they feared to incur his enmity. The result was that the posses organized by Ingram and Steelman, nominally under the leadership of the sheriff, could not move against him without warning reaching the outlaw.

The relationship between Steelman and Ingram was a stiff and formal one. But in this matter of putting the cattle thieves out of business Steelman knew there must be coöperation.

He discussed the situation with Smith-Beresford one day.

"We're not gettin' anywhere, Lyulph," he said, tilting back a chair and putting his feet on another. "Nor we won't with this Jim What's-his-name sheriff. He's got no guts. He won't go out after Quantrell an' sleep on his trail till he gets him. I had a talk with him yesterday. He's willin' to resign if we can find a good man to take his place. Well, I've found the good man."

"I wish him luck if he's going out after Bob, and at the same time I'll say good-bye to him," Smith-Beresford replied. "By the way, who is he?"

Steelman puffed at his pipe a moment or two before he answered. "What would you think of our partner, Garrett O'Hara?" he asked.

The Englishman's answer was instant. "By Jove, no! He's had enough trouble unloaded on him already. Why hand him more?"

"What kind of a sheriff do you think he'd make?"

"He'd make a bully one. That's not the point. I'm thinking of Garrett and his safety. Dash it all, I'd rather go broke from that young scoundrel Quantrell's raids on our stock."

"Someone has to stop this rustling. I'm too busy. My boy is too young. Ingram is the logical man, but he claims he hasn't time for it. I suppose you wouldn't care to be sheriff yoreself, Lyulph?"

"Thanks, no. Much obliged for the compliment, though."

"You couldn't be. Not a citizen of this country. Run yore mind over the men you know in the neighbourhood, then tell me who is best qualified for it."

"How about Steve Worrall?"

"Guts enough, but too easy-goin'."

"Ingram's partner Tom Harvey?"

"Not satisfactory to me. I don't trust him."

"Your foreman Phillips?"

"Wouldn't suit Ingram."

"Would Garrett suit him?"

"I think so. That's what I want you to find out."

"But Garrett is no trailer. He doesn't know this country well," protested Smith-Beresford.

"We'll give him deputies who can follow a trail to hell an' back. Besides, this probably won't be a trailin' job. What it needs is a man with sand in his craw who'll never quit."

"I'm against it, Steelman. If Garrett takes the job he'll get killed. That's a five-to-one shot. He's no match for Quantrell in the brush. You know that as well as I do."

"I've watched Garrett," the cattle man answered, crossing his legs, "an' I've noticed one thing about him—he rises to his opportunities. When the emergency breaks he's right on the job. By rights, if you go by logic, he ought to have been killed half a dozen times since he came to Jefferson County. Some folks say he's lucky. I don't. He's alive because he's the gamest li'l' fighting cock on the river, an' because he uses his head. That last is where he'll have the edge on Quantrell."

"I see you've already got him appointed," the Englishman said drily. "Isn't Garrett going to have anything to say about this?"

"He won't want the job, of course," Steelman admitted. "Who would? But if he thinks it's his duty he'll take it."

"I don't see that it's his duty any more than yours or mine or a dozen other men I can name. I'm against this, Steelman. He's too good to be killed by that young devil Quantrell. Thought you liked Garrett?"

The cattle man knocked the ashes out of his pipe and rose. His brown hand dropped on Smith-Beresford's and his deep blue eyes looked into those of the florid little Englishman.

"Nobody I like better. What's that got to do with it? I'd put my own son on the job if he was old enough and good enough. I'm payin' Garrett a big compliment. This country has got to be made safe from such men as Quantrell. Someone has to take the law into the chaparral, an' I believe Garrett is man enough to do it. Anyhow, he'll get a chance to say 'No.' If he makes good there's a big future for him here."

The Englishman shrugged his shoulders. "Want me to see Ingram about Garrett's appointment? Hadn't we better talk with Garrett first?"

"We'll see him right now."

O'Hara's first impulse was to refuse instantly, but he waited to hear Steelman out. Before the older man had finished he was not so sure. Someone had to take the place as a public duty. He was extremely reluctant to be the one, and he had reasons that seemed to him to have weight. He put them into words.

"Bob saved my life from Sanderson once, perhaps twice. Until he raided the Hughes place we were very friendly. If I were sheriff it would be my duty to hunt him down, perhaps to kill him. I don't want to do it. Of course he might get me instead. That's not the point. It doesn't seem quite sporting for me to go after a man in whose debt I am."

"Certainly not," agreed Smith-Beresford. "Wouldn't think of it, Garrett. Let someone else do it."

Steelman took another view of it. "He interfered with Sanderson because of a whim. They didn't like each other. You were incidentally benefited. This isn't a personal matter between you and him. He'll understand that perfectly. Say you're appointed sheriff. If he keeps hellin' around that's not yore fault. Let him go straight an' you'll not trouble him. The long an' the short of it is that here's a plain public duty callin' to some he-man. I don't say you're that man. Up to you to say whether you are or not. But I do say that yore relations to Quantrell don't figure in the case."

O'Hara thought it over and decided that Steelman was right. He had no right to pay any debt he owed to Quantrell at the expense of the public.

"Give me twenty-four hours to think it over," he said.

At the end of that time he told the old cattle man that he would take the appointment if it was satisfactory to Ingram.

Within a week the governor of the territory had appointed him.

CHAPTER XXIX: *"Quantrell Is Dangerous"*

As a YOUNG BRIDE at the Diamond Tail ranch Barbara was very popular with the riders in her husband's employ. Most of them were shy of her, but she was so pretty and so engaging that they liked to meet her even though their blushes mounted when she stopped to say "Good-morning."

None the less, she was not happy. The one man whose homage she wanted offered it rarely. Dave Ingram belonged to the old school of husbands which regards a wife as a property. He had won her, and it was not in character for him to keep on winning her. She was his woman under the law. Naturally, she would take it for granted that he was fond of her.

He never consulted her about business. He rarely told her where he was going or when he would be back. It did not occur to him to kiss her when he left or when he returned. There were hours when his passion for her flamed like tow. Yet Barbara, hungry-hearted for affection, resented these as much as his days of absorption in affairs from which she was excluded. Once she told him in a flare of anger that she was not his dog to be summoned by a snap of the fingers.

Barbara withdrew into herself, narrowing her life. A hard, fierce pride welled up in her, and bitterness lay like a lump of lead in her bosom. Not a girl given to self-pity, she did her share of weeping now when alone behind bolted doors. Sometimes she told herself that she was to blame, that she expected too much of a man. But since she was what she was this was small comfort. For she knew there could be no happiness for her in being less to a husband than his lover and his comrade.

At breakfast one morning Ingram lifted his eyes from the weekly newspaper, the *Aurora Sun*.

"See yore friend O'Hara has been appointed sheriff," he said. "If he's no better than Jim, might as well have none at all."

"Thought you favoured the appointment," she answered.

"I did. He's got guts, if he is a tenderfoot. But Quantrell's a lot more likely to get him than he is to get Quantrell."

"I noticed that everybody was urging him to take the place an' that nobody wanted it for himself," she observed sharply. "I think it's a shame. Isn't there any old-timer that had nerve enough for it?"

Her challenging eyes flashed into his. He laughed.

"Meanin' me, Barb? What d'you think?"

"You know what I think. After what you did to him Bob Quantrell will kill you unless he's brought to account before he gets a chance. You ought to make it yore first business to arrest him. If you were sheriff that's what you would do."

"Haven't time," he answered carelessly. "Too many other irons in the fire. An' I'm not worryin' any about Bob Quantrell."

She flung a reproachful look at him. "No. You'll let me do the worryin'. You know well as I do that he's burnin' up to get even with you. He'd have done it before now if he had found a chance. Some day——"

131

The passionate resentment in her voice amused him. "Some day——" he suggested, passing her his cup for more coffee.

"Saying he isn't dangerous doesn't make him less so. He may be lying out there now waitin' for you." She threw out her hand in a gesture toward the chaparral. "As for Mr. O'Hara, I do think it's a shame to let him go out against that Apache Quantrell—for that's all he is—knowin' no more about trailin' and such things than a child. You say yoreself he hasn't got a chance. I don't see what Dad was thinking about when he let him take it."

"Yore friend is a full-grown man, ain't he?" her husband asked indifferently. "An' I didn't say he hadn't a chance. I said the odds were against him if he really goes after Quantrell an' doesn't lie down on the job. Maybe he'll just make a bluff an' let it go at that."

"He won't," she said decisively. "He wouldn't have taken it if he hadn't meant to do his best."

"Hope his best is good enough. I'll sure not do any mournin' if he gets that young killer," Ingram replied, his eyes and attention wandering to other news in the paper. "See where yore father is driving a trail herd to Tuscon. Markets are lookin' up some."

O'Hara rode across to the Diamond Tail that afternoon.

Barbara came out to the porch to meet him. At sight of her a wave of emotion crashed through him. After the usual banalities of greeting he told her that he came to see her husband.

"Dave is not here. I don't know just where he is. At the beef roundup, wherever they're workin' to-day. I hear you are our new sheriff."

"For want of better," he said apologetically. "I wanted to speak to Mr. Ingram about that. I'm going to need a lot of advice. Once you called me a babe in the woods. That's about how I feel now."

"Don't be too venturesome," she begged. "You're not called on to get killed, Garrett. That wouldn't do anybody any good."

"I don't intend to be if I can help it. There's something else on my mind, Barbara. Quantrell was in Concho yesterday for a little while visiting the Gomez girl. He headed this way when he left town. It was after dark, but Steve Worrall saw him for a moment. I don't want to worry you. He's got friends on Buck Creek, an' maybe that's where he was making for. But I think Mr. Ingram ought to keep a careful lookout."

She let a flash of bitterness escape her. "Tell him. Don't tell me. I can't get him to be careful."

"He should. Quantrell is dangerous."

"Dave knows that as well as we do. But he's so sure of himself, and anyway, he is a sort of a fatalist. He says he'll not die till his time comes. I wish you'd stay an' talk to him. Maybe he'll listen to you more than he will to me. You're a man, anyhow, even though you are a tenderfoot."

"I'll stay if you like. I want to discuss my deputy with him. It's important to get a good one."

There drifted to them a sound, a faint pop that might have been the explosion of a far firecracker.

"What's that?" she cried, lifting a hand so that he would listen.

The breeze brought two more shots, and presently after an interval of seven or eight seconds three more.

The blood washed from Barbara's cheeks. She caught at her friend's arm to get strength from personal contact.

"Someone shooting at a deer, or more likely a bear," O'Hara said. But her fear had infected him. He felt no conviction that his guess was true.

Barbara ran to the hitch rack and mounted a saddled horse. It was not a side saddle but she did not wait to have a change made.

"Come on," she cried to O'Hara as she wheeled the horse and put it to a gallop.

Already he was hard on her heels. They dashed down the road in the direction from which the shots had come.

CHAPTER XXX: *A Promise Kept*

FOR ALL his apparent indifference Ingram did not take unnecessary chances. He knew that Bob Quantrell would kill him if he could, and he more than suspected that the young outlaw had lain in wait for him more than once and had been frustrated by circumstances. Ingram rode about his business as usual, but he was particular as to the trails he followed. If he went to Concho by the wagon road he returned to the ranch over the hills. Even on the home place he carried always a .44 close to his hand, and when away from it a rifle lay in its case beside the saddle.

On the day that O'Hara rode to the Diamond Tail to warn him Ingram had gone to a gather of beeves with Roche. He was rounding up a trail herd to drive to San Jacinto. To meet

133

the notes falling due ready money was necessary, and at the price offered he could begin to see his way into the clear again. Since the termination of the feud and his subsequent marriage to Barbara Steelman the bankers who held his paper had shown a tendency not to press him too hard. Three months ago the financial outlook had been very dark, but he knew now that he was going to weather the storm.

The two riders cut across the country. They jog-trotted up a hill of junipers and jack pines, crossed a mesa, and dropped down a sharp incline to a draw. Here and there the blue-spiked flowers of the larkspur caught the eye. From the uplands they could see the serrated peaks of the mountains. In the clear amber light, a hundred miles away, rose Poker Bill Butte.

They could hear the bawling of cattle in motion, and after a little, from a summit, three or four bunches of cows converging toward a common point. Behind each bunch rode one or two men. A faint "Hi-yi" drifted on the breeze to them.

"Shorty combin' Horse Prong," Roche said.

A trickle of cows emerged from a draw just below them. These merged with those already on the round-up ground, a pocket in the hills where they could be held easily while being worked. The beef herd, cut out from the herds gathered during the past week, were held apart from the stock now drifting in.

Ingram was boss of the round-up. He superintended branding and cutting, gave directions to his men, and personally kept the tally. There were few better cow men in the territory than Dave Ingram, not many as good. Most of the riders on this round-up were in his employ, though there were present representatives of other outfits to claim any calves belonging to their brands. Jack Phillips was "rep" for the Hashknife and the Circle S O ranches.

Ingram left the beef herd with his *segundo* in charge. As he headed toward home Phillips joined him. For a mile or two their way was the same. Roche cantered after them and joined the two.

"Better look out, Dave," Phillips said. "It's come to me three-four times that Bob Quantrell is layin' for you. He made his brags what he was gonna do to you in the Square Deal Saloon at Agua Caliente Saturday. One of our boys was there an' heard him."

"No news to me that he's sore," Ingram replied, with a thin grim smile. "He's got a license to be, accordin' to his way of it."

"He sure has," agreed Roche. "I never did see such a quirtin' as you gave him. I don't reckon we'd ought ever to have let him get off the ranch alive."

"If this new sheriff is any good he'll put Quantrell outa business. No use arrestin' him. Like Roche says, he's got to be killed. O'Hara has sand in his craw, but he's a tenderfoot. I've a notion to throw in with him an' clean out the gang. Trouble is I'm so pushed for time."

Phillips ruminated aloud. "If anyone was to ask me what was the most important business Dave Ingram could attend to right now I'd say it was runnin' down Quantrell. If he ever gets the dead wood on you, Dave——"

"Why, then I reckon I'll be number seventeen for him." Ingram finished carelessly.

"I've talked till I'm hoarse," Roche said to the Hashknife man. "So have the other boys. No use. Only yesterday I was tellin' the Old Man what Pesky heard Bob say. He won't pay any attention."

"Do you boys want me to shut myself up in the house?" Ingram asked impatiently. "He's nothing but a rattlesnake. Why should I be afraid of him? I'm supposed to be a grown man my own self. Seems to me someone is dinging in my ears all day long Quantrell—Quantrell—Quantrell. He's got my wife scared, too. I knew how to throw a six-shooter before that boy was born."

Phillips drew up to deflect for the Circle S O. "Well, they claim threatened folks live long. Maybe so. *Adiós.*"

The other two struck a road gait across the mesa.

They talked casually of one topic and another: the number of beeves the gather would total, the need of rain, the best route along which to send the San Jacinto drive in order to get good grass. As Ingram talked, his keen eyes searched the wooded hill slopes and the arroyos filled with scrub oak. He might appear to take Quantrell's threats lightly, but he had no intention of offering himself as an easy mark. Roche noticed that without appearing to do so he picked their line of travel, keeping as much as possible to the uplands from which one could look down upon the washes and draws where an ambusher would be more likely to lurk.

They were dropping down a hill to the road which swung around a bluff to the ranch. The horses picked their way slowly through the rubble ready to start sliding at the least pressure. Knowing how sure-footed their mounts were, both riders leaned back and gave them their heads.

They reached the red road ribbon, then turned to follow it

as it circled the base of the butte. Presently they could see the huddled buildings of the ranch and the windmill shining in the setting sun.

Three twisted cedars hugged the shale cliff close to the road. A man and a horse were in the cedars. The man had dismounted.

Roche pulled to a sudden halt. The heart in him died under his ribs. The man in the cedars was Bob Quantrell and he held in his hands a shotgun. It was a double-barrelled one. That the cartridges were loaded with buckshot the cowboy did not need to be told. The outlaw paid no attention to Roche. He looked at the man who had flogged him, and it seemed to the vaquero that a red-hot devil of rage glared out of his eyes. But when he spoke his voice was low and almost casual, yet somehow malignantly sinister.

"Like I promised you, Dave, me an' you alone."

Ingram must have known that he was a dead man. At that distance Quantrell could not miss. The young ruffian who stood there taunting him would pull the trigger long before he could drag the rifle from its scabbard, before even he could flash a six-shooter into the light. Ingram's decision was instant, and it was characteristic of the man. He took the one forlorn fighting chance that offered.

Flinging his body from the saddle head first, the cattle man's clutching fingers plucked out a revolver as he dived for the ground. A gun roared, and a dozen buckshot tore through Ingram's side while he was still in the air. His moments were to be counted on the fingers of two hands, and he knew it. But his indomitable will was for one instant stronger than death. He steadied himself on his left forearm, raised the weapon jerkily, and fired. Simultaneously, or perhaps a fraction of a second later, came the roar of the shotgun.

Before the sound of it had died away the cow man was dead.

Quantrell reached for his revolver. Roche was flying in a panic down the road toward the Diamond Tail. The killer's tusks showed in a grin, one not pleasant to see. He shuffled his bow-legged way forward, and in a sudden fury of rage flung three bullets into the dead body.

"Maybe you'll not be so handy with a quirt from now on," he spat out venomously.

The outlaw could not stay to enjoy his triumph. There was need of a hurried departure. Roche would cry the news at the ranch and saddles would be slapped on cow ponies in a hurry for the pursuit. But Quantrell took his time. It would be long before he would have another hour so full of relish as this one.

He walked back to his horse, pulled the slip knot by which it was tied, and swung to the saddle. Beside the body he stopped once more to grin evilly down at it.

From this point the road dropped slightly, in the direction of the ranch, for several hundred yards, then plunged down out of sight for some distance. Two horses were galloping toward him. He was curious to know who these two might be. Certainly they were losing no time. Delay was dangerous, but the taste of peril in his nostrils stimulated him. He waited till the riders topped the rise, turned to go, but looked back with his hand on the cantle.

"By cripes, one of 'em is a woman," he said to himself, and he swept his hat off in a rakish bow.

He plunged into a draw of scrub oaks, crashed through it, and presently was among thickets of chaparral. For an hour he rode fast, but when dusk began to fall he knew he was safe and slackened pace. He began to sing in a high cracked voice:

> "Rock-a-bye, baby,
> Bump off a bazoo,
> Daddy'll be home
> When the round-up is through."

Chapter XXXI: *O'Hara Says His Piece*

THE KILLING of Ingram aroused public sentiment more than any atrocity that had taken place during the feud. If it had occurred while the Jefferson County War had been still in progress there would have been a divided opinion, but coming as it did just after peace had been declared both factions turned on Quantrell and his gang. Posses scoured the chaparral, driving the outlaws from one camp to another. None of the bandits dared show themselves in any town. They fled into the high hills and "holed up."

The nesters on the creeks, the small ranchmen who had hitherto been friendly to Quantrell, were now among those most eager to have him run down. For Ingram had been their leader in the fight against the aggressions of Steelman and his vast herds. Moreover, the governor of the territory had put a price of three thousand dollars on the head of Quantrell dead or alive.

Even Bob Quantrell, in spite of the jaunty insouciance he assumed, was daunted by the storm he had aroused. It was not so much his enemies that he feared as those whom he was forced to trust. From half a dozen trees at lonely crossroads he tore down placards which described him and announced the reward for his capture. When he rode up to a cabin near the head of some creek, one far from any neighbours, he could never be sure that a bullet would not greet him before he swung from the saddle. He watched suspiciously the nesters who supplied him with food, and they in turn eyed him and his followers nervously. They sensed his mistrust of them and could not be sure that in a moment of acute doubt he would not resort to the six-shooter. Their apprehensions were increased because they knew, two or three of them at least, that they would have betrayed him had they dared.

At no time could Quantrell escape from the haunting dread of treachery. It was present with him when he and his men were camped far up in the pines close to the jagged peaks. He could not look into the eyes of any of his fellow outlaws without seeing the lust for that three-thousand-dollar reward gleaming out of them. Even though he knew that his imagination was getting the better of his nerves he could not be easy in mind. It was one thing to go coolly to meet danger. It was quite another to feel it lurking in the heart of every human being he met. He began to get jumpy. This was a new and disturbing condition.

One night he spread his blankets a little way from those of his companions, on the edge of the camp. After they had gone to sleep he rose very quietly, packed his roll, and carried it into the brush. He found his hobbled horse, saddled it, and tied the blankets back of the saddle. Five minutes later he was winding his way between two of the thousand precipitous hills that surrounded him.

When Deever woke in the morning he found a pencil-scrawled note weighted down by a stone beside his saddle. It read:

Adiós, boys. See you later. I'm heading for Mexico. This country is bad medicine for me. It's hotter than hell on a holiday right now.

BOB QUANTRELL.

The outlaws discussed it.

"Just as well," Deever said. "He was scared of us—scared we'd shoot him for the reward. I could see by the way he's been actin' lately. I'm plumb glad he's lit out."

"Me, too," agreed another known as Sandy. "Sure enough Bob's been on the hook lately—kinda mean actin', an' you

138

know how good-natured he usually is. I don't aim to get into any jackpot with him if I can help it. Well, I reckon the rest of us better scatter, too. Trinidad for me. I got a friend up thataway with a cow ranch."

"I aim to be an absentee for a spell my own self," the third man said. "If I ain't too late I'll take a job with a trail outfit in the Panhandle. A friend of mine's brother is foreman. Anyways, I'll shake a hoof for Tascosa, an' glad to get away at that. I been right oneasy ever since Bob bumped off Ingram."

So it happened that within six weeks of the appointment of O'Hara the Quantrell Gang dissolved and went its several ways. The new sheriff got some credit for this because of his activity in organizing and directing the posses that had kept the outlaws on the jump, but he knew he still had to justify his selection in the eyes of the old-timers.

This he proceeded to do. There were other rustlers, horse thieves, and criminals in his district. Some of these were nesters in the hills. Others had their headquarters at Concho. These latter were most of them warriors who had been drawn to Jefferson County as hired gunmen in the feud. Against these O'Hara waged continuous warfare if he could prove that they had lifted a hand to overt lawlessness since the end of the war. He was supported by a change in public feeling. Capital was beginning to come in from outside for investment and the community reacted to this in a normal fashion. Men said to each other that it was time the country settled down and quit "hellin' around."

Deever drifted down to Concho and joined the group of bad men who still hung around. He relied on the fact that there was very little definite evidence that he had been one of Quantrell's men. That he had been with them now and again he did not deny, but never while the gang had been engaged in rustling or any other lawlessness. So he claimed at the Gold Nugget, which was the chief resort of the group with whom he fraternized.

O'Hara had adopted the habit of life of those about him. He wore corduroy trousers thrust into the tops of cowboy boots, a pinched-in Stetson hat, and a gray flannel shirt. A .45-calibre Colt six-shooter sagged from a belt fastened above his hips. His face had become as brown as coffee. His muscles were hard and pliant as those of the tough buckskin peg pony he rode. But the change in him was more than physical. It extended to his mental reactions. Two months earlier, for

139

instance, he would never have taken with Deever the high-handed course he took now.

It was evening when he drifted into the Gold Nugget. The place buzzed with activity. A poker game was in progress near the back door, by which way the sheriff had entered. Some young cowboys were trying their luck with a pair of professional gamblers. A faro game was running and also one of Mexican monte. Men were lined up beside the bar drinking.

O'Hara nodded to one and another of those he knew. He was on friendly terms with a good many citizens. Most honest men liked this quiet, amiable young man who had proved unmistakably that he had nerve.

He stopped at the faro table just back of the man he had come to see. Deever looked around.

"Don't put yore foot on the rung of my chair," he growled. "I'm kinda superstitious, young fellow."

"All right, I won't," O'Hara promised pleasantly. "You about through playing?"

"What's eatin' you? Want my seat?"

"Not to-night. Don't let me hurry you. When you're through I've got a few words to say to you."

Deever slewed around in his chair. "Say 'em now."

"I had in mind private conversation."

"Speak yore piece right out in meetin', fellow. I got nothin' to say to you that can't be said before everybody."

"Just as you please, Deever." The sheriff's voice did not lose its amiability in the least. "What I wanted to say was that you are to get out of this county inside of twenty-four hours."

"Me! What for?" The squat cowboy rose to his feet and faced the officer. His hard eyes narrowed. "You got a warrant for my arrest?"

"No. If I had I'd arrest you."

"Then what's this play you're makin'? I don't have to get out on yore say-so."

"No, you can stay. But I wouldn't if I were you. Take a straight tip and hit the trail. This climate is unhealthy for you."

"Why? Because some squirt of a tenderfoot sheriff says so?" Deever's manner was menacing, his voice harsh.

Men suspended their card-playing and their drinking to watch this drama. Red tragedy might flame out of it any moment. The less hardy ones began looking for places of refuge should bullets begin to fly.

"That's it, Deever. You've guessed it first time." O'Hara still spoke gently, almost smilingly, but what he said rang out clear as a bell. "Because this tenderfoot sheriff says so."

"Fellow, do you claim you're the law an' all you gotta do is give orders?"

"I'm the law as far as you're concerned, Deever. Get out. Inside of twenty-four hours, as I said."

"An' if I don't?"

The sheriff shook his head. "No 'if' about it. You're checking out."

He was so quietly confident that Deever wavered. The outlaw knew Concho had had a change of heart. If he followed his impulse, called for a showdown and shot O'Hara, very likely he would never leave town alive. For a moment his glance sidled around the room, looking for the men who might be expected to stand with him. What he saw gave him small comfort. A score of men were watching him, but what they were thinking behind those steady eyes he could not tell.

"You got no right to drive me out when I've done nothin'. I claim my rights. You can't hand me my hat an' you can't arrest me without you got a warrant for me."

"I can't, but I'm doing it."

"You're the big auger 'round here now, are you?" jeered the outlaw. "Because Wes Steelman got you appointed to a two-by-four job. Say, fellow, don't get heavy with me. It ain't supposed to be safe."

"Safe for you?" asked O'Hara, his brown eyes never lifting from the outlaw's face. "Listen, Deever. Here's the layout. Don't try to crowd your luck here. You're bucked out in this county. Get out, or I'll throw you into jail."

He turned on his heel and sauntered to the bar. Steve Worrall was there taking a drink. He asked O'Hara to join him, then added as a postscript to his invitation a remark intended to reach Deever.

"Some of these scalawags will learn after a while to hit the pike when you give the word," he said, clapping his friend on the back. "By the great jumpin' horn' toad, you're sure one hellamiler. Betcha my bald-face mare against a dollar Mex that Concho will lose one of its sure-enough bully puss warriors right soon, say within twenty-four hours."

"I think so," agreed O'Hara nonchalantly. "How's the freighting business these days, Steve?"

"Lookin' up again, like sheriffin'," Worrall grinned. "Say, young fellow, you're sure a tonic to an old stove-up donker like me. Travellin' with you would make a jackrabbit spit in a wildcat's eye."

"Come on, Steve, I want to have a powwow with you," O'Hara said.

He slipped an arm under the tall man's elbow and the two walked out of the Gold Nugget together.

Chapter XXXII: *David Arrives*

THE PREDICTION of Steve Worrall turned out to be a true one. In the dark hours of the night Deever slipped out of town and departed for parts unknown. At the time O'Hara turned his back on him he had no intention of going. He boasted to his cronies that no tenderfoot sheriff could drive him away.

"I'm his game at any turn of the road. If he wants to come a-smokin', suits me fine. I don't scare worth a cent, not for any flop-eared hound all bark an' no bite." The outlaw patted the six-shooter by his side. "This here's my hole card, an' it's a sure enough ace. Come to that, it's five aces. The smart-Aleck has got to have a royal flush to beat it, an' I'll bet my boots he ain't got it. Me, I'll be sittin' in at the showdown he's called for."

Which was all very well when he was sitting drinking with the other ex-warriors of the Jefferson County War. They applauded his nerve, assured him that O'Hara had not a chance with him in a gun play, and flattered his vanity with fulsome compliments. Even while he accepted their plaudits Deever realized the motive back of them. His companions were more than willing to have this new sheriff, who threatened to become very inconvenient to them, shot down at no risk to themselves.

But after he had left his companions, when the drink had died down in him, the logic of cold facts pressed home. He could kill O'Hara. There was no doubt about that. But what good would that do him if the citizens of Concho arrested him before he left town and promptly lynched him? He did not like the cold silence of those who had listened to the sheriff's ultimatum. He did not like Steve Worrall's open comment, one that he would never have made if he had not felt that public opinion backed him. On the other hand, he did not like to run away after the play he had made. He had got himself in a jackpot.

Deever was game enough but he could not buck against a

whole community. He was driven to a conclusion his self-esteem hated to accept.

"Dad burn it, I got to light a shuck," he told himself. "But if I ever get a crack at this pilgrim O'Hara I'll send him a through ticket to Kingdom Come."

After which he slapped a saddle on a bronco and decamped.

This enhanced the new sheriff's reputation tremendously. The people of Concho could not follow the workings of Deever's mind. What reached them was that O'Hara had served notice on this outlaw, one of the most vicious of the bad men, to get out of town within a specified time and that the fellow had not waited to challenge the ultimatum. They deduced that he was afraid of the sheriff.

O'Hara made a discovery. If a bad man was sober it was nearly always possible to arrest him without using a gun. Back of the officer was the law, an asset intangible but powerful now that Jefferson County was emerging from its wild past.

As the months passed O'Hara, assisted by public sentiment, cleaned up the town. There were still occasional shooting affairs, but they did not have the sanction of community support.

O'Hara was kept so busy that for months he did not find time to pay more than one or two flying visits to the Circle S O. His partner, Smith-Beresford, was managing the ranch, with some advice from Wesley Steelman, and he was doing so well that it began to look as though he might escape the usual fate of wealthy Englishmen who went into cows in the West.

It was nearly nine months after the death of Ingram that a cowboy from the Diamond Tail brought the sheriff news, not entirely unexpected. Barbara had given birth to a boy, weight eight pounds.

Since the day of the funeral O'Hara had not set eyes on Barbara. His excuse had been that he was too busy to call, but the real reason was that he did not know whether he could keep his eyes from telling her what was in his heart. Now he could no longer decently stay away. At the first opportunity he rode out to the Diamond Tail.

Little Bennie Ford came running to meet him as he alighted. His mother, Mary Joe, appeared in the doorway of the ranch house. O'Hara tossed the youngster to his shoulder and came forward. He guessed that Mrs. Ford had been looking after the patient.

"Would you like to see the finest baby in Jefferson County, Mr. O'Hara?" she asked, smiling at the sheriff.

"That's why I've ridden twenty miles, Mrs. Ford," he told her.

She was a very pretty young woman, and it was certain that she would remain a widow only until the right man appeared. Perhaps she would have liked to feel that there was a reason more personal to herself that had brought him, but she was clear-eyed enough to know better. She could make him blush. That did not mean that she had ever touched his heart.

"Wait here a minute," she told him, and disappeared into the house.

Mary Joe was gone a long ten minutes before she returned. "You're to come in," she said.

O'Hara did not know that the time had been spent in making the bedroom into which he was ushered more orderly, and the young woman in the bed more presentable. At sight of her the blood rushed stormily to his heart. He knew that he was betraying himself, yet words choked in his throat and he could find nothing to say. In his brown hand he held the one she had given him, and as he looked at her a slow flush crept into her cheeks.

Each of them thought how the months had changed the other. Her quick eyes saw him another man than the tenderfoot she had met the day of his arrival. He was clean and brown and compact, of supple grace. To look at him was to understand why he had so impressed his personality upon the community. The stamp of the West was on him, its self-reliance and its quiet poised strength. She liked the grip of his bronzed hand. It was a promise.

He saw her even more changed. She was a woman, no longer a girl. The radiance of youth, almost insolent in its joyous vitality, was not now the outstanding note of her.

"So you came at last," she said. "After all these months."

He had no answer for her reproach except to murmur that he had been busy. How could he tell her that he dared not let himself come within the orbit of her attraction?

"Since you've come at last to see my baby I'll forgive you," she said, and drew back a fold of wrapping that he might get a better look at it.

"Would you like to hold him?" she asked, as though she were conferring upon her friend a precious privilege.

"If I may."

The baby whimpered a little as he held it.

144

"His name is David," she said.

"I hope he'll defeat all the Goliaths that he meets."

"Do you think he is pretty?" she asked.

He came through with the proper endorsement of its beauty.

Barbara laughed happily. "You're tellin' fibs, Garrett. I'm his mother, but even I can see that he's a homely little peanut yet. You couldn't call that little button a nose, could you? But his eyes *are* lovely, aren't they? They are his father's."

Mary Joe relieved O'Hara of the baby and carried it out of the room. "Time he went to sleep," she announced with authority. "You may sit down and talk to Barbara, Mr. O'Hara."

"Won't I tire her?"

"No. Not if you don't stay too long. Amuse her."

After Mary Joe had left them alone Barbara settled back among the pillows. "You've heard yore orders. Amuse me, Garrett." There was a faint friendly smile on her lips. She knew him of old.

"Good gracious! I can't. I never amused a woman in my life. I don't know how to talk with one."

"Then don't bother about amusing me. Interest me. Tell me all about yoreself an' what you've been doing. I've heard all sorts of things about you."

"I haven't been doing anything worth while—just the routine of office."

"Then there's nothing to what I've heard," she derided.

"I don't know what you've heard."

"Well, Dad says you're the best sheriff in the territory."

"Your father has to believe in me because he was responsible for my appointment."

"Lyulph agrees with him." She mimicked Smith-Beresford's speech and manner. "The best in the whole bally country, by Jove!"

His face was hot with embarrassment, but she had given him a way of escape. "You know, of course, that he is to be married soon—that he is going home next month to bring his fiancée out?"

"Of course I know it. I keep in touch with *my* friends."

He chose to ignore this thrust. "Hope he'll be happy. I don't know anyone who deserves happiness more."

"He'll be happy if she is like her letters. Lyulph let me read some of them."

"It will be very different here from what she is used to.

145

I've seen a picture of her father's place in Surrey. One of those fine old English houses with a lawn a hundred years old. English men and women are not so easily transplanted as the Scotch. She will be giving up a lot." He spoke doubtfully.

"The great point is that she and Lyulph seem so sure of each other. They haven't any doubts, either of them. It doesn't matter what she gives up. She'll have all kinds of new experiences—an' that's life. And above all, they'll have each other."

"Ye-es," he assented.

Her eyes flashed with gay malice. "But you're a bachelor. You wouldn't think that much."

He smiled ruefully. His modesty would not let him believe that he had in him the qualities to win the woman he wanted to such joy. What had he to offer her so compelling that she would find in the house of their life together doors opening to dear delights and windows looking upon dawns rosy with the promise of new happiness?

But what he said was lame enough, a repetition of what he had said before. "I hope they'll be happy."

"You sound faint-hearted in yore hopes," she accused. "And if we're to judge by the people we see you're right enough. It won't do for a man and a woman just to love each other. They have to fit, care for the same things, each go more than halfway to try to understand. But I'm pretty sure of one thing. You won't find happiness unless you go out expecting to get it."

"And you're not twenty-one yet," he pretended to mock.

" 'An' think you know so much,' you wanted to add. Perhaps I don't know very much, but I'm learnin' all the time. One thing I'm pretty sure of is that if you don't demand a lot of life you won't get it. If I were a man an' wanted anything in the world I'd go after it with all I had."

Abruptly she stopped. Her cheeks became the colour of a Cherokee rose, for she suddenly remembered what it was he had a few months since desired above all things. Would he think that she had been inviting him to make love to her?

Into the embarrassment of that moment walked Mary Joe, unconscious that her arrival was a most propitious one.

"The little skeezicks dropped right off to sleep," she said.

O'Hara rose to go.

Barbara shook hands with him, but she did not ask him to come again. The memory of her latest remark was still too present with her.

146

The young man carried away with him a good deal to think about. He had found out that he was still sunk fathoms deep in love. It would be this woman or none with him. But what about her? Was there a chance that after many days her heart would answer the deep silent call of his? Had she meant to encourage him? He did not think so. He was almost sure she had not. That was the frank, fearless way she talked. Nor did he forget that she had not asked him to come again.

CHAPTER XXXIII: *Bob Quantrell Offers Hospitality*

PUBLIC INDIGNATION is usually not sustained. It evaporates with the passage of time. When the rumour spread, about a year after the disappearance of Bob Quantrell, that he had returned to his old haunts the residents of Jefferson County did not bestir themselves to comb the mountains and the chaparral for him. This was strictly the business of Sheriff O'Hara and such indiscreet youth as he could induce to serve with him as deputies.

Bob had been seen one night at Concho, but he did not stay more than a few hours nor did he advertise his presence. Deever was with him. They made a fleeting visit to Agua Caliente to buy supplies. It was known they had been on Horse Creek.

O'Hara recognized that this was to be a campaign. He had to depend on information given him secretly by friendly cow men, vaqueros, and sheepherders. It was essential that he have deputies upon whom he could depend at a pinch. Quietly he set about making preparations.

He dropped in at the Longhorn Corral.

Steve Worrall greeted him. "What's new, old-timer?"

O'Hara sat down in a chair. The long freighter disposed his lank frame on two chairs and the table.

"The latest news is that Steve Worrall has been appointed deputy sheriff of Jefferson County," O'Hara said, smiling at him.

"Did you hear the rest of the story, how he said he was much obliged for the compliment but was so doggoned busy he couldn't accept?"

"No, I hadn't heard that. Anyhow, that's not the way it is. He may not know it yet, but he's practically all ready to be sworn in."

"How come? I know quite several jobs I like better than

that—safer an' more comfortable an' better pay with less hard work."

"Less hard work. Hmp!" O'Hara's eyes travelled down the long, lean body. "Getting soft. Too much loafing around the corral, too much time wasted at cards."

"Also," continued Steve, paying no attention to this gratuitous criticism, "I haven't lost Bob Quantrell any to speak of, if that's the notion that's stickin' in yore coconut. He's a slick fellow to leave lay when he's huntin' for nature's sweet solitude."

"Not what he was," the sheriff said to himself, almost in a murmur, eying the other judicially. "Have to take him from the fleshpots of Egypt before he runs to fat. And I can remember him, too, when he was a he-man. Too bad! Too bad!"

The freighter ignored the insult. "Last man in the world I want to jump unexpected. No, like I said, I'd rather leave him lay. If Bob waved me round I'd sure enough make a wide loop to duck undue proximity. '*Adiós!*' would be the word."

O'Hara continued his soliloquy. "Besides, it'll do him good. A nice vacation from the worries of business. All work and no play makes Jack a dull boy. A few pleasant camping trips here and there——"

The long man jumped indignantly at one word, then at another. "Play! Play! What's yore notion of work, young fellow, if this is what you call play? You give yoreself away. Campin' trips here an' there? By the great jumpin' horn' toad, I'll do my campin' right here in Concho. About 'steen hours a day on a horse buckin' blizzards an' ploughin' through snow two feet deep. Camp on a windy ledge below zero with the piñon so waterlogged you can't light a fire. No grub but sour beans an' hoe cake an' coffee. Not for me. I've done served my time. I'm too old an' stove up for such pranks." He stopped, then gulped out an apparently embittered question in which his friend could read surrender: "Why in Mexico do you pick on me? Got anything against me? I ain't ever done you a favour, have I?"

The sheriff grinned at his friend. "I want a long guy who can stand up in his stirrups and tell me who's over the hill a mile or so away."

"Insult as well as injury," snorted Steve, reaching for his pipe. "Fine for you. You're gonna be elected sheriff unanimous next month, an' I've heard some doggoned idiots say you'd make a good district judge. After that it'll be gover-

148

nor if you make good, like as not. Different here. Where do I get off the wagon at? Bob Quantrell ain't interferin' with me any. Why should I get all het up about him? 'Live an' let live' is my motto."

"My idea is to make haste slowly," O'Hara said, passing over the other's objections as negligible. "We'll not go ramping all over the country looking for him. Until we get a straight steer we'll sit tight and wait. No use chasing down every rumour we hear. When I follow a trail I want it to be a hot one."

"Are you aimin' to capture Quantrell's gang? Or to run 'em down an' wipe 'em out?"

"To capture them if I can. We want men with us who will do to take along. What do you think of Buckskin Joe?"

"He's a good trailer."

"So I'm told. But will he do to ride the river with?"

"I'd say he would. Don't know him very well, but he's got a good rep. Fought Apaches. I've heard army officers speak well of him."

"I've thought of Amen Owen, too. He's an old-timer, well acquainted with this country, and thoroughly reliable."

"Good man. He used to be right friendly with Bob, though."

"So did you and I, for that matter. If Owen throws in with us he'll go through."

"I reckon."

They discussed others as possibilities for any posse that might be required, though both of them realized that the personnel of any posse would be a measure to be determined by the men available at the time.

Quantrell did not keep them waiting long. A buckboard driver brought in word three days later that a bunch of horses had been stolen from a rancher named Ferril, who lived close to the Mal Pais in the western part of the county. Hastily O'Hara gathered a posse and rode to Ferril's place. With him he had Worrall, Owen, and two brothers named Brown.

It was a long ride and the weather was bitter. The snow was five or six inches deep, and the wind swept it from the ground in swirling gusts that drove it into their faces with the sting of sleet. All day they rode, and it was after dark when they reached the ranch which was their destination. Icicles hung from the eyebrows of the men, matted the beards of the two Browns, and depended from the manes of the horses. A dozen times the riders had been forced to

149

dismount in order to get circulation into their legs by walking alongside the animals.

"We'd be nice easy marks if Bob an' his crowd happen to have come back here to spend the night," grumbled Amen as they drew up outside the house.

The sheriff slipped from the saddle and walked to a window. A good fire blazed at one end of the room. Ferril sat beside it mending a stirrup leather with rivets. His wife was washing dishes.

O'Hara shouted, "Hello the house!" and knocked on the door.

The rancher called "Who's there?" then after a moment opened without waiting for an answer.

He invited the half-frozen men into the house, and they thawed out in front of the fireplace while Ferril and his son stabled the horses and fed them.

Mrs. Ferril was a bouncing, round-breasted young woman with snapping black eyes. She was twenty years younger than her husband and was the stepmother of the lad. At once she set about making supper for the self-invited guests. While she worked she flashed smiles at them and talked. Not for a long time had Garrett O'Hara seen a woman with more gusto and exuberance for life.

The sheriff asked questions enough to direct her conversation. It appeared that Phil, her stepson, had ridden out of an arroyo in time to see the rustlers round up the horses. They had caught sight of him and one of the men had fired at him before he realized that this was a raid. Phil was almost sure that the man who had fired at him was Deever. He had not been near enough to recognize any of the others.

"Which way did they go after leaving the ranch?" Owen asked.

"Toward the Mal Pais," she said. "Hank followed them for several miles. He couldn't miss their trail in the snow. They have a hangout there in a cave. The story is that they have a bunch of cattle rounded up in a valley two-three miles from there."

Her talk did not at all interfere with the getting of supper. She worked very rapidly, and in a surprisingly short time had a steaming meal ready for them. The members of the sheriff's party sat down to a table loaded with pea soup, steak, hot biscuits, corn bread, potatoes, gravy, dried apricots stewed, and honey. They fell to ravenously, for they had not stopped at noon for dinner, and after they had fin-

150

ished unanimously voted it the best supper they had ever eaten.

The men of the posse slept on the floor in their own blankets, which they first dried out before the fire.

In a few minutes they were all dead to the world. It had been an exhausting day and the sturdiest of them was tired. None of them awakened until Phil renewed the fire which had been banked for the night.

"Roll out an' roll up, boys," O'Hara shouted, and he fitted action to word by doing so himself.

Each man tied his blankets in a roll and tossed them into a corner of the room. They stamped out to the washpan, made themselves clean, and combed their hair. By the time they had fed the horses, breakfast was almost ready.

It had been agreed that Hank Ferril was to ride with them. He did not want to go, but he could not very well object. The stolen horses were his, and he knew the Mal Pais country better than any of the others.

"They're a tough layout, an' I hate to get them sore at me," he said while he was saddling.

"Why, of course, if you're raisin' stock for Bob Quantrell's benefit, Hank," said Owen with obvious sarcasm.

"Not a chance in the world of gettin' my stock back, Amen. Like huntin' a needle in a haystack. If Bob wants us to find him we will; if not, we won't see hide or hair of him. An' you can bet that if we do it'll be because he's got the dead wood on us."

Ferril's prediction was a true one. Forty-eight hours later the posse, a group of weary and saddle-worn men, dismounted at his ranch and bow-legged stiffly to the house from the corral. For a day and a night it had been snowing steadily.

"No luck?" asked Mrs. Ferril of the sheriff.

"No luck," replied O'Hara. "Bob wasn't at home when we reached the cave, but he left a note for us. Thoughtful of him."

He handed a torn fragment of a newspaper to her. On it was scrawled:

Make yourself comfortable, Sheriff. Flour under the ledge. Quarter of beef hanging from the cottonwood by the spring. Cards on the shelf. Sorry can't stay and say howdy, but I've got a hen on at the Circle S O ranch. Meet up with you and chew over old times later. *Adiós*.

The pencilled note was signed "Bob Quantrell."

Mrs. Ferril showed strong white teeth in gay laughter. "He's sure enough a case, that boy. Never saw the beat of him for impudence."

"He's certainly got the laugh on us this time," the sheriff admitted. "Bob must have had a scout out, for he hadn't been gone half an hour when we reached the cave. The fire hadn't died down at all."

"What will you do now?"

"Get back to the Circle S O fast as a horse will carry me. Then I'll probably be too late."

"You think he means something?" She pointed to the note. "There where he mentions the Circle S O?"

O'Hara smiled ruefully. "Can you name anything that would please him more than to rustle our stock while I'm down here on a wild-goose chase after him?"

She nodded. Her eyes sparkled reminiscently. "He'll get a lot of chuckles out of that if he pulls it off. He's got a sense of humour, that boy. Only last Thursday he dropped in here an' advised Hank to look after his horses closer or some rustler would drive 'em off."

"I'd enjoy his humour more if it wasn't at my expense," O'Hara said, smiling at her.

"So would Hank, but you're enjoying this more than he is, Mr. O'Hara. You're not in cahoots with Bob, are you?"

"Not exactly. I'm in a different boat from Mr. Ferril. Quantrell hasn't raided my stock yet. He has only threatened to. I'm hurrying back to try to head him off. The other boys will follow at their leisure. I'm to have your fastest horse."

"You may be lucky if you get there too late," she warned.

He agreed that there was something to that.

CHAPTER XXXIV: *"I Wish You Weren't Sheriff"*

IT WAS LATE when O'Hara dropped wearily from the saddle at the Diamond Tail and hailed the house. He wanted to see Jack Phillips, who had since Ingram's death been foreman of the young widow's ranch.

Barbara answered his call. "Who is it?" she asked.

"Garrett. Is Jack here?"

"No, he isn't. He went over to see Dad and said he wouldn't be back till late. What is it, Garrett?"

He hesitated. No use worrying her.

"Nothing much, Barbara. I'm on my way to the Circle

152

S O and I stopped to have a word with him. But if he isn't here——"

"Wait just a minute and I'll be out," she said, and drew back from the window.

Presently a lamp was lit. After a minute he saw the light pass from her room to the hall. She opened the front door.

"Come in," she said, holding the lamp high to light the way.

Still he hesitated.

"Come on in, Garrett," she insisted. "I want to see you."

He followed her into the house. She led the way into the sitting room and put the lamp on a table. One swift glance showed her that he was travel-worn.

"I'm not very presentable," he apologized. "I didn't mean to waken you."

"I wasn't asleep. Hadn't gone to bed yet. What is it, Garrett? Something important?"

O'Hara did not want to speak about Quantrell to her. The man had murdered her husband. Even the mention of his name might stab her.

"I just wanted to tell him to keep an eye out for rustlers. I've reason to think some are heading this way."

"You mean the Quantrell Gang?" she asked quickly.

"Yes. Probably they'll not show up on your range. More likely the Circle S O country."

"How do you know? Tell me about it." Again her gaze swept up from his muddy boots and leathers to his unshaven face and sunken eyes. She interrupted herself to fling at him a question. "How far have you ridden to-day?"

"From the Mal Pais."

"When did you eat last?"

"This morning. I was in a hurry to get through. Don't bother about me. I'm all right—get food at the ranch when I get there."

"You'll eat here," she told him firmly. "Lie down on that sofa while I make supper for you."

"No. You're not strong enough. You mustn't——"

"I'm perfectly strong. David is three months old to-day. How long do you want me to be an invalid?" She tossed some newspapers from the lounge and ordered him to lie down.

Reluctantly, still protesting, he did as he was told. Barbara threw a Navajo rug over him and left the room, taking the lamp with her. Through the door he could see her moving about the kitchen with the light grace that characterized

153

her. His lids drooped. He fought against fatigue. . . . She was a woman to dream about, deep-bosomed and supple-limbed; incomparably alive . . .

When she returned, shading the flame of the lamp with her hand, he was sound asleep. Barbara looked down at him, a smile in her eyes. A glow warm and tender pervaded her, a diffused happiness. Never had she known anyone at all like him. Sensitive as a girl, quick with the shyness and the generosity of youth, he was none the less as self-reliant and competent as Dave Ingram himself had been. Gentleness was an essential quality of him, but no more so than the gay courage that emergencies seemed to set bubbling in his veins. He was a bookman—liked to read classics that till lately had been only names to her—but he had flung himself into the frontier life with boyish zest and had met, often buoyantly, always unflinchingly, the stark tests that had been imposed on him.

She let the light shine on him. His eyelids flickered open and he smiled at her.

"Your supper is ready," she told him.

"May I wash my hands?"

She had not forgotten even that. He found warm water in a basin and a clean towel at hand.

While he ate she sat across the table from him, elbow on table and chin on fist, listening to the story of his hunt in the Mal País country for the outlaws. He made light of it, but she could muster only a very faint smile even when he read aloud Quantrell's note. The man was more deadly than a rattlesnake, for he struck with warning. She had lived over fifty times that dreadful hour when she had come upon her husband's dead body lying in the road.

From her throat there leaped involuntarily the thought in her mind: "Oh, I wish you weren't sheriff, Garrett!"

A wave of emotion flooded him. He dared not let himself hope that her spontaneous cry meant more than friendship. He passed quickly over it lest she explain it away.

"I'd rather Quantrell felt that way than you," he said, trying for an effect of carelessness.

"There's something—inhuman about him."

He could see that fear had risen to her throat and choked her. Therefore he spoke evenly, almost negligently. "Not at all. He's just a boy gone bad, as they say. And don't forget, Barbara, that he's at the wrong end of this hunt, not I. He's the one that has to double and twist to escape, the one who has to suspect every man he meets of wanting to betray him.

154

We on the side of the law have a tremendous advantage, a moral force that makes a lot of difference."

"What difference would it make if he ever—ever——?"

"Don't worry about me, Barbara. He's not trying to get me but to get away from me." His hand moved a few inches across the table toward her. "I understand how you must feel about him—how you fear for your friends. But it really isn't necessary. I'm taking no unnecessary risks. He may dodge me for a while, but we'll round him up in the end—and I'll not be hurt doing it."

"If you ever get a chance you ought to—to put an end to him as you would a wolf," she cried with a little flare of savagery.

The brown eyes looking into hers were grim. "Listen, Barbara," he said. "I haven't undertaken to fight a duel with Quantrell. He's a killer, an outlaw wanted because of the crimes he has committed. If I can I'll get him at advantage, and if necessary I'll do just what you've said. Our lives aren't of the same value to society. I've been chosen to put an end to his lawless career. That's what I mean to do, one way or another, if I can. I don't intend to be a chivalrous fool about this, if that's what you are afraid of."

She gathered from this what reassurance she could. "But you *will* be careful, won't you?" she pleaded. "You'll not take any chances you don't have to?"

"Not a chance," he promised. "As the boys say, I'll not throw off on myself."

Garrett O'Hara had talked to Barbara with quiet confidence of the prospects. There was, he felt, no need to alarm her unduly. But the arguments he had used did not wholly convince himself. It was true, in one sense, that the advantage in such a campaign as this lay with the officers. In another way the odds entirely favoured the hunted rather than the hunters, because the former could at one time or another choose the setting for battle. During the two days that O'Hara's posse had combed the Mal Pais for the outlaws there had not been an hour when the searchers had not been in terrain where it was possible for Quantrell to ambush them. That he had not done so was either because the young desperado had other fish to fry or because of the criminal's instinct to keep on the dodge as long as he could and avoid an open conflict with the forces of law.

It was all very well to talk about being cautious, but it was an intrinsic part of the game he played that he had to take chances even when he did not know he was taking them.

As O'Hara, on a fresh horse, ploughed through the drifts on the divide between the Diamond Tail and the Circle S O, he knew that there never had been a time when he wanted less to fall a victim to Quantrell's marksmanship than now.

Riding through the night, he rebuilt the scene, her words and manner, the inflections of her voice. Had she meant more than friendliness? He would not let himself think so. Yet there blazed in him a new and glorious hope.

CHAPTER XXXV: *The Sheriff Follows a Hot Trail*

WHEN O'HARA reached the Circle S O he found that Bob Quantrell had made his threat good. In the darkness he and one other companion had slipped up to the stable and taken two blooded horses that belonged to Smith-Beresford. In place of them they left two leg-weary geldings branded with the sprawling H F used by Hank Ferril.

Quantrell left also one of his characteristic notes. He had nailed it to the top of the feed bin.

Only a short visit this time, Mr. Tenderfoot Sheriff. Business in Concho, so I can't stay. Much obliged for the horses. They say an even swap is no robbery. Tell Wes not to feel slighted. I'll drop in on him soon. See you later.

BOB QUANTRELL.

Tired though he was, O'Hara stayed at the ranch only long enough to have another mount run up and saddled for him. He did not doubt that Quantrell would keep his word and go to Concho. What deviltry he had in mind to do there, if any, the sheriff could not guess. In any case it was his duty to follow the young outlaw to town.

The ride to Concho was a long, cold one and O'Hara was drooping with fatigue. His hands clung to the horn of the saddle. His head nodded. More than once the jolting of the horse's motion awakened him with a start. It was nearly four o'clock when he slipped into town by way of the pasture back of the Concho House. Here he dismounted and hobbled the horse, hiding the saddle in a clump of scrub-oak bushes. The pasture was a large one and the odds were that the animal would not be noticed. As it chanced, the brand on it was a P D Bar. Smith-Beresford had bought it from a Buck Creek nester and the Circle S O riders had not yet rebranded it. Even if anyone observed the horse he would not associate it with the sheriff. This was important, because O'Hara did not

156

want advertised the fact that he was in town. That was why he had not gone direct to the Longhorn Corral.

O'Hara left the pasture, crossed the road, climbed an adobe fence, and passed down a slope to the creek. He followed this for two hundred yards, then moved up through the brush to a little log cabin set well back from the street.

He tapped on the only window and called in a low voice, "Grogan—you there?"

At first there was no answer, but after he had spoken the name again he heard a stir inside, followed by a husky demand, "Who's wantin' me?"

"You alone?"

A momentary pause followed, then a curt reply. "Yep. Now tell me what I asked."

"Garrett O'Hara. Let me in."

The man in the house could be heard moving about the room. He did not light a lamp, but presently he came to the door and opened it. The sheriff stepped inside and Grogan at once closed and bolted the door.

"Kinda early, or late, one or the other, to be drappin' in on a fellow, ain't it, O'Hara?" the owner of the cabin suggested, yawning.

"Do you know whether Bob Quantrell is in town?" the sheriff asked.

Grogan dropped his arms, still stretched in the yawn. He was a man of medium height, bow-legged and muscular. His hair was a yellowish red, and his face and wrinkled neck were sprinkled with freckles. At the mention of Quantrell's name his lax figure starched to rigidity.

"Why no? What makes you think so?"

"I've been sleeping on his trail for four days. He's either here, or he's heading this way."

"You sure?"

"Not sure, Buck. But he told me he'd be here."

"Told you?" Grogan's forehead knotted in a frown. "You an' Bob gettin' to be side-kicks these days?"

"Listen, Buck. I've got to have some sleep. In forty-eight hours I've hardly had a wink—been in the saddle ploughing through drifts most of the time. I don't want it known I'm in town. While I sleep find out for me if Quantrell is here. Last night he stole the two Kentucky horses of my partner. If the horses are in town it ought not to be hard to locate them. Bob may be staying at the house of Manuel Gomez. They say he's in love with Dolores. Not likely he'll stay at the Gomez house, though. He's too wily for that. Find out what you can, but be careful nobody suspects what you're after. When you get back wake me if I'm asleep."

Buck Grogan was a brother of the Texas Kid, who with Shep Sanderson had been killed on the main street of Concho a little more than a year before this time. In his heart he cherished a bitter hatred of the outlaw.

"All right, Sheriff," he said. "You sleep. I'll find out what I can. Hadn't I better let you lay till ten or eleven o'clock?"

"No. If he's here he may hit the trail at daybreak. Soon as you get back wake me up."

O'Hara took off his boots, his coat, and his vest, and settled himself on the bunk. In two minutes he was sound asleep.

When he opened his eyes it was broad daylight. Grogan was standing over him.

"He's here."

"Have you seen him?" asked O'Hara.

"No."

"Who told you he was?"

"You did. I've seen the horses he an' some other guy rode in on. They're stabled in the barn back of Delgado's house."

"Do you know where Bob is?"

"No, I don't. Down in the Mexican quarter, I'd say. I met Gomez on the street an' edged round the subject the least li'l bit. But you know how greasers are. They won't tell a thing they don't want to."

"You didn't let him know I was here?"

"Do I look like a plumb fool?" Grogan wanted to know. "Of course I didn't. What I said to Gomez was that I'd heard Dolores' friend was in town, an' when he looked at me real quick I added kinda casual, 'Maria Garcia.' She is, too. Came up from Agua Caliente Tuesday. Manuel was right there with the 'Si, si' stuff, but he was just a mite too late. He'd done give himself away, though I didn't let on for a minute."

"You feel sure Quantrell is in town, then."

"I'd bet six fat three-year-olds against a plug of tobacco that he's not four hundred yards from us right damn now."

"If he hasn't lit out."

"Tell you I saw the two Kentucky horses."

"He might leave them here to fool me while he's making tracks for parts unknown."

"What would be the sense in that when he could just as well take 'em along? You know how he loves a good horse. No, sir. When he goes those horses go, too. Wouldn't surprise me if he lies low here three-four days. There won't be more than half a dozen folks know he's here. He can trust his

158

Mexican friends. They like him, an' they're not civilized enough to betray him."

The last sentence Grogan offered with an ironic grin. Common opinion to the contrary, it is quite true that the Mexicans are as a people very loyal to their friends. During the past year or two as much could not be said of the white population of Jefferson County. While the feud had been in progress most of the ranchmen had stood to their colours, but the hired warriors had not felt any compunction about shifting sides. It was, for instance, not at all remarkable that O'Hara was now depending upon Buck Grogan to help him capture Quantrell, although the two cowboys had fought together against him in the battle at the Circle S O ranch. Yet Grogan was no traitor. The circumstances had changed, and with them his allegiance.

"That sounds logical," O'Hara admitted. "But Quantrell isn't very dependable. He doesn't always do what you'd expect him to do."

"That's so, generally speakin'. But he'll stay put here two-three days an' give his saddle a rest. He's been on the dodge a long time, an' he's right fond of Dolores Gomez. I'd say he'll want to stick around for a while, an' he most always does what he wants to do. He ain't what you'd call a prudent guy. His friends will be keepin' a lookout to see he's not trapped. Yes, sir. He'll be plumb tickled to lie right here in Concho an' fool you."

"Yes, that would be like him," O'Hara agreed. "Will you find out for me whether Steve Worrall has reached town yet? I want to see him."

"Got in late last night—him an' Amen Owen. Their horses were sure whipped out, too."

"Good! Ask him to drop in and see me. He'd better come along the creek and in the back way. Some of Quantrell's friends may be watching him."

"All right. Breakfast first. No, sir. You lie right there. I'll fix us up something."

A couple of hours later Worrall reached the cabin. He and the sheriff talked the situation over. It was decided to keep an inconspicuous watch on the Delgado stable from a side window of the Steelman store. Probably Quantrell would not stir out until night. After dark the Gomez house was also to be kept under observation.

"If his gang is here with him some of the bunch will poke their noses from where they're holed up soon as it gets dark," said Worrall. "Good thing to have quite a few men ready for emergencies, don't you reckon?"

"I think so. See Buckskin Joe and Amen and the Browns. You might speak to McCarthy, too, Steve. Tell them trouble is brewing and may break, but don't let them know what's up. If too many people know a secret it's not one any longer."

O'Hara did not leave the cabin until darkness fell. By a back way he went to the Steelman-McCarthy store where Worrall and Grogan were to meet him. He was eating a supper of cheese and crackers and sardines when Owen joined him.

" 'Lo, Amen," he said. "Get all rested from your long ride?"

"Umpha! Say, boy, there's a Mexican *baile* to-night at the Montez place. If you're all het up to meet Bob you might find him among those present."

"What makes you think that?" asked O'Hara.

"You mightn't think it to see me such a stove-up old donker as I am now, but once upon a time I was a kid my own self. As I come down the street I met the Gomez family dressed in their war paint headed for the dance. Includin' Miss Dolores of the black, black eyes. She sure is a right pretty señorita an' I wouldn't blame Bob for wantin' to shake a leg with her. Course I don't say he'll be there. All I'm sayin' is that he might."

"So he might," agreed the sheriff reflectively. "Well, I'm not too old to enjoy a dance. I'll give myself an invitation to be there, too."

Amen Owen grinned. He thought perhaps he had started something. "Uninvited guests ain't always so doggoned welcome," the old cowboy said. "If you go you're liable to get in a jackpot, don't you reckon?"

"It wouldn't surprise me."

"Bob is top hand with his shootin' irons. I'd say take four or five of us with you."

O'Hara cut a piece of cheese and put it between two crackers. "Can't take a posse into the barn with me. That would mean trouble right away if Bob was there, and I can't risk promiscuous shooting with a lot of women present. If Bob wasn't there, word would reach him in ten minutes that we were hot on his trail. No. I'll leave two or three of you outside and go in alone. I'll take you and Grogan and Baldy Brown. Worral and McCarthy and Jess Brown will watch the Delgado stable to cut Quantrell off from the horses if he tries for a getaway."

160

"Is it yore notion that there won't be trouble soon as Bob sees you?" asked Owen with obvious sarcasm. "Guess different. When you go in there right then you're playin' yore hole card—if Bob is at the *baile*. Now if I kinda drifted in maybe he'd let it ride. Far as we know, he ain't hep to it that I rode on the posse to the Mal Pais. *Quién sabe?*"

"Dollars to doughnuts that he knows. You rode into town last night with Steve, didn't you? If he's here the info was passed to him almost before you had unsaddled. No, it's my place to go into the barn and see whether he is there. So I'll go."

"You're cock-a-doodle-do of this outfit, Garrett. All I got to say is, look out you don't buck yore luck onct too often."

"The Lord loves the Irish, Amen," answered the sheriff, his gay smile flashing. "Far as this curly wolf goes, he's just a man like you or me. Don't forget that he has his weaknesses, just as all criminals have. One of Bob's in his vanity. He has to make grandstand plays so that people will fear and admire him. Some day he'll come a cropper on account of it. Maybe that some day is to-night."

"Hmp! Bob ain't the only grandstander in our midst. Right now I'm close enough to spit on another guy who is a hell-poppin' team his own self. Don't tell me you're against advertisin', boy. I ain't ever noticed that you ride into the *encinal* to pull off the plays that make folks talk."

The sheriff protested. "I've been driven into doing spectacular things I didn't want to do, but I never did any of them to make people talk. Or if I did the reason was not vanity, but to increase respect for the law."

Owen shrugged his shoulders. "I'll backtrack on you being a grandstander, Garrett. You're not that, an' you're there, boy, both ways from the ace. But that won't keep you from playin' on a golden harp if you're so doggoned careless. Some low-down cuss will plug you one of these days when you walk up to him with no gun in yore fist an' say, 'Consider yoreself under arrest.' I'm warnin' you."

"Maybe you're right and maybe you're not, Amen." O'Hara rose and brushed the crumbs from his clothes. "But I've got to play the hand the way it's dealt. One might as well be cheerful about it as melancholy. How does that song go that Texas Jim sings?

> "Roll your tail and roll her high,
> We'll all be angels by and by."

"Hmp! I've heard preachers deny that, but even if so I

161

aim to postpone my angelin' for a while. Well, let's mosey along."

\Chapter XXXVI: *Through a Window*

OUTSIDE of the Montez barn four or five young Mexicans were grouped. O'Hara moved forward out of the darkness and greeted them casually. He had seen a bottle passing from one to another, but at sight of him activities became suspended. They were surprised to see him. This was a private *baile;* at least Americans had not been invited. If the sheriff attended it must be in the way of business.

Then on what business? The Mexicans held together against the *gringos*. If one was wanted by the law his countrymen hid and shielded him. They were suspicious of the administration of justice as worked out by the ruling race.

O'Hara passed into the building. The sounds of stamping feet and the strains of the music filled the barn. Most of those present were dancing and did not observe him, but the men standing near the door expressed in their looks a surprised hostility. This was their demesne. *Gringos* were not welcome, especially officers of the law.

The sheriff refused to understand the resentment. His smile remained pleasant and friendly though it was a little absent-minded. His eyes were already searching for the man he had come to find. The first survey of the floor failed to find him. There were only Mexicans.

He saw Dolores Gomez. She was dancing with a slender young vaquero in the costume of a caballero. Ranged against the wall were her father and her mother, the latter wearing a black lace mantilla. Juan Garcia was on the floor. In the room were two Hashknife riders. But no Bob Quantrell.

A shift in the position of the dancers brought Dolores and her partner into the foreground. Carelessly O'Hara's gaze rested for a moment on the young man with the girl. He was in velvet bell-shaped trousers and a short vest elaborately fringed with gold braid. A wide red sash was fitted tightly to his slim waist. From the costume the sheriff guessed this gallant a vain young man. He was light on his feet, but he went through the figures of the dance hesitantly, as though he had not practised them very much. Yet he was not abashed when he made a slight mistake but quite self-possessed. A smile lit the swarthy face, and at sight of the two buck teeth that showed above the retreating chin

162

O'Hara's heart lost a beat. In spite of the disguise he knew that the dancer was Bob Quantrell.

And even while the sheriff watched him a man sidled up to the outlaw and dropped a word in his ear. O'Hara knew what the man had said as well as though he had heard him. For Quantrell's glance swept instantly to the door and found the officer. Hard and unwinking, the eyes of the two men met and clashed.

Quantrell knew he had been recognized, and the sheriff knew that he knew it, though the man's feet still kept time to the music. What would he do? O'Hara did not for an instant lift his eyes from the bandit. The price of a moment's inattention might be death.

There was only one door to the barn downstairs and one window. To reach the stairway in the loft it would be necessary for Quantrell to come within eight feet of where the sheriff stood. O'Hara knew the outlaw was thinking furiously. He would guess that the barn was surrounded, that the sheriff had his posse outside. Otherwise his course would be simple, to shoot the officer down and escape in the darkness.

Quantrell murmured something to Dolores. The girl's startled eyes flashed toward the door. She lost step, her mind distracted, then joined her partner and walked beside him from the floor.

The sheriff noticed that she was between him and her lover; that her body protected Quantrell against the chance of gun fire. A quick suspicion shot into his mind. He moved toward the man he wanted, brushing aside those who were in the way, dodging the dancers as he crossed the barn.

O'Hara was too late. He saw the outlaw's teeth flash in an impudent grin, caught a mocking wave of the hand. A streak of color dived through the air. There was a crash of glass. Quantrell had flung himself through the window head first.

Confusion instantly filled the room, which became vocal with screams, imprecations, and the lift of excited Spanish vowels. Men and women pushed this way and that, so that O'Hara found himself caught in the press as he fought his way to the window. The soft bodies of young girls impeded him no less than the muscular ones of lean vaqueros.

From outside came the sound of shots, staccato reports of battle. The sheriff drew closer to the exit, though in his eagerness to reach the open it seemed to take many minutes rather than moments. He found himself flung against a señorita face to face, so closely that her bosom rose and fell against his heart. Dark, liquid, long-lashed eyes lifted to his.

163

The firm brown flesh of bare arms brushed his cheeks and fingers laced themselves together back of his neck. Dolores Gomez had found another way to serve her lover.

O'Hara tried to push her away. She hung there heavy as a sack of meal. He reached back, caught her wrists, and dragged at them to break the hold. The girl clung desperately to him. Even after he had freed himself she snatched at his coat to detain him.

At last he was at the window. Protecting his face with his arms, he plunged through it to the ground outside.

Someone shouted, "Who is it?"

The voice belonged to Amen Owen. O'Hara called aloud his name. The cowboy ran to him, revolver in hand.

"He got away—that greaser who came through the window. Who was he?"

"Bob Quantrell." The sheriff was already on his feet, his six-shooter out. "Which way did he go?"

"Thataway." Owen waved his hand into the darkness. "He took us by surprise. We didn't know at first but what it was you—not till after he came a-shootin'."

"Anybody hurt?"

"No. Too dark to see. All of us pluggin' away for general results. The boys followed him a little ways, but I called 'em back. Figured it might be a trick to draw us off from the barn. Here are the boys."

Grogan and Baldy Brown joined them.

The sheriff sketched briefly the situation while he hurried down the street with his men.

"That was Bob Quantrell who made the break through the window. He out-generalled me. No question of either of us shooting from where we were. Too many women around. So he came out through the window while I watched the door. He knows we're hot on his trail and he'll try to get away at once. Chances are he'll head toward the Delgado stable for the horses. If so, we'll have another brush with him."

A voice hailed them.

"That's Jess," said Baldy Brown.

It was. Worral had sent him to find out the cause of the firing.

"Nobody been for the horses yet?" the sheriff asked.

"Not yet. Pankey showed up an' took a look at the horses to see they were all right, then came out again. We didn't even chirp."

"Pankey, eh?"

"Steve was right sure it was Pankey. Couldn't see his face much, but the fellow limped like Pankey does."

Within five minutes they had joined Worrall and McCarthy, who were hidden behind an adobe wall across the road from the stable. They held a hurried low-voiced consultation.

"I've a notion to take a scout around the Gomez place," O'Hara said. "Likely the family won't stay at the dance now, and Bob will try to meet Dolores before he leaves town. Steve, you come with me and look around there. We'll be back soon."

Owen rubbed dubiously the unshaven bristles on his chin. "You're crowdin' that boy consid'rable, Garrett. I done told you he's got more sting to him than a sidewinder. You better stick around here with the rest of us, don't you reckon?"

"When you call for a showdown with Bob you wanta be sure you've got an ace in the hole," Baldy Brown said, drawing a plug of chewing tobacco from his pocket. "He can sure make a busted flush go a long way. An' most usually you'll finds his cards are all red when they're flipped over. Now my idea is to sit here an'——"

O'Hara cut curtly into Baldy's discourse. "Not a debating society we're holding. I'm here to capture Bob Quantrell. The way to get him is to go after him. Come along, Steve."

Worrall grinned at Owen and Brown. "String along with Garrett here an' you'll have lively times, boys, long as you have any. My last words are that if I'd lived a better life I· wouldn't of been here. All right, Sheriff. Scratch gravel."

O'Hara and his long lean deputy moved away and were lost in the darkness.

"There's a lad, that Garrett O'Hara, who's had more bullheaded luck than a nigger with a rabbit's foot," Baldy drawled, a little resentful. When he was making oration he did not like to be cut off so abruptly.

"Luck yore foot!" scoffed Owen. "He makes his own breaks, Garrett does. He's got guts an' horse sense."

"So have you, old-timer, but I ain't heard anybody shoutin' about what a wonder you are. Coupla years ago this O'Hara was a tenderfoot—didn't know sic' 'em. You wouldn't of said he would be worth a barrel of shucks as sheriff. Now he's the white-haired lad of Jefferson County. Tell me why, if it's not luck."

"Sure I'll tell you why, Baldy. It's because he never quits —goes after bad men like the Watsons. Lights on 'em all spraddled out. On top of that he's straight as a string. That's its shape."

Baldy agreed, still grumbling.

CHAPTER XXXVII: *The Sheriff Makes a Capture*

GOMEZ LIVED in a large one-story adobe house on the outskirts of the town. He was one of the original settlers. He had driven his longhorns up from Mexico and settled on the creek in the days when the Apaches were still troublesome. Within a few years the town had grown up almost at his doorstep. For a Mexican he was well off. His cows and horses had increased in number. More rooms had been added to the house. He entertained hospitably and was a political leader of his race locally. Dark-eyed sons and daughters, eleven all told, were growing up around him and his still handsome wife. They were attractive young people, devoted to their father and their mother. The gods, it was generally felt, had been very good to him.

Manuel himself was usually inclined to agree with this verdict. He did not worry about the morrow. *Mañana* was another day and would take care of itself. But just now he was somewhat disturbed. He was a law-abiding peaceful citizen who liked to work in harmony with the leading Americans in the county. The reappearance of Bob Quantrell made a shadow on the sunny outlook. The young outlaw's popularity was great among the countrymen of Gomez. A dozen times Quantrell had stolen cows or horses, driven them far, and made a present of them to the poor natives who sheltered him. His name was becoming a legend among the poor. Gomez could not, without sacrificing his position as leader, turn his back on the bandit.

Moreover, the relation of Quantrell to his daughter Dolores complicated the situation. The young people were in love with each other, and he knew that there could be no happiness for the girl with such a man.

After Quantrell's escape from the dance hall Gomez reproached Dolores for having hindered the sheriff. It had been neither wise nor ladylike, he told her. The girl's answer ignored argument, went through his protests to the quintessential fact.

"I love him," her low, sweet voice said in liquid Spanish, and against that emotional reaction her father's logic beat in vain.

The natives buzzed like excited bees. Their sympathies were all with the wild young scamp wanted by the law. He must be helped to escape.

Gomez knew he was expected to assist Quantrell. His prestige was at stake. As soon as he had got his wife and daughter home he set out to find Quantrell and to arrange for horses upon which he and his men could make their getaway. The outlaws must lie hidden until such time as mounts could be gathered for them and brought to the cabin where they were keeping under cover.

As Gomez moved down the walk in front of his house two men rose from the shadow of a plum tree where they had been lying and confronted him.

"Just a moment," one of them said.

The speaker was O'Hara.

Gomez made the most of his English. "You weesh to see me?"

"I want you to take me to the place where Bob Quantrell is hidden."

The Mexican shrugged his shoulders and shook his head. To simulate ignorance of English is an old Mexican trick. O'Hara repeated what he had to say, in the best Spanish he could muster.

"But, señor, I do not know." Gomez fell back on his own tongue and poured out a flood of protest. Was he not a good citizen? Did he not pay taxes to establish law and order? Had he not campaigned for the election of Señor O'Hara?

Worrall murmured a suggestion to his friend. "No luck, Garrett. You're wastin' yore time. Manuel won't spill a thing."

A quick light step sounded on the hard-packed snow.

The sheriff caught at Gomez's arm, whispered an imperative in his ear, and drew him back into the shadows.

They waited, listening. The crunching of the boots on snow had ceased. Presently they could hear someone wading through the drifts in the orchard. Whoever he was, the man was moving warily. More than once he stopped, as though to make sure he was not walking into a trap. He circled the house toward the rear.

O'Hara gave quick directions to his deputy and vanished. He ran along the walk and around the house in the opposite direction to that taken by the prowler. At the back corner, close to the adobe wall, he once more stopped to listen. Someone, not ten feet from him, was whistling to attract attention. It was the low, shrill whistle of a man who wants only one person to hear.

To the sheriff there flashed a plan. He remembered Pankey's lameness and his stutter.

"B-b-bob," he called, and limped around the corner of the house. "B-b-bob, the s-s-sheriff——"

Quantrell's six-shooter seemed to leap to his hip as he crouched like a cornered wolf. It was the first instinctive reaction to the surprise of the other's presence.

The point of the revolver dropped. "What about him?" the outlaw snapped.

"D-d-delgado's s-s-stable——"

"Spit it out, man!" Quantrell's voice showed irritation.

O'Hara had been moving forward as he struggled with speech until he was close enough to touch the other. Not before he plunged at Quantrell did the latter realize his mistake. A startled oath leaped from the killer's lips as he jerked up his six-shooter.

He was too late. O'Hara's fingers closed on his wrist. An arm locked around his body. His feet were swung into the air and he was flung heavily to the ground, the sheriff's weight pinning him down.

Quantrell struggled furiously. He tried to free the hand with the revolver. He thrashed to and fro, using hands and feet as levers to throw off the incubus clamped to him.

Almost he succeeded. In the struggle the revolver went off, flinging a wild shot skyward. O'Hara was not a large man, but he had fifteen pounds' advantage of his opponent, and he needed every ounce of it to keep the outlaw's right arm extended from the body that tossed itself about so violently. The sheriff knew that if for one instant Quantrell could flex the muscles of that arm a bullet would crash into his brain. To keep his place astride of that writhing torso was like riding a bucking bronco. The officer clamped his knees and spread his feet to give him more purchase. He burrowed his face into the sloping neck of his foe and with all his strength clung to the wrist he had gripped.

The man underneath of a sudden relaxed, ceased his struggles. O'Hara became aware that someone had intervened. Sinewy fingers gripped the outlaw's throat.

A voice said, "I've got the gun, Garrett."

Steve Worrall had heard the shot and had arrived in time to decide the issue. A bony man of great strength, the deputy soon had Quantrell helpless. He held him trussed while O'Hara fastened handcuffs to the prisoner's wrists.

Now that he knew it to be useless Quantrell made no further effort to resist. The fury of fight had apparently gone out of him. He was still panting from his exertions, still swallowing to get breath through the throat Worrall had manhandled, but when he could speak there was no rancour in his voice, rather a note of ironic derision.

"Better—iron my legs—too," he gasped.

"If necessary I shall," O'Hara answered. "Now I've got you I mean to keep you."

"How long, fellow? Those may be yore notions. Different here. I'm with you only for a short visit."

O'Hara did not bandy words with him. "Where had we better keep him?" he asked the deputy.

Worral considered. The jail would not hold a child. It was built of soft adobe, and the last prisoner had dug his way out.

"How about the Concho House?" suggested Quantrell. "You want to treat me right or I'll not stay."

"There's that log *hogan* where Two-Ace Burke usta live —only it ain't half furnished. I reckon Bob's idea is about as good as any. We've got to keep him guarded, anyhow. The food would be right handy."

O'Hara nodded. "All right. We'll keep him at the hotel. It won't be for long. I'll take him to Aurora. They've got a new jail there."

"I'm not going to Aurora," the outlaw announced. "Never did like the town. It's a two-bit burg. I'll stay right here till I get ready to say '*Adiós.*' See you get me a good room."

Gomez came around the corner of the house and joined them. In Spanish he asked Quantrell reproachfully why he had come back when he knew the officers were so hot on his trail.

"Don't worry about me, Manuel," the manacled man answered gaily. "I kinda want to stick around awhile, anyhow. Might as well let the county feed me till I'm ready to go."

"We'll be on our way," O'Hara said curtly.

"That's the major-domo crackin' his whip," explained Quantrell impudently. "The li'l' tenderfoot sheriff blowin' off steam."

He went jauntily to confinement as though it were a joke.

CHAPTER XXXVIII: *A Round-up*

BRAD HELM eased his massive body up from the chairs he was occupying. His astonishment at the sight of Bob Quantrell in handcuffs had not yet had time to subside.

"Why, I can fix you up with a room, Sheriff. I would of liked to of kinda fixed it up some, but that doggone Chink is up to the Gold Nugget playin' the wheel."

"A room with two beds," O'Hara said.

"There's that south room. How would that do?"

"I want a nice, warm, comfortable room, Brad, the best you've got in the house," Quantrell said, with his gay impudent grin. "Price no object. This is particular company you're havin', understand. Guest of the county."

The fat innkeeper grinned nervously. He had no intention of slighting this dangerous guest. "It's a good room, Bob, with a fireplace in it," he wheezed. "We'll keep it nice an' warm. If anything don't suit you, just holler."

"Have Charlie cook me some of that rice puddin' tomorrow, with lots of raisins in it. The county has got to feed me good if I stay."

"I'll sure see you get it, Bob."

"No objection to that, Brad," said O'Hara. "But understand that orders come from me and not from Bob. He's just a prisoner. I'd put him in the jail if it would hold him."

"Just a prisoner, is he?" Quantrell asked with mock politeness, looking down at his slim, long girlish hands. "An' how long will he be one, Sheriff?"

Brad had picked up a lamp to lead the way to the room. He stopped to listen. There had come the sound of shots, a scattered fusillade of them.

"What's up, do you reckon?" he asked.

The sheriff turned to Worrall and spoke quickly. "Take Bob to the room, Steve. Tie him with a lash rope to the bed. If he tries to escape shoot him down. I'll be back soon as I can."

He ran out of the hotel and down the street in the direction of the Delgado stable. He passed people emerging cautiously from saloons and gambling houses. One called to him.

"What's the fireworks about, Sheriff?"

He did not answer. His business was to get to the scene of action as soon as possible.

Someone in the road hailed him. "Hold on there. Not so fast. This road's closed."

O'Hara recognized the voice of Amen Owen and pulled up. "What's wrong?" he asked. "This is O'Hara."

A little group of men were standing in the road back of Owen.

McCarthy spoke. "They tried to get the horses from the stable. Four of 'em. We yelled to throw up their hands an' they started shootin'. Course we let 'em have it, an' when the smoke cleared away two of 'em had lit out. The other two we got. One of the birds is ready for Boot Hill. Pankey had got a pill in his arm."

The sheriff stooped and looked at the face of the dead man. He recognized the man as the cowboy who had been known as Mac, one of those who had been with Quantrell when he raided the Hughes place a year or two before this time.

Pankey spoke up coolly. "D-dead as a s-stuck shote, Sheriff. Yore boys drilled him thorough. Y-you k-k-kinda outsmarted us that time, looks like."

Someone laughed. Pankey was a bad egg, but he was no quitter. In the current phrase of the time and place, he played his cards the way they were dealt him. The little man walked lame, and would as long as he lived. He owed that to Garrett O'Hara, a memento of the battle at the Cress ranch,· but he cherished no grudge on that account. His wound had been given him in fair fight.

"Hadn't been so dark we would have got Deever an' Sommers an' maybe Quantrell too," said Owen casually.

Almost too casually, in fact. It was Pankey who spoke, after a moment of silence.

"C-claimin' they were in this, are you, Amen? G-guess again, old-timer."

"We know who were in it, Pankey. Don't fool yoreself about that. An' in good time we'll round 'em up like we did you an' Mac."

"You don't s-say," jeered the little rustler. "A li'l' luck sure goes to some folks' heads."

"Did they get the horses?" asked O'Hara.

"Nary a bronc," replied one of the Browns.

"Good! You and Baldy stay here and make sure they don't come back. Not much chance of that, I'd say." O'Hara turned to Owen and McCarthy. "Will you have someone get this body? But first we'll carry Pankey to the Concho House if he's not able to walk."

"I can w-walk all right." The outlaw spoke up.

171

"Good! We'll have Dr. Holloway look after you." Again the sheriff spoke to his allies. "Get together a dozen good citizens and patrol the roads out of town. Maybe we can catch Deever and Sommers as they try to slip away."

"An' Bob Quantrell—what about him? Ain't he worth gatherin' in?" Owen asked, with an ironic little grin.

"He's already gathered," the sheriff said quietly.

The look of blank surprise on the faces about O'Hara gave place to amazement. There was a chorus of exclamations.

"How gathered?" asked McCarthy.

"Arrested."

"You mean you've got Bob Quantrell under arrest?"

"That's what I mean."

"An' he didn't kill you? Nor you him?" Baldy Brown asked.

"Nothing like that."

"Didn't put up any kind of a fight?"

"We got him to see reason."

"Where's he at now?"

"Being guarded by Steve Worrall at the Concho House."

"Well, I'll be teetotally doggoned!"

"How did you arrest him?" Amen asked.

"Oh, just explained he was under arrest. We found him outside the Gomez house. Need any help, Pankey?"

"I can m-make out to get along." The little outlaw looked at the sheriff with reluctant admiration. "I n-never saw the b-beat of you, O'Hara. You look about as dangerous as a b-brush rabbit, but you certainly take the watch. When you hit this country you didn't know s-sic' 'em, but you sure lit all spraddled out. I got to say you're a top hand."

Inside of half an hour every road out of town was guarded. Men watched the trails that wound over the hills. The houses of suspected Mexicans, those known to be friendly to the rustlers, were searched by a posse of deputies sworn in for the occasion. But no sign of either Deever or Sommers was found. They had not got away on horseback, for no horses were missing. O'Hara, Owen, and Worrall decided that they had probably slipped away immediately after the fracas and were hiding in the chaparral. The one sure thing was that they would try to raid some ranch for mounts upon which to escape.

172

CHAPTER XXXIX: *Quantrell Furnishes Melodrama*

O'HARA COULD NOT leave Concho for a few days on account of official business. Judge Warner was holding court and it was necessary for him to be present.

The sheriff knew that Bob Quantrell was slippery as a weasel and dangerous as a wolf. Every moment he had to be watched. Give him half a chance and he would find some way to escape. Therefore O'Hara chose his guards with great care. He selected three: Steve Worrall, Amen Owen, and Buck Grogan. They were to divide the day and night into relay periods. The first two men he picked because they were the best available. Grogan was slower witted, and O'Hara hesitated about appointing him. But the man could be relied on not to relax his vigilance. He hated Quantrell too much to give him any opportunity of getting away.

The instructions given by O'Hara to his deputies were definite. He warned them, too, against letting the prisoner for a single instant get his hand near a weapon.

Owen nodded approval. "Do like the boss says, boys. If Bob ever gets a half a chance you're gone. He's a wonder with a six-shooter. I've seen men with as quick a pull as Bob's. They claim Jesse James was chain lightnin' on the draw, an' I know Ben Thompson was for I've seen him. Others I've known with as rapid fire, an' still others as accurate. Maybe more so. Take Wild Bill. He was more deliberate in gettin' his guns into action. Fact is, he was so kinda easy about it he looked slow, but, gents, hush! when he onct started nobody could pump lead faster or straighter. He sure was a wonder. But this Kid Quantrell—take it from me that no man ever lived who had the edge on him in combination quick pull, rapid fire, an' straight shootin'. I'm talkin' about a .44 or a .45, you understand. I can name a dozen fellows in town can beat him with a rifle."

"The long an' short of which is that if any of us throws down on his job he's liable to go to the Happy Huntin' Ground pronto," Worrall said. "Speakin' for Number One, I'll say I think too much of myself to get careless."

O'Hara had further doubts as to the wisdom of his choice of Buck Grogan when he saw the man with the prisoner. The bow-legged cowboy could not keep from gloating over Quantrell.

"Not long now," he jeered. "We're gonna try you down

at Aurora for killin' that kid Turner at the Indian agency, an' then we'll hang you by the neck till you're dead. This country's plumb tired of two-gun men who go struttin' around with notches on their six-shooters, so we aim to make an example of Mr. Bob Quantrell right soon."

"That'll do, Buck," ordered O'Hara. "Bob hasn't been tried yet, and anyhow you're not here to devil him. If you can't be civil I'll take you off and put someone else on."

It was final as far as O'Hara was concerned but not with the others. Quantrell was more to blame than Grogan. He enjoyed stirring the anger of the guard. It helped to pass the hours. Moreover, he was watching always for a chance to escape and he felt that Grogan simmering with rage might offer opportunities that would not be given by the same man unmoved by passion.

So when O'Hara asked the prisoner a day or two later whether he had any complaints to make about the treatment he was receiving Quantrell grinned and shook his head.

"Nary a one, Sheriff. Grub's O. K. I been improvin' my mind with the books you brought. The boys you leave me so's I won't get lonesome suit me fine. Especially Buck here. We're gettin' to be real tillicums, ain't we, Buck?"

Grogan flushed but made no comment. Quantrell was far more nimble-witted than he, and had completely turned the tables on him. It was the prisoner now who jeered at him, angered him, and led him into verbal traps that made him furious. Yet he did not want to be relieved, exasperating though the situation was. He found in it the same savage pleasure that one with a toothache has when he is impelled to grind upon the throbbing molar in resentment.

Nor did Quantrell want him relieved. He knew there was very little chance of escape during the shifts of Worrall or Owen. Both of these were old-timers who had a healthy respect for his prowess. Neither of them ever gave him any opportunity for a snatch at freedom. They watched him like hawks. Quantrell felt that if he was to make a getaway it would have to be while Grogan was in charge of him.

In the darkness of the night shift the outlaw had made a discovery. He was small boned, and he could slip his long narrow hands out of the cuffs at considerable pain to himself. When the right moment came he intended to do so. But he had to be sure of his moment. If there was any slip-up, if he did not succeed, O'Hara would see that he never had another chance. Every moment that he was awake, no matter whether he was eating, reading, or devilling Grogan, his mind was busy with the problem, planning the best way to divert the guard's mind and make him for one instant careless.

Quantrell played the long shot he had planned one morning soon after Worrall went off duty. He had been playing solitaire at a little table, handling the cards awkwardly with his manacled hands. Now he was apparently tired of the game. He began instead the more attractive one of rowelling Grogan's temper.

The guard was sitting opposite him at the table less than three feet away. Quantrell dropped his arms into his lap and leaned forward to jeer at Grogan. He showed his buck teeth in a grin and murmured insults at him. Meanwhile his wrists had slipped down and he was using his knees for a vise to hold the iron while he worked his right hand out of the cuff.

". . . you an' yore whole family, Buck. Pore white trash, I been told. An' yellow. Every last one of 'em. Kicked outa yore own state for stealin' sheep, the way I heard it."

Grogan, flushed to furious anger, lost control of his temper entirely. With an oath his right hand reached across the table and caught the lapel of Quantrell's coat.

Instantly the lad's left hand made a backward circle through the air, the handcuff still attached to the wrist. Before Grogan knew what was happening the swinging iron struck the side of his head. Almost at the same moment Quantrell rose, leaned forward, and with his right hand snatched the revolver from its holster beside the guard's hip.

Eyes staring incredulously, dazed from the blow, still uncertain of what had occurred, Grogan staggered back a step or two. He stared vacantly at the smiling, derisive face of his enemy. Then he understood—and woke too late to violent action. Like a wild bull he charged the menacing gun.

Two shots rang out, so close together that they sounded like one. The guard's body plunged down on the table, upset it, and slid to the floor.

Quantrell stood there, feet apart, wolfishly wary, the hand with the smoking .44 resting on his hip. His shallow cold blue eyes held to the body of the man he had just shot down. He wanted to be sure that his work was thorough. There was no doubt about that. After the first spasmodic twitching of the muscles the huddled figure lay still.

Slowly a grin creased the face of the outlaw. "O'Hara *will* send a boy to mill, eh?" he murmured.

The killer wasted no time. Someone would hear those shots and the alarm would be spread. He put his hat on, tilted jauntily to one side, and walked out of the room into the lobby of the hotel.

As usual Brad Helm was sitting there with a couple of cronies.

"He was a wiry hook-nosed guy with eyes set too close together," wheezed the hotel keeper, "an' I noticed his claybank had sack hobbles tied around its neck. Says I to him, kinda careless—— Goddelmighty!"

The last startled exclamation, not at all careless in its inflection, was wrung out of the fat man by the sight of Quantrell emerging from the hall.

"Mornin', Brad, an' gents all," the outlaw said lightly, his glance stabbing at first one and then another.

The fat man's heart died under his ribs. "W-where's Grogan?" he quavered.

"Grogan!" Quantrell's smile was thin and cruel. "Oh, he's back there in the room. Did you want to see Grogan?"

Brad Helm knew now the meaning of the shots he had heard. Until now they had not even disturbed him. He had thought his boy was practising at a target back of the hotel.

Swiftly Quantrell stepped back of the home-made office counter and lifted from a nail a belt containing cartridges and a revolver. He broke the Colt's and saw that it was loaded.

"Much obliged, Brad," he said. "Since you're so pressin' I'll borrow the loan of this for a while."

"Help yoreself, Bob. You're sure welcome. If there's anything else——"

"Where's O'Hara right now?" broke in the young desperado.

"At the courthouse. Judge Warner's holdin'——"

"An' Steve Worrall?"

"Why, Steve's asleep down at the Longhorn Corral, I reckon."

"Amen?"

"I dunno where Amen's at, Bob."

Again Quantrell's shallow eyes, a deadly threat in them, passed from one man to another. "Stay in yore chairs for fifteen minutes. Don't rise. Don't call anyone. If you don't stay put you'll have to settle with me. Understand?"

He passed into the hall, down it, and out the back door. His glance slid to right and left to make survey of the prospect. Nobody was in sight except Brad Helm, Junior, and he was too busy roping a post even to notice him. The boy had

176

that moment arrived from the Longhorn Corral, where a vaquero had been taming a wild horse.

Quantrell moved swiftly in the direction of the Gold Nuggett. There would be horses, he knew, at the hitch rack in front of the gambling house. How soon the news of his escape would be flung broadcast he did not know. It could not be long. He had to get out of town before O'Hara closed the roads and trails, but he had no intention of leaving without first demonstrating his coolness. That the manner of his achievement, as well as the fact itself, be talked about was demanded by his vanity.

Into the back door of the Gold Nugget he slipped. At once his haste appeared to vanish. He sauntered forward to the bar past the gaming tables and the roulette wheel, a young man very much at his ease. Quantrell's eyes were busy as he moved toward the front of the building. They picked up Hank, the town drunkard, dirty and unshaven as usual, two cowboys whom he did not know, a man sleeping on a bench with his hat over his eyes, and two cow men discussing business over a mug of beer. Nobody else was in the Gold Nugget except the bartender, for this was the hour of the day when the place came nearest to being empty.

The bartender had his back toward the newcomer. He was dusting the bottles on the shelves. A sound of clanking steel made him turn abruptly. Quantrell had dropped on the bar the loose cuff still attached by its neighbour to his left hand.

"Service, Mike," the escaped prisoner said quietly.

Mike stared at him, astounded. The town was full of rumours about Quantrell, but he had not seen him for more than a year.

"You durned old alkali, wake up an' gimme a whisky straight," Quantrell ordered.

The outlaw's senses, despite his casual manner, were highly keyed. His ears were alert for any unusual sound there might be on the street. Already his eyes had registered the fact that Hank and the two cattle men had now recognized him. Hank had risen and in another moment would be making for the back door. This did not suit Quantrell .

"Drinks on me. Everyone this way. You, too, Hank," he called.

All but the sleeping man came forward, the cowboys with no urging, the others reluctantly. For those who knew Quantrell were aware that some drama was working itself out, probably a highly dangerous one. He had escaped. The jingling handcuff told them that. Why had he come here? What did he mean to do?

One of the cowboys caught sight of the handcuffs. "Holy smoke, pard! What kind of jewellery is that you're wearin'?" he asked.

"Compliments of Sheriff O'Hara. Name yore own poison, gents, an' drink to the long life of yore host, Bob Quantrell. To hell with the law."

The jocose cowboy took one quick look at him and became serious.

They drank, nervously.

Back of the bar four or five revolvers hung suspended from nails driven into the wall. They had been left there by cowboys visiting town, in accordance with the new custom instituted by O'Hara, and they were to be returned to their owners when the latter were ready to go back to the range.

"I'll take a look at those," Quantrell said, and he stepped back of the bar. After swift examination he selected a .44 and tossed aside the one he had taken from Helm. He helped himself to a belt filled with cartridges, and to a pint bottle of whisky.

"The bill goes to the sheriff," he said to Mike. "I'm the guest of the county. If he doesn't pay it let me know an' I'll have a li'l' talk with him."

"That's all right, Bob," the bartender said hastily. "Anything you want."

Quantrell yawned and stretched himself. "Well, I got to say '*Adiós!*' boys. You know how the old sayin' goes, that the best of friends must part."

He turned his back on them audaciously and swaggered to the door. Back to them came the sound of a high unmusical voice raised in song. It was Bob Quantrell's favourite ditty.

> "Hush-a-bye, baby,
> Punch a buckaroo,
> Daddy'll be home
> When the round-up is through."

The drumming of a horse's hoofs reached them. Mike looked out of the window. The outlaw had flung himself astride a saddled cow pony and was galloping out of town.

"I'll be doggoned!" one of the cowboys said. "An' that was Bob Quantrell." He spoke as one awed by the nearness of one greatly famous.

"Himself," Mike corroborated. "He broke loose. I told

'em he would. I heard shots. You don't reckon he's killed O'Hara, do you?"

"Not O'Hara," one of the cow men said. "We saw him at the courthouse not five minutes ago. We better get the news to him right away."

Already there was the hum of excitement in the air. Men could be heard running along the street shouting to each other that Bob Quantrell had got away.

It was news as exciting as that of his capture had been three days earlier. Food had been furnished for a hundred debates that would be waged furiously by the partisans of the young desperado and of the sheriff. For a time O'Hara's stock had been above par. Now it had been driven down again. His friends still had faith in him, but the general opinion was that, good sheriff though he might be, he had met more than his match in Bob Quantrell.

The sheer melodrama of Quantrell's getaway stirred the imagination and sent a thrill of horror through the community. His capture by O'Hara had been done inconspicuously, though the sheriff's posse had one dead and one wounded bandit to its credit. Their leader had played down the achievement, as an affair all in the day's work. But Quantrell, with his sure instinct for the limelight, had magnified his. Handcuffed and closely watched, he had managed to kill the guard and walk out of prison, to saunter carelessly about town, to ride away when he was ready, all with the spectacular gesture that differentiated him from ordinary bandits and killers. Bob Quantrell at least had personality.

CHAPTER XL: *A Hot Trail*

To GARRETT O'HARA at the courthouse came Brad Helm puffing from rapid travel. He waddled up to the sheriff's desk and wheezed out his startling tidings.

"Bob Quantrell has done killed Buck an' made his getaway."

The heart of O'Hara went down like a plummet in ice-chilled water. But even at this shocking news he wasted no words in lament or incredulity.

"Has he left town?" he asked.

"Don't know. He held me up an' took my gun. We found Buck dead in the room."

"Get Owen and Worrall and bring them here. If I'm not in, tell them to wait till I come." O'Hara turned to Judge

Warner, who was seated in the office. "Judge, I'll have to use you as a messenger. Go to the Fair Play Saloon and ask for Buckskin Joe. Find him, please; and ask him to outfit a pack horse with grub for a week in the hills. I'll want him to go along. We'll start inside of an hour."

Already the sheriff was buckling on the belt that held his guns. He passed out of the courthouse and down the hill to the main street of the town. He could see men gathered in knots. They were discussing the news excitedly.

O'Hara reached them and asked a question. "Is Quantrell still in town?"

The man who had doubted him looked embarrassed. "No, sir. Jumped a horse in front of the Gold Nugget an' lit out. Helped himself to all the guns he wanted first. Made all the boys there drink his health an'——"

"Which way did he go?"

"Took the east road. Looks like he might be——"

The sheriff had turned on his heel and was on his way. He had all the information they could give him and he was too busy to listen to surmise.

Within the hour he and his posse were following the escaped bandit. He had with him Worrall, Owen, a cowboy known as K. C., and Buckskin Joe. The latter was an old scout who had trailed after the Apaches with Al Sieber. His sobriquet came from the fringed leggings and the hunting shirt he wore. Both of these were made from the hide of a buck. He was by way of being a character. His language fell easily into the pungent speech of the frontier.

"He's p'intin' for the hills, that lad, looks like. Betcha he meets up with Deever an' whatever other pardners he's got. Likely they've got a hangout somewheres to hole up in. He'll be travellin' light, with no extra dufunnies, so we got no show to catch him right off. Being as you've drug me into this, take yore time, says old Joe. See them tracks. He's going lickety split. 'Make haste slowly,' Al Sieber usta tell us, an' it was sure good medicine."

"He's more slippery than an eel, and he'll outguess us if he can. I'd like to come up with him as soon as possible."

"Don't wear out yore spurs, young fellow. You'll come up with him one o' these days, maybe sooner'n you're lookin' for it," the scout said drily.

They were following a diagonal trail up the side of a rough, steep hill. The sheriff fell back behind the guide.

Owen spoke. "Well, here we are again, as the fellow who had been reprieved twice said to the hangman. Out for a nice long ride. Bob hops around worse than a Mexican flea. He certainly gives you a reasonable amount of variety."

"He keeps my official life from being decorously and damnably dull," admitted O'Hara. "My fault this time. I had a feeling I ought to take Grogan off as a guard, but I hadn't anybody to put on in his place."

They camped the first night on the other side of Powder Horn Pass, well up in the snow. Jack pines and cedars broke the sweep of wind that whipped the divide. For their camp fire they used a dead and down juniper and some young pines. Though the crackling wood roared, one side of their bodies froze while the other broiled. They did not linger long around the fire after they had eaten, but rolled up in their blankets and fell asleep. During the night one or another of them rose to fling on more logs. It was so cold that they were glad to be up early and stirring about.

There had been fresh snow in the late afternoon of the day before and Quantrell's trail had vanished, but the last they had seen of it he had been heading down into the foothills again.

"Came this way so he wouldn't meet anyone, looks like," Owen suggested. "Betcha their shebang is on Horse Creek somewheres. Bob always did kinda favour that country when he was on the dodge."

"Deever has been seen there since he escaped from town," Worrall added.

"Whatever we do will probably be wrong," O'Hara said. "Might as well try Horse Creek as anywhere."

The sky was clear and the sun shining. As they dropped down from the rugged peak country the temperature became perceptibly warmer.

About noon O'Hara came to a decision. "Think I'll ride over to the Diamond Tail and find out if anything has been seen of our birds. You fellows meet me at the Circle S O before supper. We'll stay there to-night. You might work the creek on the way down."

Steve Worrall looked at him and grinned. A little later, when the two were out of hearing of the others, the deputy made an innocent proffer.

"Kinda hard ride to the Diamond Tail an' back to the Circle S O. If you'd like me to scout that territory for you why of course I'd reluctantly consent, old-timer."

O'Hara flushed. "No, I'm younger and ought to do the hardest work," he said, tongue in cheek.

"It wouldn't be hard work for me," Worrall said, "an' I'll bet you won't find it so doggoned hard yore own self."

"Anyhow, it's my duty," O'Hara said drily.

"Hmp! Duty—that's a right mean word. Wonder what Barbara will say when I tell her you feel she's a duty. It ain't ever been a duty for most young fellows to ride clear acrost the county to say 'Howdy!' to her. They claimed it was a pleasure."

"Did I say it wasn't?"

"No, sir, just hinted it. You tell her I'll be along one o' these days, after I get through being dragged around by the guy who thinks she's a duty, an' it'll be strictly a pleasure visit."

"I'll tell her. That will keep her cheered up till you come," his friend retorted.

O'Hara rode across rough country and dropped down along the creek to the Diamond Tail. He came up to the house from the rear and rode around to the front.

Barbara was holding a low-voiced conversation with Jack Phillips, her foreman. A few feet from them was the baby buggy, tenanted.

She caught sight of O'Hara and her eyes became quick with life. As she moved toward him he felt that strange flash in them that set his blood tingling.

"Oh, Garrett, we're so proud of you!" she cried softly, for the mother in her could not forget that David was asleep. "I've been afraid—didn't know what he might do to you. But now you've taken him and destroyed his gang. We're so happy about it. You've been wonderful, and now the danger is past."

He shook his head, smiling ruefully, as he held her hand in his. "You haven't heard the latest: I couldn't keep him. He killed his guard and escaped."

He could see the chill shock of his tidings sink in her.

"Killed his guard—not Steve?"

"No. Buck Grogan. We don't know just how it happened. He must have grown careless. But it's my fault. I had a feeling Buck might not be the man for a guard. But my fear seemed ridiculous and I let him stay."

"That's absurd, to say it was your fault," she demurred instantly. "It wasn't, in the least. Was it, Jack?"

"Do you know where he headed for?" asked Phillips.

"Across Powder Horn. We lost his tracks this side of the pass."

Phillips looked serious. "We'll have to keep a sharp lookout for our stock."

"Yes. Deever and Sommers have been seen on Horse Creek. We think Quantrell will probably join them, if he hasn't done so already. Far as we know, both Deever and Sommers are still afoot. They'll have to rustle horses to get away."

"Are you out after them? Where's yore posse?"

"I'm to meet the boys at my ranch before supper. Thought I'd better ride over and warn you." He felt the heat pricking into his face and knew he was blushing. This annoyed him. Couldn't he ever get over that fool girl trick of flying a flag of embarrassment?

The foreman nodded. "I'll see the boys right away and have what horses are around the ranch close herded." He turned and strode away.

Left alone, both the man and the woman found themselves empty of words for a moment. This meeting had stirred in each of them an emotional disturbance.

"Mayn't I see His Royal Highness?" he asked lamely.

"If you don't wake him."

They tiptoed to the buggy and looked down at the sleeping babe. His eyes lifted—and his blood leaped. In her starry eyes he found the gift his heart desired.

CHAPTER XLI: *The Sheriff Plays Second Fiddle*

MARY JOE FORD came out of the house, a worried look on her face. She nodded greeting to O'Hara, then spoke to Barbara.

"Have you seen Bennie anywhere? I've been all over the place lookin' for him. Tim put him on that little piebald pony an' went into the stable to do something. When he came back Bennie had gone. Tim thought he had come up to the house, but he's not here."

"He must be around somewhere, Mary Joe," Barbara said.

"Not unless he's hidin' from me." Mary Joe's next remark showed that she was anxious. "I'll warm him if he is. I've called an' called to him."

"He can't be up the creek, because I've just come down it," O'Hara said. "I'll take a look and see if he's below the ford."

"I wish you would, Mr. O'Hara—an' I'll certainly paddle him proper when I get my hands on him."

O'Hara remounted and rode to the creek. He found no sign of the truant below the ford. As he rode back up the creek Barbara came riding to meet him.

"You didn't find him?" she asked.

"No."

"He isn't around the place. Tim says he spoke about Round Cliff. Bennie's crazy to ride. Maybe he started for it."

"If he did he'd have to pass through that snow patch at the edge of the timber and we can pick up his tracks," O'Hara answered.

In the snow they found tracks evidently made by the little piebald pony. Somewhere between them and Round Cliff, which rose on the rock rim to dominate the ranch, they would no doubt catch up with the young adventurer.

There was no reason for frantic haste. Their horses would travel much faster than the pony, and the youngster could not have had more than fifteen or twenty minutes' start of them. In less than an hour he would be back at the ranch in the disciplinary hands of Mary Joe.

O'Hara's chance had come. He knew he must make the most of it, must fling into words the emotion that engulfed him. But his old shyness rose up and took him by the throat. He looked at the gulch they were about to enter, at Round Cliff's dome shining in the sun, anywhere but at the brown beauty riding beside him, the slender figure of sheathed loveliness tempered like a blade.

As for Barbara, she would go no farther to meet him. Her eyes had made confession when they stood opposite each other over David's buggy. It was for him to storm the last fortress of her defenses if he wished it to be so.

He swallowed hard, found words, rejected them, and got as far as "Barbara!" gulped out desperately.

They were in the cañon's mouth. Her eyes met his expectantly, a shining courage back of the diffidence that fluttered in them.

A cool and mocking voice interrupted. "An' here we are again, old friends all of us."

Barbara's heart died within her. Bob Quantrell had ridden out from behind a large boulder. Little Bennie Ford sat in front of him. In the outlaw's hands rested lightly a Colt revolver.

He did not raise it. He did not order O'Hara to throw up his hands. With a thin, grim smile on his face he sat there watching the man who had hunted him from one cover to another, broken up his gang, captured and shackled him.

"Not lookin' for me, are you, Sheriff?" he continued derisively.

Out of her terror Barbara spoke quickly, in a desperate plea for mercy. Her tortured memory swept back to that other day when he had once before despoiled her life.·

"We were lookin' for Bennie. He was lost."

"An' now he's found. Ain't you, Bennie?"

"I was gonna ride to Round Cliff an' I met Bob," the little fellow piped. "But I wasn't lost, not the leastest bit."

O'Hara had not yet spoken. He did not speak now. His eyes rested on the face out of which a mocking devil leered at him. At sight of Quantrell his heart had jumped and then his vitals had grown chill. But he was not in panic. His brain functioned logically as he estimated the chances.

He could not take the luck of battle, not with little Bennie sitting in front of the outlaw. Quantrell had not put the youngster in front of him, O'Hara knew, because he feared the issue if it came to bullets. With his six-shooter already out he could drill the sheriff through and through before the latter could even lift his weapon. Why, then, was he using Bennie as a shield? Was it because he wanted to hold the officer inactive while he enjoyed his chagrin and terror?

Again Barbara voiced her agonized plea to the young desperado. She must save her lover who was so near to death. Somehow—somehow—she must stand between Garrett and impending doom.

"If he had been lookin' for you would he have brought me along?" she cried.

"Are you claimin', ma'am, that he knew Bennie would get lost an' that he came from Concho so as to be here to find him?" Quantrell asked, his shallow light blue eyes not once lifting from his trapped hunter.

"He came to see me. We—we're going to be married," Barbara explained. She had no time to think out the most effective way to reach this young killer's heart. But she had heard he was in love. A woman's appeal might touch him.

"If nothing happens first," he added with smiling suavity. "I sure wish you heaps of joy, Miss Barbara, *whoever you marry.*"

"He's sheriff," she pushed on. "He had to do his duty, but he has no feeling against you. Why don't you go away again while there's time? Let him go, an' he'll let you go."

"That's real good of him," Quantrell murmured ironically. "Let me go, will he? Yes, ma'am, I'd call that right kind of him."

"Don't you owe me something?" she begged. "You killed my husband and left my baby without a father."

A spasm of hatred twitched his face. "I'd kill him again if he was alive."

"But not Garrett," she pleaded. "He's just sheriff. It's nothing personal. You wouldn't want to spoil my life again just when—when——"

Quantrell laughed, not without bitterness. "Sheriffs are like outlaws, ma'am. They hadn't ought to be lovers. Pick a preacher if you want a real safe one. What's yore idea? Am I to let this fellow chase me around an' shoot up my friends an' then let him go when I've got the dead wood on him? I notice he didn't let me go the other day."

"He only did what he had to. You didn't suffer any personal damage from him."

"I heard some talk about a hangin' from one of his crowd," Quantrell answered cynically. "I got nothin' against yore friend here. Maybe I had onct, a year or two ago. But that's in the discard. Point is, it looks like it's got to be him or me, one. He sleeps on my trail too clost for comfort. Well, I don't allow it's gonna be me."

"But if you'd leave the country, go to Mexico——"

"I'm not aimin' to leave the country. Neither him nor anyone else can drive me out till I get ready to go."

"We used to be friends, kinda," she said, smiling at him with pitiful eagerness. "Don't you remember? I called you 'Bob.' We had our little jokes together. For the sake of old times and because of my little fatherless baby, won't you let Garrett go this time?"

The outlaw smiled, a friendly, amiable smile, and his eyes met hers. "All right. You win, ma'am. Yore silent friend gets off—this time. But if you've got any influence with him you tell him real earnest to quit crowdin' Bob Quantrell. A whole lot of things are supposed to be safer than that."

O'Hara spoke. "Let's understand each other, Bob. As long as I'm sheriff I've got to keep after you."

"You've had yore warnin', fellow. Next time there won't be a nice young lady to beg you off. Right now you hit the trail back to the Diamond Tail." Quantrell lifted Bennie from the horse and lowered him to the ground.

Bennie ran back of the big boulder and returned a moment later with the piebald pony. O'Hara helped him to get into the saddle.

The outlaw sat motionless, revolver in hand, while the other three filed out of the cañon, O'Hara bringing up the rear. When they were no longer in sight he wheeled his horse and followed the winding of the gulch as it cut deeper into the hills.

He was pleased with himself. It suited his whim to-day to be merciful. Even if Barbara Ingram had not begged for mercy he would not have killed O'Hara, he told himself now. But he was glad she had sued for her lover's life. It ministered to Quantrell's vanity to feel that she recognized that the power of life and death had been in his hand. Because he had come off best he felt a certain amiable kindliness rather than animosity toward Garrett O'Hara.

Unmusically but jocundly he assured the hills that Daddy would be home when the round-up was through.

CHAPTER XLII: *All Happy But Bennie*

BENNIE PROUDLY LED the homeward-bound party. Unaware of a rod in pickle for him, he wanted to be the first to reach the ranch with the story of his adventure. That two lovers lagged behind was to him an unimportant trifle.

The strain of peril relaxed, Barbara had to fight against a wave of faintness. She caught at the saddle horn with both hands to steady herself.

"I think you saved my life," O'Hara said in a voice unsteady with emotion. "I couldn't lift a finger to help myself, not with Bennie sitting in front of him, and if Bennie hadn't been there it wouldn't have done any good for me to try."

"I thought—I was afraid——" she murmured.

"He couldn't stand out against what you said. There's a human streak in him. And he likes children. When you spoke about the baby——"

"I didn't know what I was saying. I was sick with fear." A shiver of reminiscent dread ran down her spine.

"I'll never forget what you said," he told her; then flung at her the question in his mind: "*Are* we going to be married, Barbara?"

"Are we?" she echoed, her voice colourless.

With a sudden jubilant singing of the blood he knew they were. "We are," he cried.

Bennie was fifty yards ahead of them when they reached the creek. He put his pony to a canter as he mounted the slope.

O'Hara slipped from the saddle at the edge of the willows and caught the bridle rein of Barbara's horse.

"We'll have to hurry if we're going to save Bennie from a spanking," she protested, rather faintly.

"Bennie will have to take his chance," he said with decision. "He needs that paddling, anyhow. Get down."

"You're very masterful, aren't you?" she said, her eyes both tender and mocking. But, obediently, she dismounted and found herself in his arms.

A happy little laugh welled from her throat as her eyes turned to his.

It was fifteen minutes later that she reminded him of their errand. "We came to find Bennie."

"He can't be lost again already, can he?" her lover laughed.

But he submitted to walk with her to the ranch house, leading their horses by the bridles.

Bennie, his face tear-stained, made a public announcement, one influenced by recent events which had cast more than a shadow behind.

"I'm gonna live at your house, Barb'ra, after you 'n' the sheriff get married, 'n' when I grow up I'm gonna be a noutlaw like Bob Quantrell."

Mary Joe looked quickly at Barbara and observed confusion. "He says you met Bob Quantrell," the mother said by way of diversion from an embarrassing subject.

"Yes," confirmed O'Hara. "He turned Bennie over to us."

"No gun plays?" Phillips asked quickly.

"No."

"Barb'ra told him she was gonna marry the sheriff," Bennie contributed. "An' she is, too, an' I'm gonna live with 'em."

The eyes of the lovers met. Barbara smiled permission for O'Hara to tell the news. He did so, and created no sensation.

"I knew it all the time," Mary Joe said calmly. "Ask Jack if I didn't tell him so three weeks ago."

"I expect you've been telling Jack more interesting things than that," Barbara replied, smiling at her foreman.

Whereupon more news came out.

"We'll make a double wedding of it," Mary Joe suggested gaily.

"Can you ride with me, Jack?" O'Hara presently asked him. "I've got to follow Quantrell's trail while it's hot."

"I reckon so," Phillips answered. "Soon as I'm caught an saddled."

"I want to see you, Garrett, just a minute, in the house," Barbara said. Inside, she turned swiftly on him, catching a

188

the lapels of his coat with an eagerness almost savage. "Do you have to go—right away, when I've had you such a little time? Can't you forget that man just for to-day an' stay here with me?"

"I wish I could, sweetheart." The word of endearment fell shyly, as did the caress accompanying it. "But I can't. I've got to follow him at once."

"He might have killed you to-day, Garrett—and he didn't," she reminded him.

"I'm an officer, not a private citizen, Barbara. It's my business to capture him because he's a criminal. I've got to stay with the job."

"I suppose so," she conceded reluctantly. "But you'll be careful, won't you? You'll come back to-me."

"I'll be very careful, and I'll come back to you," he promised. "When I finish this one job I'll resign."

She clung to him, as though she would never let him go, kissing with feminine ferocity the ardent lips that met hers.

Her whispered confession just reached his ears.

"I've loved you, Garrett—always, always, and didn't know it."

She pushed him from her and ran down the passage into her bedroom.

As he strode out of the house to his horse there was a light in Garrett O'Hara's eyes that never had been there before.

CHAPTER XLIII: *A Job Finished*

BOB QUANTRELL approached with the greatest care the old dilapidated cabin where the outlaws had been accustomed to hole up. The price of life for him was wariness, and he had no intention of running into a trap for lack of adequate precaution.

When at last he opened the door noiselessly and looked inside it was to see the crouched figure of a man confronting him, a man with a six-shooter in each hand.

"Throw 'em up," a hoarse voice ordered excitedly.

In that fraction of a second during which Quantrell's .44 flashed out the two men recognized each other. The two-gun man was Deever.

"Thought O'Hara had you in the calaboose," the squat rustler said in surprise. "That's the story I heard."

"Do I look like the kinda bird that would stay in a cala-

189

boose?" asked Quantrell boastfully. "I bumped off Buck Grogan an' said *'Adiós!'* "

"That must be why there's a posse on Horse Creek."

"I reckon that's why," Quantrell admitted casually. "But I served notice this afternoon on O'Hara not to crowd me."

"On O'Hara? Where?"

"Above the Diamond Tail, at the mouth of the Box Cañon. I had the drop on Mr. Sheriff, an' for two cents I would have bumped him off."

"Was he mounted?"

"Sure." Quantrell looked at his companion in surprise. "Ain't everybody mounted in these hills?"

"I'm not." The younger outlaw noticed an odd glitter in Deever's eyes. "I got no horse an' I'm starved an' wore out climbin' these damned hills an' wadin' through snow. You fool, why didn't you kill O'Hara an' get his horse for me?"

"Don't talk thataway to me. fellow," Quantrell snarled. "How d' I know you wasn't fixed with a horse by this time? Took me about the flick of a cow's tail to get one."

"Where is yore horse?"

"Back in the pines where we always tie."

"We'd better get outa here," Deever said. "O'Hara's posse bumped into me half an hour ago an' took two-three shots at me. I ducked into the big rocks an' crawled up here. But they're after me hotfoot."

"Where's Sommers?"

"He left me at Squaw Crossing. He's aimin' to lie low with a cousin of his near Agua Caliente. Wisht to God I'd gone with him." There was a hunted look in the man's eyes. His hardy confidence had deserted him. "They'll get us sure. They're armed with rifles an' we ain't, an' I ain't tasted food for 'most three days."

"Buck up, Deever. They've not got us yet, an' they're not gonna get us—not without a real dog fight first."

"Thought old Rim Rock Hanson would gimme food an' a horse, but his place is deserted. What'll we do, Bob?" whined the tormented man. "Tell you I haven't eat or slept either one. I'm bucked out, an' this posse liable to be here any minute."

"Keep yore shirt on, old-timer," advised Quantrell. "We'll try to slip over to Bear Creek an' down it. We can ride an' tie till we pick up another horse. We both been in a lot tighter holes than this one. Sure have."

A voice from outside hailed the house.

Deever started. His sunken eyes went wildly to those of the other outlaw. "It's the posse."

"I reckon you're right. Old Amen Owen's voice, I'd say. We better sneak outa the window an' try a run for the bronc. We'll make it fine through the big rocks more 'n likely."

"With one horse for the two of us we can't make a getaway. I got a good mind to surrender."

"An' you with a gun in each hand. Fellow, you're yellow. Slide outa that window an' do like I say. If you've got any sand in yore craw I'll pull you through."

"Tell you I'm sick," Deever protested. "I been through hell these last two-three days an' nights."

Yet he did as Quantrell told him. The two crept from rock to rock. Not till they were close to the pines did one of the posse catch sight of Deever and fire. Other shots sounded, but the outlaws had reached the timber.

Deever caught his foot in a projecting root and fell. As Quantrell ran past him to the horse Bob called, "Keep a-comin', Deever."

The bandy-legged man had fallen into a panic of fear. Either he thought that Quantrell was about to desert him or else he feared both of them could not escape on one horse.

As the younger man pulled the rein from the slip knot he heard the pounding feet of his companion.

Quantrell turned. "All set, old-timer, for——"

Deever's six-shooter roared twice.

Bob Quantrell staggered, fired once blindly into the ground, lurched against the trunk of a tree, and slid along it to the snow.

A moment, and Deever was in the saddle galloping for safety.

Twenty minutes later, still riding hard, he swung around a curve in the trail. He dragged the horse to its haunches. For he was face to face with the sheriff and Jack Phillips.

He followed his first instinctive reaction and fired at O'Hara. Before the echo of the shot came back from the cañon wall the guns of O'Hara and Phillips were in action.

Deever dropped his weapon and clutched at the saddle horn. He slid to the ground.

"Don't shoot again," he gasped. "You've got me."

Almost before they reached him he was dead.

The officers looked at each other.

"Something drivin' him in a hurry," Phillips said. "Do you reckon he met yore boys?"

"He's riding the same horse Bob Quantrell was two hours ago. That is, he was a minute ago."

"Then we better go slow. Bob is liable to be around somewhere."

In a little while they met O'Hara's posse and learned the news of Deever's treachery to Quantrell.

"Scared they couldn't both make it. So he plugged Bob twice through the heart," Owen explained.

They carried the bodies of the outlaws to the Circle S O ranch where they were to spend the night.

O'Hara did not wait for supper. He ate a couple of sandwiches and drank a cup of coffee. On a fresh horse he struck across to the Diamond Tail.

It was dark long before he reached the ranch.

When he knocked on the door Barbara opened it for him. At sight of her lover she caught her breath sharply.

"Is it—is everything—all right?"

He caught a glimpse of the outline of her bosom beneath the wrap she had caught up and thrown on.

"My job is finished," he told her.

From her throat came a little sobbing sound of joy.

THE END